Praise for
Lady in Waiting

"*Lady in Waiting* is sheer beauty set in two time periods, both equally captivating stories. Meissner writes characters I care for, root for, and pine alongside—and she does so while weaving enticing, heart-wrenching plots. This book proves why I'm an ardent Susan Meissner fan."

> —MARY DEMUTH, author of *Life in Defiance*

"*Lady in Waiting* by Susan Meissner: The pacing, perfection. Transitions between centuries, seamless. Capturing the nuances of relationship, flawless. Put anything written by Susan Meissner on your "must read now!" list, right beside Barbara Kingsolver and Elizabeth Berg. I couldn't put this elegant novel of love and choice down. A completely satisfying read."

> —JANE KIRKPATRICK, award-winning author of *A Flickering Light* and *An Absence So Great*

"A novel about decisions long regretted and decisions yet to be made, *Lady in Waiting* resonates with the great hope and exhilaration that come with the realization that there is always a choice."

> —SIRI MITCHELL, author of *She Walks in Beauty*

"Artfully blending past and present, Susan Meissner weaves the stories of two different women into a rich tapestry of love, disappointment, and ultimately the power of standing up for what you believe in. The subtlety of her storytelling makes *Lady in Waiting* both delightful to read and impossible to forget."

> —NICOLE BAART, author of *The Moment Between*

Praise for
Susan Meissner

"As raindrops become mighty rivers, Susan Meissner's words seem simple in the beginning, but one thought builds naturally upon another, phrases and sentences flow together with effortless fluidity, and before you know it, you are totally engrossed by the powerful undercurrents of her story. To read Ms. Meissner is to put yourself into the hands of that rarest kind of author: an artist working in the medium of words."

—ATHOL DICKSON, Christy Award–winning author of *The Cure* and *Winter Haven*

"Writing as incandescent as pure flame. Susan Meissner delivers again with a family story that wraps you up and stays with you long after the last page."

—JAMES SCOTT BELL, best-selling author of *Deceived* and *Try Fear*

"I loved *The Shape of Mercy* from beginning to end. Ms. Meissner's prose sings, and her characters captured my interest from the start. As the story unfolded, those same characters captured my heart. I won't soon forget Mercy, Lauren, or Abigail."

—ROBIN LEE HATCHER, award-winning author of *Wagered Heart* and *When Love Blooms*

"With a deft hand, Meissner blends an intriguing storyline, artful writing, and memorable characters for a truly delicious read. This one's a keeper!"

—DENISE HUNTER, author of *The Convenient Groom*

"*White Picket Fences,* with its wonderful cast of characters, offers hope to all of us who live less than perfect lives behind our own white picket fences. Susan Meissner skillfully weaves together parallel storylines to show how healing can come when we risk sharing our secret pain with others."

—LYNN AUSTIN, author of *Until We Reach Home*

Lady in Waiting

Lady in Waiting

SUSAN MEISSNER

Author of *The Shape of Mercy*

WATERBROOK
PRESS

LADY IN WAITING
PUBLISHED BY WATERBROOK PRESS
12265 Oracle Boulevard, Suite 200
Colorado Springs, Colorado 80921

Scripture quotations are taken from the King James Version.

Apart from well-known real people and real events associated with the life of Lady Jane Grey, the characters and events in this book are fictional and any resemblance to actual persons or events is coincidental.

ISBN 978-0-307-45883-4
ISBN 978-0-307-45884-1 (electronic)

Published in the United States by WaterBrook Multnomah, an imprint of the Crown Publishing Group, a division of Random House Inc., New York.

WATERBROOK and its deer colophon are registered trademarks of Random House Inc.

Library of Congress Cataloging-in-Publication Data
Meissner, Susan, 1961–
    Lady in waiting : a novel / by Susan Meissner. — 1st ed.
        p. cm.
    ISBN 978-0-307-45883-4 — ISBN 978-0-307-45884-1
    1. Self-actualization (Psychology) in women—Fiction. 2. Grey, Jane, Lady, 1537–1554—Fiction. I. Title.
    PS3613.E435L33 2010
    813'.6—dc22

                                                                        2010009570

Printed in the United States of America
2010—First Edition

10 9 8 7 6 5 4 3 2 1

For Bob,
the one my heart beats for.

LADY JANE GREY'S ROYALS & NOBLES

Henry Grey
Marquess of Dorset, Duke of Suffolk
Lady Jane Grey's father

Frances Brandon Grey
Marchioness of Dorset, Duchess of Suffolk
Fourth in line to the throne after Henry VIII
Jane's mother

Lady Jane Grey
Fifth in line to the throne after Henry VIII

Thomas Seymour
Lord Admiral
Married Henry VIII's widow, the Queen Dowager, Katherine Parr
Uncle to Edward VI

Edward Seymour
Duke of Somerset and Lord Protector to Edward VI
Brother to Lord Admiral Thomas Seymour
Uncle to Edward VI

Edward Seymour the younger
Son of the Lord Protector, the Duke of Somerset

Henry VIII
King of England

Edward VI
First in line to the throne
Son of Henry VIII and Jane Seymour

Princess Mary
Second in line to the throne
Daughter of Henry VIII and Catherine
of Aragon

Princess Elizabeth
Third in line to the throne
Daughter of Henry VIII and Anne Boleyn

John Dudley
Earl of Warwick,
Duke of Northumberland
Lord Protector after Edward
Seymour the elder

Guildford Dudley
Son of John Dudley

I saw the angel in the marble
and carved until I set him free.

—MICHELANGELO BUONARROTI

Lady in Waiting

Jane

Upper West Side, Manhattan

One

The mantel clock was exquisite, even though its hands rested in silence at twenty minutes past two. Carved—near as I could tell—from a single piece of mahogany, its glimmering patina looked warm to the touch. Rosebuds etched into the swirls of wood grain flanked the sides like two bronzed bridal bouquets. The clock's top was rounded and smooth like the draped head of a Madonna. I ran my palm across the polished surface, and it was like touching warm water.

Legend was this clock originally belonged to the young wife of a Southampton doctor and that it stopped keeping time in 1912, the very moment the *Titanic* sank and its owner became a widow. The grieving woman's only consolation was the clock's apparent prescience of her husband's horrible fate and its kinship with the pain that left her inert in sorrow. She never remarried, and she never had the clock fixed.

I bought it sight unseen for my great-aunt's antique store, like so many of the items I'd found for the display cases. In the year and a half I'd been in charge of the inventory, the best pieces had come from the obscure estate sales that my British friend, Emma Downing, came upon while tooling around the southeast of England looking for oddities for her costume shop. She found the clock at an estate sale in Felixstowe, and the auctioneer, so she told me, had been unimpressed with the clock's sad history. Emma said he'd read the accompanying note about the clock as if reading the rules for rugby.

My mother watched now as I positioned the clock on the lacquered black mantel that rose above a marble fireplace. She held a lead crystal vase of silk daffodils in her hands.

"It should be ticking." She frowned. "People will wonder why it's not ticking." She set the vase down on the hearth and stepped back. Her heels made a clicking sound on the parquet floor beneath our feet. "You know, you probably would've sold it by now if it was working. Did Wilson even look at it? You told me he could fix anything."

I flicked a wisp of fuzz off the clock's face. I hadn't asked the shop's resident-and-unofficial repairman to fix it. "It wouldn't be the same clock if it was fixed."

"It would be a clock that did what it was supposed to do." My mother leaned in and straightened one of the daffodil blooms.

"This isn't just any clock, Mom." I took a step back too.

My mother folded her arms across the front of her Ann Taylor suit. Pale blue, the color of baby blankets and robins' eggs. Her signature color. "Look, I get all that about the *Titanic* and the young widow, but you can't prove any of it, Jane," she said. "You could never sell it on that story."

A flicker of sadness wobbled inside me at the thought of parting with the clock. This happens when you work in retail. Sometimes you have a hard time selling what you bought to sell.

"I'm thinking maybe I'll keep it."

"You don't make a profit by hanging on to the inventory." My mother whispered this, but I heard her. She intended for me to hear her. This was her way of saying what she wanted to about her aunt's shop—which she'd inherit when Great-aunt Thea passed—without coming across as interfering.

My mother thinks she tries very hard not to interfere. But it is one of her talents. Interfering, when she thinks she's not. It drives my younger sister, Leslie, nuts.

"Do you want me to take it back to the store?" I asked.

"No! It's perfect for this place. I just wish it were ticking." She nearly pouted.

I reached for the box at my feet that I brought the clock in along with a set of Shakespeare's works, a pair of pewter candlesticks, and a Wedgwood vase. "You could always get a CD of sound effects and run a loop of a ticking clock," I joked.

She turned to me, childlike determination in her eyes. "I wonder how hard it would be to find a CD like that!"

"I was kidding, Mom! Look what you have to work with." I pointed to the simulated stereo system she'd placed into a polished entertainment center behind us. My mother never used real electronics in the houses she staged, although with the clientele she usually worked with—affluent real estate brokers and equally well-off buyers and sellers—she certainly could.

"So I'll bring in a portable player and hide it in the hearth pillows." She shrugged and then turned to the adjoining dining room. A gleaming black dining table had been set with white bone china, pale yellow linen napkins, mounds of fake chicken salad, mauve rubber grapes, plastic croissants, and petits fours. An arrangement of pussy willows graced the center of the table. "Do you think the pussy willows are too rustic?" she asked.

She wanted me to say yes, so I did.

"I think so too," she said. "I think we should swap these out for that vase of gerbera daisies you have on that escritoire in the shop's front window. I don't know what I was thinking when I brought these." She reached for the unlucky pussy willows. "We can put these on the entry table with our business cards."

She turned to me. "You did bring yours this time, didn't you? It's silly

for you to go to all this work and then not get any customers out of it."
My mother made her way to the entryway with the pussy willows in her
hands and intention in her step. I followed her.

This was only the second house I'd helped her stage, and I didn't
bring business cards the first time, because she hadn't invited me to until
we were about to leave. She'd promptly told me then to never go anywhere without business cards. Not even to the ladies' room. She'd said it
and then waited, like she expected me to take out my BlackBerry and
make a note of it.

"I have them right here." I reached into the front pocket of my capris
and pulled out a handful of glossy business cards emblazoned with
Amsterdam Avenue Antiques and its logo—three *A*'s entwined like a Celtic
eternity knot. I handed them to her, and she placed them in a silver dish
next to her own. *Sophia Keller Interior Design and Home Staging.* The
pussy willows actually looked wonderful against the tall, jute-colored wall.

"There. That looks better!" she exclaimed, as if reading my thoughts.
She turned to survey the main floor of the town house. The owners had
relocated to the Hamptons and were selling off their Manhattan properties to fund a cushy retirement. Half the décor—the books, the vases, the
prints—were on loan from Aunt Thea's shop. My mother, who'd been
staging real estate for two years, brought me in a few months earlier, after
she discovered a stately home filled with charming and authentic antiques
sold faster than the same home filled with reproductions.

"You and Brad should get out of that teensy apartment on the West
Side and buy this place. The owners are practically giving it away."

Her tone suggested she didn't expect me to respond. I easily let the
comment evaporate into the sunbeams caressing us. It was a comment for
which I had no response.

My mother's gaze swept across the two large rooms she'd furnished,
and she frowned when her eyes reached the mantel and the silent clock.

"Well, I'll just have to come back later today," she spoke into the silence. "It's being shown first thing in the morning." She swung back around. "Come on. I'll take you back."

We stepped out into the April sunshine and to her Lexus parked across the street along a line of town houses just like the one we'd left. As we began to drive away, the stillness in the car thickened, and I fished my cell phone out of my purse to see if I'd missed any calls while we were finishing the house. On the drive over, I had a purposeful conversation with Emma about a box of old books she found at a jumble sale in Cardiff. That lengthy conversation filled the entire commute from the store on the seven hundred block of Amsterdam to the town house on East Ninth, and I found myself wishing I could somehow repeat that providential circumstance. My mother would ask about Brad if the silence continued. There was no missed call, and I started to probe my brain for something to talk about. I suddenly remembered I hadn't told my mother I'd found a new assistant. I opened my mouth to tell her about Stacy, but I was too late.

"So what do you hear from Brad?" she asked cheerfully.

"He's doing fine." The answer flew out of my mouth as if I'd rehearsed it. She looked away from the traffic ahead, blinked at me, and then turned her attention back to the road. A taxi pulled in front of her, and she laid on the horn, pronouncing a curse on all taxi drivers.

"Idiot." She turned to me. "How much longer do you think he will stay in New Hampshire?" Her brow was creased. "You aren't going to try to keep two households going forever, are you?"

I exhaled heavily. "It's a really good job, Mom. And he likes the change of pace and the new responsibilities. It's only been two months."

"Yes, but the inconvenience has to be wearing on you both. It must be quite a hassle maintaining two residences, not to mention the expense, and then all that time away from each other." She paused, but only for a moment. "I just don't see why he couldn't have found something similar right here in New York. I mean, don't all big hospitals have the same jobs in radiology? That's what your father told me. And he should know."

"Just because there are similar jobs doesn't mean there are similar vacancies, Mom."

She tapped the steering wheel. "Yes, but your father said—"

"I know Dad thinks he might've been able to help Brad find something on Long Island, but Brad wanted this job. And no offense, Mom, but the head of environmental services doesn't hire radiologists."

She bristled. I shouldn't have said it. She would repeat that comment to my dad, not to hurt him but to vent her frustration at not having been able to convince me she was right and I was wrong. But it would hurt him anyway.

"I'm sorry, Mom," I added. "Don't tell him I said that, okay? I just really don't want to rehash this again."

But she wasn't done. "Your father has been at that hospital for twenty-seven years. He knows *a lot of people.*" She emphasized the last four words with a pointed stare in my direction.

"I know he does. That's really not what I meant. It's just Brad has always wanted this kind of job. He's working with cancer patients. This really matters to him."

"But the job's in New Hampshire!"

"Well, Connor is in New Hampshire!" It sounded irrelevant, even to me, to mention the current location of our college-age son. Connor had nothing to do with any of this. And he was an hour away from where Brad was anyway.

"And you are here," my mother said evenly. "If Brad wanted out of the city, there are plenty of quieter hospitals right around here. And plenty of sick people for that matter."

There was an undercurrent in her tone, subtle and yet obvious, that assured me we really weren't talking about sick people and hospitals and the miles between Manhattan and Manchester. It was as if she'd guessed what I'd tried to keep from my parents the last eight weeks.

My husband didn't want out of the city.

He just wanted out.

Two

Sometimes, during those first few weeks after Brad moved out, I'd wake in the middle of the night and forget I was now alone in my bed. I'd instinctively move toward Brad's side, and when I'd feel the emptiness there, a strange kind of vertigo would come over me, and I'd grab hold of the sheets to keep from falling.

It happened every night the first week. I'd lie awake afterward until the alarm went off hours later, unable to stop contemplating why Brad wanted distance from me. And why it took me by such stinging surprise. By the third week, I wasn't waking up in the middle of the night with vertigo anymore; I was just waking up. Sometimes at two in the morning. Sometimes at three. And I'd still be awake when dawn broke.

I hadn't known Brad was suffocating in our marriage. That's the part that made me shudder as sleep skittered away from me night after night. Brad had felt like he was suffocating, and I hadn't seen it. Sometimes doubt kept me awake. Sometimes grief. Sometimes anger. And sometimes a messy mix of all three.

We were sitting at our kitchen table the morning Brad told me he was leaving. The Sunday paper was strewn among our coffee mugs, and the aroma of the western omelet I had made for us still lingered. Onions, peppers, and diced ham. It was mid-February, but the sun was bold that morning, and its flashy tendrils spilled across our shoulders from our bal-

cony windows as if it wanted in. Brad said my name. I looked up, thinking he perhaps wanted me to pass the french press to freshen his cup.

But he was looking off toward our front door, not at me.

"There's a position in radiology at a hospital in New Hampshire," he
said.

Several seconds passed before I realized this was a circumstance that
mattered to him. "New Hampshire?"

He looked at his coffee cup and stroked the ear-shaped handle.
"Manchester. It's in diagnostics, working alongside oncologists. Part of
the job involves research and clinical studies. I was asked to consider it."

He raised his head, and his eyes slowly met mine.

"You were?" Scattered thoughts ran through my head. I hardly knew
which question I really wanted to ask. *Why are you telling me this?* seemed
like a good place to start, but he spoke before I could decide.

"Actually, I was specifically approached. They've read my articles in
the *Journal,* and they want me to come on staff."

Perhaps I should've said something affirming, something that would
let him know that I was proud he'd been handpicked for something, but
all I could think was that Brad might actually take this job and we'd be
leaving New York. Just like that. I was already wondering how I'd tell my
mother and Aunt Thea I wouldn't be able to manage the antique store
anymore. Thea, tucked away in her assisted-living apartment in Jersey
City, would probably insist my mother take over the store, since she
wouldn't trust it to anyone but family. My mother wouldn't be happy
about that. Antiques were not her thing. And the very idea of moving, of
leaving everything that was familiar, was unsettling.

"But it's in New Hampshire," I said.

He resumed stroking the arc of the mug handle. "It's a great career
move." His gaze was on his mug.

My thoughts zoomed to my parents. They'd probably see this as a stellar promotion, even if it did mean leaving Manhattan. My dad would anyway. My parents adored Brad. They always had. Perhaps they wouldn't flip if I told them we were moving. But my mother would definitely be annoyed about my leaving the store...

"So, are you going to look into it?" I finally asked.

My question was met with what seemed like a long stretch of silence. When Brad finally looked up at me, I knew.

He'd already accepted the job.

My elbow knocked my mug. A tiny wave of coffee winked out and dotted the sports section. "You already said yes? Without even checking it out?"

"I interviewed last Thursday. They flew me up for the day."

My face instantly warmed with a weird jumble of embarrassment and surprise. Brad had been to New Hampshire and back, on a day I assumed he'd been in Manhattan working a twelve-hour shift.

"Why didn't you tell me?" I murmured.

He pushed his mug away. "I really wanted to check this out on my own."

The air in the room seemed to still. "Why?"

Brad rubbed his hand across his morning stubble. "Because...because I knew I would not be asking you to make any changes for me."

My mouth dropped open. "What do you mean?"

But I knew. He meant he wanted to go to New Hampshire alone.

He sighed the tired exhale of someone who has to explain something that shouldn't have to be explained. "I think it's time we were both honest with each other." He said it like he'd already imagined saying it a hundred times. "I think we need a little break."

My first thought was that he was joking. But no one jokes about something like this. The worst of it was he thought I was in the know. He thought I also felt the need for distance, that our marriage had hit a dead zone, and that we needed some time away from each other, and that I'd been pretending I didn't see it. He must've been feeling this way for quite a while. And I had no idea.

The tears formed immediately. Two slipped out and slid down my face. Brad looked away.

"A break from what?" I whispered. "You want a break? From me?"

"Jane—," he began, and it suddenly occurred to me, with nauseating force, that he was having an affair.

"Is there someone else?" I blurted. "Are you seeing someone? Are you having an affair?"

"No."

He said it quickly. But in that same tired voice.

"You're not having an affair?" I wanted to believe him but was afraid to.

"I'm not having an affair."

For a split second, I wished he was. I wished he was having an affair, that someone had stolen his attention away from me. Then there would be someone else to be angry at. Someone to blame for yanking him away.

More tears slid down my face. Brad reached for a tissue on the breakfast bar behind us and held it out to me. I ignored it and wiped the tears away with the sleeve of my bathrobe.

"I don't understand any of this," I said.

He tossed the tissue onto the table. "Can you honestly tell me you think everything is fine with us? Don't you know it's not? I shouldn't have to spell it out. I never wanted to hurt you."

"Well, how did you think I would feel when you told me this?" Resentment rose within me, fueled by hurt and bewilderment. "How did you think I'd feel when you told me you wanted to leave me?"

"I didn't say I was leaving you. I said we needed a break."

"But you're leaving me!" I put my hands in my lap to try to still them.

"I just think we both need some time apart to see if there's anything that is keeping this marriage alive."

My face stung as though I'd been slapped. "What?"

"I think maybe Connor has been the only thing keeping us together. When he went away to college, it's like he pulled out the last nail. It hasn't been the same for us. And I think you know it."

I opened my mouth to protest, but there were no words ready. In that instant I knew I had done nothing to address the void in our lives when Connor packed his bags for Dartmouth. And neither had Brad. For the last eighteen months, we'd been holding our breath in between Connor's semester breaks and visits home. Well, at least I had been. Brad had apparently been doing something else—imagining life without me. But what he was suggesting made no sense.

"How will being apart help us see what's keeping us together?" I asked.

"Because being together isn't doing it."

This, too, stung me. I reached for the tissue, and he handed it to me. "Shouldn't we try counseling?"

He hesitated a moment. "Maybe. In a little while. Right now I just need some space. I think we both do."

I grabbed the french press and rose from my chair. I stepped into the open kitchen and slammed the press onto the counter. Coffee sloshed onto our breakfast dishes.

"Jane?"

"For how long?" I kept my back to him.

"I…I can't answer that."

"What about Connor? What are we supposed to tell him?"

"We tell him as much as he needs to know. That I've been offered a great job in New Hampshire and I am taking it while we see if it's a move we both want to make."

I turned around and stared at him, my radiologist husband who spent his days looking inside people. "Is this really what you want to do?"

He closed his eyes, as if I had asked the wrong question and he was trying to find an answer that would make the question work. "It's what I need to do."

For a long stretch of seconds, neither one of us said anything. Then he methodically told me, as if he'd rehearsed it, that he'd rented a furnished condo near his new hospital, that he'd given notice at Memorial and asked for an early out so that he could start on Tuesday. Memorial had granted it. He asked me if he could take the car, even though it was his anyway. Then he told me we'd use the time away from each other to see where our hearts were headed.

"What am I going to tell my parents?" My cheeks were wet with tears, spilled as he spelled out the arrangements he'd made.

Brad stood. "This has nothing to do with your parents."

"What am I going to tell them?"

"Tell them this is my fault."

He started to walk past me, probably to start packing. I reached out to touch his arm, and he stopped.

"You made love to me last night," I whispered.

When he said nothing in return, I looked up at him. He was looking down on me, at my arm on his arm, waiting for me to let him go.

He didn't say it, but I suddenly knew his thoughts.

What we had shared the night before was the most visceral vestige of our oneness. He had considered it, and it wasn't enough.

We'd been sharing the same house, the same car, the same friends, the same bed for twenty-two years. And it was Connor who'd kept the loose threads tied together.

I let my hand fall.

❧⊱⊰❧

I had missed the signs that Brad was bored with our life. Surely they had been there. But I'd missed them. My best friend, Molly, upon whose shoulder I'd leaned daily after Brad's departure, said I perhaps distracted myself with managing Thea's shop, because I didn't know what to make of the signs, didn't know how to address them, so I'd pretended they weren't there. But there had been no pretending. I just didn't see them.

After he left, I had no choice but to consider them. The signs that I didn't see morphed into the reasons he left. My empty bed coaxed me into pondering them night after night while the rest of Manhattan slept. Morning would come and I'd drag myself down to the shop, woozy as a victim of malaria. The week Brad moved out, I hadn't hired Stacy yet. It was still just me and blunt, Hawaiian-shirted Wilson, the retired high school history teacher and self-taught repairman who'd been Thea's only other full-time employee.

"You hung over?" he asked, the first morning Brad was gone, appalled at my morning stagger.

"No, Wilson. I didn't sleep well."

"Pity. I'll make you coffee."

"Thanks."

"My pleasure, of course. You know, if you didn't consume so much refined sugar, you wouldn't be up at night, Jane."

I slowly took off my coat and hung it on the hall tree by the cash register. "I'm sure you're probably right."

He had stared at me. "I am totally kidding. Want an éclair with your coffee? I picked up some on the way in."

Over dark roast and pastries, I'd quietly confided in gray-haired Wilson. I told him Brad had taken a job in New Hampshire and wanted to move there alone for now.

"So he left you." Wilson wiped a bit of cream from the corners of his mouth.

"Not exactly. But that's sure what it feels like."

He stood and tossed the wax papers that had been around the éclairs into the trash. It was nearly nine. Time to open. "That's because that's what it is."

I flipped on a table lamp at the register. "Remind me not to come to you for sympathy."

He began walking toward the front door, keys jangling in his hands. "Oh! Is that what you wanted? You wanted sympathy? Do they sell that here in New York?" The key went into the lock and he turned it.

"Tell me again why Thea hired you?" I called over to him, enjoying the slight grin he'd extracted from me. It had felt good to smile, even for just five seconds.

Wilson began walking back toward me. When he got close, I could smell his favorite pipe tobacco in the fabric of his tropical shirt. The many wrinkles in his seventy-five-year-old face stretched into arcs as he grinned. "I was her paramour, of course."

The phone had rung just then, and he picked up the handset to answer it. A set of customers came in the next moment, and I didn't have the courage to ask him later if he'd been totally kidding.

My mother and I arrived at my shop from the East Village town house, and she double-parked while I dashed inside for the gerbera daisies. A late morning sun was warming the busy street, and cars zipped past her left and right. Someone honked at her as I opened the passenger door and positioned the vase on the floor of her car.

"Don't forget we're celebrating Leslie's birthday next weekend. And get some sleep, for heaven's sake. You don't look well, Jane," she called to me and then added that my sister didn't want any nasty black balloons or milk of magnesia or denture cream for her fortieth birthday. I assured her I'd find something in the shop that Leslie would like and that wouldn't suggest she's an old woman.

"Too bad that clock back at the Village house doesn't work!" my mother yelled as another car honked at her. "She'd love that."

I closed the door and waved her off.

That clock was mine.

Three

Wilson was brewing a fresh pot of coffee at the far counter when I stepped back into the shop after my mother left with the daisies. Stacy was with a customer at the jewelry case, showing a well-dressed woman a glistening pocket watch with a French inscription. I could hear Stacy speaking the beautiful foreign words, and I again thanked heaven I found her. Stacy was the daughter of missionary parents and spoke four languages, including French and Italian. She was a graduate student at New York University and worked for me twenty hours a week. As I joined Wilson in the back, Stacy was telling the woman that the inscription read: "What has never been doubted has never been proven." Wilson, sporting a tweed jacket with his banana yellow Hawaiian shirt, looked like I could ask him anything and he'd either know the answer or could easily assure me it didn't matter.

When I reached him, he nodded toward Stacy and whispered, "Diderot."

"What?"

"The inscription on the watch. That's Diderot. He was an eighteenth-century French philosopher. A radical. You are out of cream." He handed me a cup of coffee. "A strange thing to engrave on a watch."

"Must have been inscribed by a fan of his." I took the cup and brought it to my lips. Wilson's coffee was dense, woody, and dark. Always the perfect antidote to a late-morning slump.

"He probably gave it to himself," he quipped, and we both laughed.

He pointed to a collection of cardboard boxes near the alley entrance, all bearing UK postmarks. "Those came while you were gone."

Emma's latest acquisitions. She'd told me on the phone that morning that they'd probably come today. She also said she hadn't had time to organize the contents. The collection of clothes she had gotten from the same sale was a veritable gold mine, but in deplorable shape, and she hadn't time to tidy my share of the inventory. So I wasn't allowed to give her grief over the condition of the contents. She'd paid two hundred pounds for the lot, and she'd split the cost fifty-fifty.

"Want me to open them for you?" he asked.

I knelt down to look at the customs form slapped to the first box. Emma had marked the form "books, decorative tins, and trinket boxes" and given every item a value of ten pounds each. The boxes were giving off an odor. Mildew.

The odor of regret.

I was never around antiques growing up. My mother didn't like them. Everything in the house I grew up in was contemporary. The moment the décor began to feel dated, Mom reinvented the house. New furniture, new paint, new curtains, new pictures on the walls, always color coordinated and trendsetting. As an interior designer, she was able to rationalize her decorative mood swings to my dad, at least most of the time. There was one time growing up, however, when Dad came home from a long day at the hospital and his favorite chair was gone, replaced by a clunky impostor. He exploded. There were words that night. Lots of them. Leslie and I hunkered down in her bedroom and played Yahtzee while our parents had it out over that chair.

In the end, Mom got her way. I don't know how she did it. Somehow she convinced Dad the new chair was better than the old one. It stayed. For a few years, anyway.

My fascination with old things began the summer I was twelve. I spent ten days in Manhattan with Mom's aunt Thea, at her invitation. She'd had the shop for a few years, opening it after her British husband had died and she'd returned to the States a moderately wealthy woman. She never had any children, and my mother was her only living relative. Thea let me poke around in the back of the store that summer, took me on buying trips, and thoroughly convinced me that every piece in Amsterdam Avenue Antiques had been a part of someone's past—each piece could tell a story or two, if it could talk. That intrigued me—that the odds and ends of a person's past could find their way to a new person's present and everything would begin all over again. I think it pleased her that I had an interest in the things that she cared about. I spent another week with her the following summer.

In high school I took a job working weekends for a couple who owned an antique jewelry store near my parents' home on Long Island. David and Lila Longmont were an odd sort of couple. They didn't seem to get along very well, yet they couldn't stand to be apart from each other. Both of them seemed off balance if the other was away from the store, even if just for a few minutes. David was an expert on antique stones and settings, almost arrogantly so, and Lila, who couldn't say a kind word to David's face, was ferocious in her defense of his expertise to dubious customers. I loved how every piece in their store—every necklace, every brooch, every ring—had been worn by someone. I used to make up stories about the previous owners on slow Saturdays. I imagined that Thea might be doing the same thing.

Much later, when Connor was a baby and I had stopped teaching to be at home with him, the attraction to old things returned. We were living in Connecticut then; Brad was in his residency, and Connor and I spent a lot of time on our own, strolling streets and looking in shop windows. It's impossible to live in New England and not sense a connection to the past. Even my mother feels this connection, though she won't decorate with it. I began buying a few antiques here and there and going to auctions and estate sales, and by the time Connor was in junior high and we were living in Manhattan, I knew more about antiquities than some of the dealers I bought from. But I never imagined I'd go into retail. I always figured I'd go back to teaching when Connor graduated.

About the time Connor realized he could run faster and longer than just about anybody, I began spending my afternoons at cross-country and track meets, cheering for my son, hitting the Record button so that Brad could watch the meets later, and planning my return back to the classroom.

It was my mother's idea that I take over managing the store instead of her when Thea's health began to fail within a week of Connor's leaving for Dartmouth. Not only did my mother quickly have my great-aunt's blessing but also Thea's insistence that if my mother wasn't going to manage the store in her absence, it had to be me.

My mother came to my apartment the day she and Thea decided this, with the shop keys in her hand, effusing joy that the perfect solution for my empty nest had just presented itself, and I alone was Aunt Thea's answer to prayer.

"But I was thinking I'd go back to teaching," I'd said, staring at the keys she had placed in my palm.

"But you love antiques. And for heaven's sake, you haven't been in a classroom in eighteen years. Besides, Aunt Thea needs you."

"I don't know anything about running a business, Mom."

"Thea didn't either when she started. She'll tell you everything. And you'll have Wilson there to help you." She flipped her sunglasses down onto her nose and reached for the front doorknob.

"You're leaving?" She had been there less than ten minutes.

"I'm staging a house in Westchester. I have to go or I'll get stuck in traffic. Talk it over with Brad. It's the perfect solution."

She opened the door and took a step out.

"Perfect solution for what?" I called after her.

My mother turned her head but kept walking. "For you, Jane. For everyone."

Brad had come home tired and overworked that night. I told him over lasagna that I'd been asked by Mom and Thea to take over the management of the antique store.

"Do you want to do it?" he'd said.

"Thea's kind of insistent that it be me."

"But is it something you want to do? I thought you wanted to teach again." He chewed slowly.

"Do you think it's a good idea?" I asked.

He raised another forkful to his mouth. "I guess if it's really what you want to do..."

I realized later that I never asked him if he thought I'd be good at it.

As we cleared the table, I told him I thought it might be good for me to take on a challenge like this one, since Connor was away at college and everything seemed so different at home. He had agreed with me.

Subconsciously, I guess I knew something was different.

Something wasn't quite right.

I watched Brad pack the day he left for New Hampshire.

He'd suggested I take a walk so that I wouldn't be in the apartment while he emptied his closet, but that's not what I did.

As long as I was there, watching him fold his T-shirts and socks, it was like he was just packing for a long trip. It put him on edge, my sitting on his side of the bed, arranging a shirt now and then so that it wouldn't wrinkle. I could tell he didn't know what to make of my wordless assistance.

When he was nearly finished, he pulled his ties off the pegs in his closet. They dangled like long, happy snakes. I had bought nearly every one of them at one time or another. He always said I knew how to pick out a stylish tie.

He folded the lengthy bundle in half and laid it on top of his robe and pajama pants. Brad had closed the lid on the suitcase, and the zipper made a harsh sound as he tugged it closed. He lifted the suitcase and set it next to two others that were already full. A garment bag lay over the top of one of the other suitcases, and next to that, a gym bag full of shoes.

Then he sat down on the bed next to me. "I'll call you after I've talked with Connor."

"Are you sure we shouldn't just tell him together?" I had blushed. It embarrassed me to picture Connor finding out that Brad and I were at odds. I felt childish. Like I was in trouble.

"I think it should be just me," Brad replied. "He needs to know this has nothing to do with him."

The heat on my face had intensified, but with frustration, not shame. "Of course this has to do with him. How can this not have anything to do with him? We're his parents."

"You know what I mean, Jane. I mean this is not his fault."

"So whose fault is it?" I looked up at him. I really wanted to know the answer.

He looked at his suitcases. "I guess it's mine."

We sat there, quiet, for several moments.

I finally broke the silence. "I don't know what I'm supposed to do while I am waiting."

"This is not about waiting," he said slowly. "It's about figuring out where we're headed. And if it's where we want to go."

He stood and grabbed as many bags as he could to take down to the Jeep. I reached down to help him, and he simply said, "No."

I'd sat in silence and watched him struggle with his load through the narrow doorway.

The woman bought the pocket watch emblazoned with Diderot's quote. While Stacy completed the sale, I wrapped the watch in folds of tissue paper. A few feet away, the aroma of Emma's boxes began to permeate the back corner of the shop.

I slipped the watch into a bag, handed it to Stacy, and moved away from the fragrance of age gone wrong.

Four

The shop was empty of customers an hour after our lunch break, and both Stacy and Wilson headed to the back of the shop with me to open Emma's boxes.

I'd met Emma at an antiques show in Boston the previous summer. She was visiting a sister, a woman who'd married an American years before, and she'd come to the show to check out hats and purses for her London costume shop. She was single, though was once married, in her late fifties, and had been involved with London theater since she was five. Emma hadn't acted since she was in her twenties, but she told me she'd always been more captivated with the costume than the role. Emma's shop was a trove of odd and unique accoutrements, and I had the impression the professional stage costumers didn't take her very seriously. But yet they always came to her when they needed an off-color bowler hat or a chartreuse feather boa studded with rhinestones or a size zero flapper dress, because she usually had it. I'd only been to her store once. Last fall Brad let me have his frequent flier miles so that I could visit Emma and discuss our idea that she would seek out inventory for my store and I would do the same for her. I left her place four days after I arrived, confident she and I could help each other out. Over the past ten months, she had found nearly half of my jewelry, trinkets, and book inventory, and every set of antique darts and hat pins I carried. In turn I sent her Las Vegas showgirl headdresses, poodle skirts, and Texas wrangler chaps.

Wilson used a box cutter to slice through the packing tape while Stacy and I flung a sheet of plastic over a heavy oak table I use for acquisitions.

The first box revealed a 1920s era tea set, wrapped in sections of an old blanket—the source of the moldy smell—a pair of heavily tarnished candlesticks, a heart-shaped box filled with delicately embroidered hand-kerchiefs, and an enameled globe of the world depicting when Great Britain still controlled half of it. I asked Wilson to unwrap the tea set and take the blanket pieces outside to the Dumpster at once. He was happy to oblige.

The second box contained two broken vases—perhaps whole when Emma bought them—a lace tablecloth, eight intact Royal Doulton dessert plates covered in dust, a pair of spectacles in a leather case, a fire-place bellows that wouldn't open but that Wilson said he could repair, and several framed photos of men and women in turn-of-the-century outfits. There was also a set of salt cellars and their tiny silver spoons.

As we began to open the last box, the front door jangled, and Stacy rose to assist the customer. The third box was smaller than the other two and heavier. Atop the packing material was a folded note from Emma:

Jane,

I shall try to ring you up before these boxes arrive. I was unable to sort through them and clean anything up. I bought the lot at an outdoor jumble sale in Cardiff that was made miserable by a driving rain. I am not sure of the condition of the books in this box. They look old to me, very old. But they do not appear to have been kept very well. People can be such dolts. Sorry about the mess. You can feel free to owe me three untidy boxes.

Yours affectionately,

Em

Underneath her letter was a tumble of books, all of them smelling of age and neglect. The first one I drew out was a 1902 copy of *David Copperfield* with the title page missing. The next four were in better shape and slightly less aromatic. One was a book of poetry by John Keats, dated 1907. Another, a slim copy of Rudyard Kipling's *Just So Stories,* and still another, Chaucer's *The Canterbury Tales*—the oldest one yet in the box, dated 1756. At the bottom of the box, wrapped in burlap, was a metal lockbox tarnished to a marbled, sooty green. It was no bigger than a toaster, with melted hinges turned gangrenous. It was locked. I shook it gently, and I could hear something moving inside. I reached into a drawer in my work desk where I had a key ring of tiny picks that Thea and Wilson had used to open many an old lock.

I worked at it for several minutes, prying and prodding. When at last the lock sprung free, the corroded hinges clattered to the table in pieces. An audible sigh seemed to escape the box as fresh air crawled inside for the first time in who knows how long. Wilson had rejoined me, and he heard the sigh too. It was as if the box was whispering, "At last…" I lifted the lid and peeked inside. The contents were covered in filaments of straw that disintegrated at my touch.

Inside the folds of a loosely woven bit of fabric was an onyx rosary, a small hand mirror blackened with age, and a book in such decrepit shape, its back cover hung by fibers in several places. I lifted the book from the box and gently opened it, but the pages threatened to fall away from the spine. I gently laid it on the acquisitions table, wishing I had put on a pair of gloves before attempting to pick it up.

"Good Lord. That book must be three or four hundred years old!" Wilson squinted at the script. "Look at the lettering!"

I peered at the first page, but the ink was too faint. I couldn't make out anything other than its title: *Book of Common Prayer.* "You think so?"

"Definitely. This should have been in a museum somewhere, instead of some farmhouse attic," Wilson grumbled. "Where did Emma say she found it?"

"At a jumble sale in Wales."

I touched the edge of the spine that was halfway connected to the back cover and ran my finger along the inside. It felt like finely stretched leather. A bump under the lining caught my attention, and I rubbed my fingertip back over it. The raised portion was about the size of an American nickel, slightly round and lumpy. Whatever it was, I knew it would have to be removed if the book was to be repaired.

"Think you can fix it?" I asked Wilson.

He shrugged. "Maybe a professional could do something with it. They will charge you a pretty penny, though. And no one will likely pay what it's worth with the shape it is in. It's too bad, really." He fingered the rosary. "This is in lovely shape, though. Not as old as the book, I'm sure."

He held up the dangling crucifix. The black beads shimmered under the recessed ceiling lights, practically calling out for hands to touch them in prayer, and I wondered how long it had been since anyone had touched them. I looked at the shiny black stones in Wilson's hands, and I pondered for a moment what it might be like to hold them in my fingers, the tiny form of the obedient Christ dangling from my palm.

Stacy returned to the back of the store. "So what did I miss?"

"This lovely rosary. A hopeless hand mirror. And a very old prayer book that someone should've taken better care of." Wilson laid the rosary next to the tattered *Book of Common Prayer.*

"Wow," Stacy rubbed a finger over the rosary's beads. Then she leaned over the book, gently turned a page, and her eyes widened. "This thing is ancient. And it's a Protestant volume. Look. It was printed by the Church of England. And omigosh, did you see this date?"

Wilson and I leaned in, but the ink was too faint for me. Stacy's young eyes were bright. "Sixteen sixty-two! It's, like, three hundred and fifty years old!"

I'd never owned anything as old as this. Never.

"A Catholic rosary placed in a box with a Protestant book of prayer." Wilson laughed.

Stacy bent over the book again, and I saw her notice the lump in the spine. "What is that?"

"I don't know," I answered. "Maybe the remains of an insect or something. I'm sure it's the reason the spine has started to separate. We're going to have to find a way to get it out. I won't be able to reattach the spine as long as that bump is there."

"Are you going to try and fix it yourself?"

"Wilson said it would cost a mint to get it fixed professionally."

Stacy nodded. "Might be worth it, though. You could probably sell it to a collector for some good money."

Something about the book was comforting to me—like the clock that didn't tick—and the thought of selling it and the rosary made me frown.

"What?" Stacy noticed.

"I don't know. I just... I might hang on to these for a while."

Stacy smiled. "They are kind of cool, actually. Like little pieces of God from hundreds of years back. You know, when we didn't even exist and he was who he's always been."

She walked over to the tea set that Wilson unpacked. Ivory china edged in gold filigree and decorated with lavender asters. "These dishes are cool." Her spoken thoughts on the Divine had been a mere stepping stone to a comment about dishes.

Most of the time I could forget Stacy was the daughter of missionary parents. Then there were moments, like that one, where I would almost hear a swishing sound as I brushed up against her confident faith.

I reached for the rosary and the prayer book and placed them gently back in the ancient box that they came in.

Instinctively I set them by my purse to take home with me; the little pieces of God that seemed to resonate with my little broken world.

Five

I heard from Brad a few times after he left. He called after he broke the news to Connor, and again, two weeks later, when he phoned to make sure I had enough money to cover the bills. He made one trip back to Manhattan to pick up the canoe he had in storage and the panini sandwich grill, but he came while I was at an auction in Newark. He left a note on the breakfast bar saying he hoped I didn't mind him taking the sandwich maker and that he was sorry he missed me.

Sorry he missed me.

Each of those tender intrusions—the two calls, the note—left me wavering on the edge of hope and doubt when I crept into bed at night. Brad's voice and his handwriting, so familiar to me and so absent now from my day-to-day life, kneaded my thoughts like a masseur pressing against taut muscles. Sleep never came on those nights.

His first phone call came on the heels of his conversation with Connor, the same day he left. He told me he and Connor had met at the Ben & Jerry's near the Dartmouth campus. While eating ice cream, he told Connor he was trying out a new a job at a hospital in New Hampshire. And taking a little break from Manhattan.

I had paced the quiet apartment during the hour I knew he was meeting with Connor. I thought of the things Brad had said to me when he told me he was leaving. I wondered which of any of those things he was telling Connor.

That Brad and I needed some time away from each other to think.

Time to ponder.

Time to review.

Time to decide.

Brad had been insistent that this time away from each other wasn't about waiting. But time is often about waiting.

I'd thought perhaps Connor would call me after Brad left him. Surely he had questions. Was he mad? sad? confused? Was Connor disappointed in us? How much time did he need before I should talk to him?

Connor didn't call until nearly ten that night. There had been a queer, disapproving tenor to his voice, the kind of tone a cop uses when aiding a stranded driver who should've known better than to slam on the brakes when driving on ice. I told him I was going to be okay. Everything would be fine in the end. Dad needed to check out the New Hampshire job alone for a lot of little reasons, none that he needed to worry about. We didn't talk long. He clearly didn't have a clue as to how to process the situation. And that actually made me feel somewhat vindicated. Connor hadn't seen it coming either.

I had left the shop a few minutes before six. It was Stacy's night to close. I had just kicked off my shoes in my apartment and was sorting through the mail when my cell phone trilled. It was Molly inviting me over for dinner; Jeff was at a Yankees game, and it was just her and the girls. I declined, but she kept after me until I finally said yes. She didn't like me eating alone every night.

We hung up, and I changed into jeans and a sweater. Coming back through the kitchen, I sifted through the contents of the bag that I took to the store every day, looking for a tube of lipstick. My fingers brushed up against the flannel-wrapped package that contained the prayer book and the rosary. I gently removed them and placed them in the center of the table. I stared at them as I painted my lips a plummy red. Then I grabbed a bottle of wine and began to walk the seven blocks to Molly and Jeff's apartment.

I'd known Molly since my freshman year at Boston University. Her older brother, Tom, knew Brad before I did, and it was at a birthday party for Tom that I met Brad. Molly had often said if it wasn't for her, I would never have met the man I married.

She hadn't offered any advice on my dilemma, other than to reassure me that women aren't mind readers. I told her I felt foolish for not picking up on Brad's signals that he was unhappy.

"What signals?" she had said.

What signals indeed?

Molly and Jeff had moved to Manhattan before Brad and I did, coming here as newlyweds a few years after Brad and I got married. Jeff was an investment broker, a loyal fan of the Yankees, and had a hard time talking about anything other than stocks and baseball. Molly was the principal at the private school her twin twelve-year-old daughters attended and where Connor had graduated two years before.

Brad and Jeff were, I suppose, as close as two men could be with few interests in common. Brad enjoyed reading biographies and preferred the water—sailing, canoeing, fishing—to any televised sport. Brad and Jeff weren't close, but they'd spent time together; they'd talked. I hadn't, to that point, asked Jeff if he knew how frustrated Brad was with our marriage. And I was glad he was going to be at a baseball game because of that. I was somewhat afraid Jeff had known Brad was leaving me before I did.

Twilight was turning Seventy-eighth Street into an amber palette of shining colors. The evening commute was still in full swing as I stepped into the swell of pedestrians—some in suits, some in denim—as they made their way out of the heart of downtown to quieter streets and boroughs.

Brad didn't find any poetic charm in the human sea that is the streets of Manhattan. Embracing the persistent press of people was one of the concessions he made when we moved to Manhattan the year Connor turned thirteen. As I walked, brushing up against the elite and the ordinary, it occurred to me that the year Connor turned thirteen was the last time Brad made a decision that changed everything for us. The extended hours at Memorial and the hourlong—sometimes longer—commute home to Long Island had been keeping Brad away from Connor and me for too many hours of the day. Brad decided to move to the Upper West Side without even tossing the idea around with me. He wanted to be home more, and I wanted the same thing. It was easy for me to rationalize that he'd made that decision for me and Connor.

As I rounded the corner to Molly and Jeff's apartment building, I couldn't help but wonder if Brad had been feeling a disconnect with me, even then. And had made a rather impulsive move to reverse it.

I didn't mind the move to Manhattan; in fact, I was excited about it—more so than Brad. But it felt strange to tell my parents that Brad and I had decided to relocate to Manhattan, when I hadn't decided anything at all. My parents pressed me for reasons, and I listed them all as if the move had been my idea.

They had, of course, heartily praised Brad for wanting to spend more time with his family, even though the move meant we wouldn't be living fifteen minutes away from them anymore.

My parents had been charmed with Brad since the moment I brought him home to meet them, practically congratulating me for falling for a medical student who would one day be able to provide for me in ways my parents could not. My dad envied the doctors he shared the hallways with at Long Island General. He and they both worked long hours and wore beepers on their belts and had the same pale yellow name tags. They both were called away from warm beds at 2 a.m., from Christmas dinners, and into driving snowstorms to respond to emergencies. But the doctors scurried to save lives, and my dad to respond to a stalled ventilation system or leaking water tank. Dad didn't draw the same respect or paycheck as his co-workers in scrubs and white coats.

As an up-and-coming doctor of radiology, Brad was like a white-horsed knight to my parents. He was all that my father wished he had been and all that my mother wished for him.

I had dated only a few guys before Brad, including my high school sweetheart, Kyle, an easygoing soul whose aspirations to build houses in third world countries utterly failed to impress my parents. They nearly threw a party when Kyle and I reluctantly agreed to see other people after high school graduation, since I was moving to Massachusetts and he to Virginia.

I really wasn't looking to begin a relationship when I met Brad a year later. I was still getting occasional letters from Kyle, who had finished a vo-tech course on carpentry and was working with a relief organization in Kenya.

Brad was so unlike Kyle in so many ways, it's odd that I'd been attracted to both. Kyle thrived on adventure; Brad appreciated steadiness and dependability. Kyle liked surprises; Brad liked knowing details up front. Kyle was unpredictable; Brad was constant, reliable. One man made me feel like I was on the edge of the unknown; the other made me feel secure. In the end, I chose security.

I wondered, up until the day I married Brad, if that's what true romantic love was like—not the pulse-quickening, dopey-eyed fascination I'd had for Kyle, but this deeper, steadier attraction for Brad that had more to do with what I knew than what I felt.

The night of my bridal shower, I confided in Leslie that I was struggling to let go of the last traces of attraction to Kyle, even though I hadn't seen him in two years, and that I had moments when I wondered if I was making a mistake. She asked me, without even looking up from the punch she was mixing, if I could imagine myself happy in a hut in the African wilderness, peeing behind bushes, running from poisonous snakes, and sleeping under a mosquito net. I started to laugh.

"I'm serious." She was laughing too, but then she looked up from the punch bowl. "I'm serious, Jane. That's what your life would be like."

Leslie had reminded me of that conversation at our parents' fiftieth a year ago, when again she was making punch and teasing me for once wishing I had married Kyle instead of Brad and how I'd be chasing centipedes on my earthen floor with a switch if I had married Kyle.

I'd looked over at my parents, standing close as a photographer snapped their picture. I told Leslie that Mom would've swept centipedes for Dad. She laughed and said, "No, she would not." But she looked up at them too, and her laughter ebbed.

Mom would've found a way to lay down tile in her third world hut.

Molly called a taxi for me after we and her girls polished off several little white boxes of Chinese takeout and watched a couple of reruns of *Friends*. As we waited at the curb outside her building for my ride home, she asked me how much sleep I was getting.

"I don't know."

"Jane, honey, you look exhausted."

I shrugged a wordless reply.

Molly's voice took on a near-maternal tone. "It's been over two months. Don't you think maybe it's time to go see somebody? You can't continue to operate on three or four hours of sleep a night."

I stiffened a bit. "I don't want to take sleeping pills."

"I didn't say start taking pills, I said go see somebody. Somebody who can help you sort this out so you can sleep at night."

Sort this out. Sort *me* out.

"You mean a psychiatrist."

"No, I mean a counselor. You're not crazy, Jane. You're hurting. You're afraid. You're lonely. You're frustrated. You're unsure."

"Thanks a lot."

She ignored my relaxed sarcasm. "That's a lot for one person to deal with. It's no wonder you're not sleeping well. You need to talk this over with somebody. A professional."

My unspoken wish floated in between her words and my silence. I just wanted to wait it out, not sort it out. Some people hate waiting. I wasn't one of those people.

Molly filled the sound void. "There's a guy here in my building who's a psychologist. A counselor."

I turned from her words. They smarted.

"Not a psychiatrist, Jane. A *counselor.* I ride the elevator with him all the time. He seems really wise and balanced. He's got a good sense of humor. And he does this for a living, Janie."

She pulled a business card out of her front pants pocket and handed it to me. Jonah Kirtland, PhD. Licensed Counselor. She was prepared.

"You always walk around with his business card in your pocket?"

"You're my best friend. I asked for it in the elevator this morning. I told him I was going to give it to you."

I touched the letters of his name. "Jonah. Like the whale."

"No. Jonah, like the guy who got swallowed by a whale. And then got out of it."

The wide stripe of easy cornflower blue above Jonah Kirtland's name was soothing. The font below it was soothing too. Capitals that didn't shout; not an easy artistic element to pull off.

"You told him my name?"

Molly exhaled quietly. "Yes."

"Did you tell him anything else?"

"I told him you're going through a really tough time. That you're not sleeping at night."

I rubbed my finger across the slick corner of the card. "And I suppose you told him why."

Another exhale. This one a little louder. "Yes, I did. I told him your husband moved out and you hadn't seen it coming. I am sorry if you rather I hadn't done that. But I did. He told me he'd be happy to work you into his schedule."

I slipped the card into my pocket, my cheeks warm from the reminder of my naiveté; that I hadn't seen it coming.

"You mad at me?" Molly asked.

"No."

"Will you call him?" she asked.

I nodded.

"Promise?"

I nodded a second time.

Molly smiled and the relief on her face was obvious. "Good." A tiny crease formed above her eyes. "Just one thing. He's...," but she didn't finish.

"He's what?"

A yellow cab pulled up to the curb.

She shook her head and the crease disappeared. "Never mind. I think you're doing the right thing. The smart thing."

"I suppose. Thanks for dinner." I hugged her good-bye and got into the cab.

"Call me and let me know what happens, all right?" she called out as I closed the car door. I waved good-bye.

❖❖❖

I'd forgotten to leave a light on, so the apartment was dark and cheerless when I unlocked the door. I made a cup of tea and sat down at the kitchen table. I slid into Brad's chair without even thinking about it and placed Jonah Kirtland's card against a vase of straw flowers at the center of the table. I had never been to a psychologist before. Contemplating making an appointment with one prickled me with tiny doubts. Was this really the only way to get a good night's sleep while I adjusted to marriage limbo? Was I going to have to spill every secret of my soul to this person to get it? Maybe pills would be easier...

In front of me, the ancient prayer book and rosary rested next to the vase where I left them. I reached for the beads and rubbed the smooth stones. They felt like they held a million secrets and wishes. My fingers slid down to the tiny silver form of Christ, stretched and bowed.

"What am I supposed to do?" I whispered half to myself and half to the quiet Savior.

Brad had said we needed time to figure out where our marriage was headed. In the eight weeks Brad had been gone, my only observation was it wasn't headed anywhere. There was no momentum to evaluate. I was in Manhattan. He was in New Hampshire.

"What am I supposed to do?" I whispered again, and I felt hot tears forming in the corners of my eyes. I blinked them back. With my other hand, I reached for the prayer book and let it fall open. The faint but legible words in the middle of the book called to me: *Lighten our darkness, we beseech thee, O Lord; and by thy great mercy, defend us from all Perils and dangers of this night; for the love of thy only Son, our Saviour, Jesus Christ. Amen.* I pulled the text closer. The knobby bump underneath the lining and beneath my fingers was suddenly an annoying interruption. Without stopping to consider the consequences, I grabbed a letter opener from the breakfast bar next to me and slid its point under the top edge of the fragile leather lining. I was amazed at how easily it came away—as if it had been waiting for that moment for centuries.

I slipped the blade gently inside and probed the knobby bump, turning the book upside down.

Threads that had at one time been woven together fell out like confetti. And then a circle with a flash of blue landed on the table with a tender tinkling.

A ring.

I set the book and the opener down and reached for it. The band, though dulled with age, was gold. The single blue stone in the middle was flanked on both sides by two red stones and clusters of tiny white ones. I didn't know a lot about gemstones, but I was fairly certain the stones were a sapphire, rubies, and diamonds. In the light of the single bulb glowing above the table, I could see the stones' brilliance, even with the fog of deep sleep that still seemed to cling to them.

I turned the ring over in my hands, breathless with surprise and curiosity. Emma surely had no idea this ring had been encased inside the box with melted hinges and no key. The previous owner probably hadn't known either.

As I turned the ring, I noticed tiny etchings on the band's underside. The markings were too small and faint to make out. I hunted for a magnifying glass in my desk just off the kitchen. It seemed to take far too long to find it.

When I did, I flipped on my desk lamp and leaned in to peer through the lens. My eyes struggled to focus on the tiny script, and when I finally made out the words, I whispered them. *Vulnerasti cor meum, soror mea, sponsa.* They meant nothing to me.

But then I could see that something else had been inscribed just after the Latin words. I centered the glass on the other set of etched letters.

My breath caught in my throat. This word I knew.

Jane.

Lucy

Six

J ane waited for me at the window, her wee head bowed as if something lay beyond the glass that she could not bear to look upon. Her small hands rested on the sill, folded one over the other in the relaxed pose of someone who has no appointment to keep. Beneath her line of vision, I could see the sweeping lawn at Sudeley Castle and the tracks in the dirt my carriage made. A faint swirl of dust caught up against a bit of black as the carriage disappeared from our view, on its way back to Bradgate.

I should have made my presence known, but I stood at the threshold as one struck dumb. The little lady was lost in sadness, this I could see even from the doorway where I stood, and this was foreign to me. In the two years that I had been in the employ of the wealthy, I had not seen such raw sorrow. In my arms I held a garment soft as down and black as pitch. The lady's mourning gown, which the marchioness insisted I carry on my lap the entire two-day journey from Leicestershire so that her daughter's dress wouldn't be crushed in the trunk. The marchioness did not tell me this directly; Bridget relayed the marchioness's demands, and it was plain in her eyes and in her tone that it would be foolishness to let the dress out of my sight for even a moment. The little lady was to be chief mourner at the funeral of the Queen Dowager, Katherine. The gown couldn't be anything less than perfectly appointed.

Already I could see that the dress would have to be altered to fit the wee maiden. And I instantly wondered if I had the skill to do it. Bridget must've thought I did. She would not have sent me if she did not.

I was amazed the marchioness believed the gown would fit her daughter. Lady Jane must not have grown much in the months she had been living with Lord Admiral Seymour and the widow Queen here in Gloucestershire, at least not as much as her mother expected.

Or perhaps in her haste, the marchioness selected the wrong dress to be brought. Bridget had wondered if perhaps the marchioness borrowed the dress because there hadn't been time to make a new one. No one expected the poor Queen Dowager would succumb to childbed fever. No one expected the household of Sudeley Castle would be wearing black that day. Not black. Somewhere in the castle, the Queen's healthy newborn daughter lay in the arms of a wet nurse. Bridget told me not to ask about her.

I took a step into the room, cautiously, and the dress in my arms swished my name. *Lucy.* The Lady Jane at the window did not turn her head toward the sound. I poked my head farther into the room, letting my eyes adjust to the vastness of the room's size and the absence of the warming rays of the sun.

Lady Jane and I were alone in her sitting room at Sudeley Castle, a great home whose exterior stones were the color of toasted bread and which were festooned with emerald vines that would soon turn copper, crumple, and skitter away. The maid who escorted me to this room had left to see after the trunk the marchioness had me bring for her daughter, as well as my own small case. I was not accustomed to stepping into a room where the only other occupant was of nobility. I hesitated.

I had asked Bridget, as I prepared to leave, how long the Lady Jane had been away from her parents, since she was already gone from Bradgate when Bridget made me her apprentice. In truth I wanted to know *why* the Lady Jane was living away from Bradgate. Lady Jane had eleven years, naught but a year older than my sister, Cecily, who at that moment was at our Haversfield home in Devonshire, surely combing wool one moment and chasing butterflies the next. I did not think the Lady Jane had chased a butterfly in many years. Perhaps never. I had only been in the employ of one other nobleman, and his children remained at home until they married. They had not chased butterflies either. But they were not whisked away to other households. Bridget told me that it was no concern of mine why the Lady Jane left Bradgate to become the ward of Lord Admiral Seymour.

Then Bridget told me a nobleman like our esteemed Marquess of Dorset—the lady's father and my employer—has much to consider when God gives him daughters, and that I was not to be listening to gossip below stairs while at Sudeley or she would hear of it and have me dismissed. She very nearly winked at me.

So it was because the Lady Jane was a girl that she was sent to live with Lord Seymour. It was because she was a daughter whose betrothal was a matter of politics and posturing that she lived in a castle more than a day's carriage ride from her home.

On the long journey here, I'd wondered how the Lord Admiral figured into the marquess's betrothal plans for his eldest daughter. The Lord Admiral was himself already married when Jane came here, having wooed and won the widowed Queen Katherine four scandalous months after King Henry's passing. And the Lord Admiral had no sons. I didn't know the Lord Admiral personally. I only knew that he was brother to the Lord Protector, the man who managed the affairs of the young King Edward, Henry's only living male heir.

Bridget had supposed it was for marital prospects that the marquess placed his daughter in the household of the lord whose brother directed our sovereign's associations. Young King Edward was nearly eleven, like Jane, and not yet betrothed. Also like Jane.

It would not be the first time a monarch married a cousin. And Bridget told me the Lady Jane was fourth in line to the throne, in her own right. The marchioness, her mother, was King Henry's niece.

But as the carriage had rolled along, I endeavored to imagine myself eleven years old—not so hard, as I was not much older at fifteen—shuffled about in clandestine marriage campaigns, handed over to a man I perhaps did not esteem and made to share his bed and bear his children, all for the prosperity of the young male heir that I simply must produce.

I'd fingered the delicate beading in the mounds of black organza and silk in my lap and wondered what it must be like to wear a dress so heavy, bejeweled, and bedecked, and which, if sold, could feed a family in a croft for nigh a whole winter. Could have paid for my father's medicine. Could have paid the doctor who cared for him, while my mother and I did what we could—she at my father's tailoring shop and I at the marquess's household—to keep him well. I had once thought I would sew happily alongside my father until the end of his days, perhaps marrying late, if I married at all. But there I was, many miles from my childhood home in Haversfield, my parents, and what I had thought would define my quiet life. Everything that mattered to me waited for me in another place.

And now that I stood gazing at the young maiden who would wear the dress I'd carried—a wisp of a girl whose melancholy filled the cavernous room—the gown weighed like lead in my arms, holding me fast.

I took another step, and at last she turned her head.

She had her father's eyes and her mother's Tudor bearing. Her hair under her hood was brown like mine, unremarkable like mine. The dress she wore was the deepest green, very nearly black. Whispers of white lace peeked out from the sleeves and neckline. A gold sash at her waist glittered in the only spill of sunlight penetrating the dark stillness of the room. At her throat lay a necklace of pearls and tiny emeralds. Her cheeks were wet.

I fell to a curtsy.

"Beg your pardon, my lady. Shall I come back later?"

She didn't answer, and I slowly raised my head.

The Lady Jane was looking at the folds of fabric in my arms. Staring at them. Willing the dress, it seemed, to fill itself with bones and muscle and walk out of the room to find some other person to trifle with.

"You came from Bradgate?" she finally said. Her voice was thin and smooth. Cultured. But immature.

"Yes, my lady."

"Did my mother send that gown?" Her eyes were still on the dress. The room was not so dark that I could not see her unease.

"Yes, my lady."

"She is not coming."

It was not a question. But I answered as though it was. "No, my lady."

She turned back then, back toward the window. She hadn't dismissed me, so I stood there with the yards of fabric wanting to spill out of my arms like buckets of water and waited for her. Her head was cocked in a childlike way, as if she was wondering when she would wake up from this dream.

It was inconceivable to me that one so young should be the chief mourner at the funeral of the Queen Dowager, King Henry's widow. Bridget told me protocol forbade the presence of the widowed Queen's new husband, the Lord Admiral Seymour, at the funeral. King Henry's younger daughter, the Princess Elizabeth, who had lately lived here at Sudeley and who had left amid troubling rumors, would not be in attendance either, nor would the young King Edward, nor the Princess Mary, King Henry's eldest daughter.

Instead, an eleven-year-old girl would lead the procession to the chapel, wearing the borrowed gown I held in my arms.

From behind us, deep within the castle, I heard the faint sound of an infant's wail. A faraway door opened and closed, and the sound disappeared. Jane raised her head, and her gaze traveled past me to the hallway and the other rooms.

"There will be no one to love her," Jane whispered.

"My lady?"

"The Queen's child."

"Beg your pardon, my lady?"

"Lord Thomas won't even look at her."

"L-Lord T-Thomas?" I stammered.

"Lord Admiral Seymour. He won't even look at the babe."

I repositioned the dress in my arms. I could not tell for whom she grieved. A moment earlier, I thought her sadness was due to missing her home and family. Then, no, it was the unnamed baby. And now, was it the Lord Admiral's sorrow that clutched at her heart?

I said nothing else. I didn't know what to say.

"You need for me to try on that dress?" she said languidly.

"Yes, my lady. I am afraid I do."

"Why didn't Bridget come? I do not know you."

I did not tell her Bridget was losing her eyesight and couldn't travel alone as the dressmaker. Bridget needed to stay at Bradgate where she could blend in with the rest of the wardrobe staff. No one but me knew she struggled to see her own stitches.

"I am new to Bradgate, my lady. Bridget sent me. And the marchioness."

"What is your name?" Her young voice rang with subtle authority.

"Lucy Day, my lady."

"I like that name." But her voice was sad.

"Shall we?" I hefted the dress in my arms.

She nodded, turned, and we headed to her wardrobe room, which adjoined her sitting room.

I helped her remove the green dress she wore. As I began to lift the black dress—so she could step into its skirt—Jane, with the folds of the black dress now all around her, began to tremble. I held the dress open and waited. Her eyes misted over and her trembling increased, and she stepped away from the ballooning fabric.

"My lady?" I said.

"I cannot stain it!" she gasped, savagely wiping away tears lest they should fall onto the material.

She grasped at her heaving chest, flat and narrow underneath her chemise, as grief silently pounded its way out of her. She sank to her knees as a sob erupted from deep within.

I dropped the dress I had carried on my lap for one hundred miles and knelt down by her, sisterly instinct sending me there before I could think clearly. Jane leaned into me, and I nervously slipped an arm around her and patted her shoulder, vaguely aware that if anyone came into the room, I would surely be dismissed for not knowing my place.

Her tears and anguish were innocent and raw.

"I miss her," she whispered.

"Your mother?" I whispered back. Lady Jane shook her head.

The child grieved for the Queen.

Seven

The seams lay open on the curved bodice as I slid the whittled whale-bone stays back into their tiny pockets. Lady Jane's nurse, Mrs. Ellen, stood over me, sipping a tisane as I worked to resize the black mourning dress to fit a girlish bosom.

Her presence made me uneasy.

She had come into the room earlier as I assisted Lady Jane to her feet, after my lady's tears had all been spilled. When she saw us, Mrs. Ellen rushed, aghast, to the lady's side as if I'd poisoned her.

"What have you done?" Mrs. Ellen had exclaimed, wrenching the girl from me.

Before I could answer, Jane spoke. "She has done nothing except show kindness to me. Leave her be."

Mrs. Ellen, so I'd heard, had been my lady's nurse since the day Jane was born and was quite protective of her. She proceeded to fuss about us as I took the lady's measurements, unnerved, I think, that I had been the one to witness my lady's outpouring of grief and not her. She kept asking my lady if she was quite well, and Lady Jane finally asked her to fetch her a bit of syllabub from last night's supper.

"She worries over me," Jane said as Mrs. Ellen left to find a maid to send to the kitchen.

I bunched the skirt at her waist and nodded.

"She knows I dread going back." Jane's gaze sought the doorway where Mrs. Ellen had left us, and she seemed to be speaking to no one. But then she turned to look at me, and I knew I had been spoken to. She waited for me to comment.

"Back, my lady?" I said.

"To Bradgate." Jane said the name of her home with equal parts longing and dismay.

"You…you don't like Bradgate?"

She'd sighed quietly. "I love Bradgate."

I made a mark on the skirt where I would need to take it in and waited. I didn't know what to say to her.

"But I was happy here with the Queen. She was happy too. Even with everything…everything that had happened." Jane stopped for a moment as if she had said too much. Then she went on. "The Queen loved the Lord Admiral, and she loved this child…and she even loved me. At Bradgate it is…different."

She tipped her head and looked at me. "How long have you been at Bradgate?"

"Since the new year, my lady."

"And where were you before then?"

"In London. At Whitehall."

She seemed then to work out an equation in her head, measuring the odds of my understanding what it was like to live as a child of privileged birth inside your parents' home. And outside it. It occurred to me we were not talking about the home itself but the expectations within its walls. I do not know if she arrived at a satisfying conclusion. Mrs. Ellen stepped back into the room, and Lady Jane fell silent.

"Are you still at it, lass?" Mrs. Ellen had frowned at me, clearly disappointed that Jane still stood, dwarfed by yards of fabric, while I tucked and pinned. "Could not Bridget have come?"

I straightened and then whispered to my lady that I would help her out of the gown. "Miss Bridget felt constrained to manage the rest of the wardrobe staff at Bradgate," I said as I helped Lady Jane step out of the skirt. Mrs. Ellen had said nothing, so I curtsied and left the room with the dress before she could ask me anything else.

Now, an hour later, Mrs. Ellen had come to the wardrobe room to inspect my progress.

I slipped the last bone into place and began to thread the needle to sew the seam shut.

"Have you news of Bradgate?" she finally asked me.

Not knowing Mrs. Ellen, I did not know if she was asking for below-stairs gossip, of which there was surely plenty. Since I worked above stairs, Bridget had endeavored as best she could to shield me from it, lest I spill something unpleasant in front of the marchioness or Jane's little sisters. But there is always whispering on the stairs. Those of us who work above stairs pretend we do not hear it. Those below stairs know we do.

I responded that the marquess and marchioness were very well and had been entertaining hunting guests.

She set her cup down. "Who were the guests?"

I poked my finger with the needle as I tried to remember who had been guests of late. There had been several. They had had no wardrobe needs that I was charged with meeting. Bridget had seen to those. Mrs. Ellen cocked her head, waiting.

"The Lord and Lady Darlington were guests the week before last. And...and a nobleman from Leeds. His name escapes me now." Mrs. Ellen looked down at her cup, bored.

And then I remembered.

"Oh. And the young Edward Seymour, the Lord Protector's son, and his mother were there."

She raised her eyes to me at this and set her cup down. "The Lord Protector's son? Are you quite sure?"

"Yes, madam."

"He and his mother were hunting-party guests?" Mrs. Ellen frowned.

"I believe so, yes."

It was clear she wished to ask me what conversations I had been privy to, but she could not. She did not know me yet either.

I did not tell her that talk in the kitchen on the days that the Seymours were at Bradgate revolved around the Lord Admiral's and the Lord Protector's insane sibling rivalry and that since the admiral had not been able to advance the Lady Jane's prospects, her father, the marquess, was entertaining the notion of a marriage between Jane and young Edward Seymour. The admiral's nephew.

The jealousy between the two Seymour brothers was legendary. Mrs. Ellen already knew this. We all did. And she guessed young Edward Seymour's reason for being at Bradgate without my even hinting at what I'd heard below stairs.

"Poor Jane," she whispered, but I heard it. I'd observed the young Edward Seymour as a guest at Bradgate. He was polite to the staff, gracious to the marquess and marchioness, and respectful of his mother. He seemed a gentleman. I chanced a question to let Mrs. Ellen know she could speak freely if she wished.

"Is Edward Seymour not a kindly young man?" I dared not to look up from my stitches.

Mrs. Ellen did not answer, and I raised my eyes to see if she was forming a reprimand for my boldness. I saw not anger there, but disquiet, as if she could already see that we were to be paired, she and I, intertwined with the life of the young Lady Jane as her destiny was decided—and that neither one of us would be able to do anything to hold back its progress.

"He is a fine young man." Her answer was slow and measured, inviting me into our partnership, albeit begrudgingly. "But you and I both know that is seldom a consideration of betrothal for young women of royal blood."

She waited for me to nod my head, to acquiesce that I knew whomever Lady Jane married, it was no concern of mine or hers, or even Jane's, for that matter.

"Yes." I held her gaze a moment and then fell back to my stitching.

She stood there a moment longer, and then I heard her turn and leave the wardrobe room. I raised my head just as her skirt swished out the door.

I looked at the curved bodice before me, thinking of the tiny bosom that would fill it and wondering what Jane thought of her father's strategies to first have her wed to the King and now possibly the son of the King's Protector. Did she even know of these campaigns? Bridget told me the Lady Jane was all the time reading, writing, and translating texts. Her tutors were brilliant men. The young lady could speak five languages. She was intuitive and clever. Surely she knew.

My thoughts naturally flew to my sister, Cecily, the same age as Jane, whose marital prospects were of no consequence to anyone.

Like my own.

Eight

My mother, a dressmaker also—and a fine one—told me once that black is the color that whispers. Crimson shouts, yellow laughs, blue and green sing, white heralds, and violet woos. But black is always hushed, and at times silent. I asked her what does black whisper, and she told me when you are victorious, it whispers applause, and when you are grieved, it whispers condolences. What if you are neither? I asked. And she said that is when you wear a different color.

When the alterations were finished on my lady's mourning dress, I hefted it into my arms to hang the wrinkles out. And as I did so, I knew my mother was right. The dress whispered to me, "She weeps, she weeps, she weeps."

It was nigh unto sunset when I laid the needles down, and I was alone in the wardrobe room. I made my way down the servants' stairs to the kitchens to see if supper was still being served to the household staff. The staff dining room was nearly empty. A few were finishing their meals, but my entrance was barely acknowledged. The Queen Dowager had been loved in this house. A cloak of sadness hung even in here, a room she likely hadn't ever set foot in.

I sat down next to a girl about my age, whom I'd seen earlier in the wardrobe room repairing a pair of men's breeches. An older woman, who had also been in the wardrobe working on a length of black velvet, now sat on her other side, and she scowled at me as I sat down. They had left

the wardrobe long before me. Mrs. Ellen had called the scowling woman
Alice. Another woman sat a few chairs away, her head resting in an up-
turned palm. She looked tired. A bowl of broth and a plate of joint and
potatoes were set before me.

Presently, Miss Alice stood and clucked her tongue. "Finish up then,
Nan!" she growled at the younger girl. "The admiral wishes to be off."

The girl named Nan took a tiny bite of potato. "Yes, madam."

Alice moved away from us, and Nan watched her leave, chewing
slowly.

She turned to me. "I'm Nan Hargrave."

"My name's Lucy Day."

Nan tipped her head toward the doorway that Alice had disappeared
into. "Miss Alice can't decide if she is vexed or relieved you were sent for.
She doesn't like outside dressmakers using her needles and threads. But she
wouldn't have been able to come up with a dress for Lady Jane on such
short notice. And she knows it. Pay her no heed."

"You been at Sudeley long?" I asked.

"I've been with the Seymours since I was twelve, but they only spend
the summer months here in Gloucestershire. The admiral prefers Chelsea.
He likes to be near court, if you know what I mean."

"Since you were twelve?"

"First with his mother, Lady Margery, then with the admiral. My
father was the admiral's primary tailor. Papa died two years ago. The admiral kept me on, though. He likes my even stitches. Better than a man's,
he says."

The woman near us raised her head from its resting place in her palm
and stared at Nan. One eyebrow arched upward like the back of a startled cat. Nan disregarded her.

"How long have you been at Bradgate?" Nan asked me.

"Just since January."

"Ah. So you'd not met Lady Jane before today. She's a sweet thing. Quiet. So different than the Princess Elizabeth, as I am sure you know. They were all together at Chelsea earlier this year. Those two are like night and day."

I knew she meant Elizabeth, the unfortunate Anne Boleyn's daughter. I nodded. The woman in the other chair cleared her throat, and again Nan ignored her.

"I rather miss having the Princess's dresses to attend to," Nan mused.

"Didn't the Princess have her own seamstress?" I asked.

"She had several. But she was always tearing and ripping her clothes on one thing or another." Nan smiled at me as if she was letting me in on a secret. "I sewed more than one ripped seam on her chemises," she continued, but in a voice not much more than a whisper.

The woman across from us pushed her plate away and stood. "If I were leaving tonight, I'd be finishing up my meal and packing my things." This, she said to Nan.

Nan turned to look at the woman, but she said nothing. After an uncomfortable moment of silence, the woman turned and left. We were now alone in the room.

Nan turned back toward me. "That one has the unpleasant task of looking after the nursery. I hear the Queen's babe cries for hours at night, and the wet nurse can't soothe her. 'Tis no wonder the woman is ill-tempered."

"What…what will happen to the babe?"

Nan shrugged. "The admiral won't care for it, you can be sure of that. She'll be sent to distant family, no doubt. He wanted a boy, you know."

"So…you are leaving tonight?" I was unsure which topic of conversation to attempt to continue.

"Aye. The admiral cannot be here for the Queen Dowager's funeral.

Even though he was married to her. She was King Henry's *widow*, after all. It would be unseemly, or so I have heard. As if all had been proper until now."

Nan seemed to be waiting for me to press her for more information. I wiped my chin. "So you are going back to Chelsea?"

"Well, of course. Although," and she leaned in, though there was now no one else in the room, "I am sure the admiral will send for Jane straightaway."

"But Jane told me she is to go home to Bradgate."

"Yes, but that does not mean the admiral has not asked that she be allowed to continue on as his ward. Or maybe as something else…"

She cocked her head as if waiting for me to finish her sentence. I honestly did not know what she was suggesting.

"Something else?"

"His wife, of course!"

I gasped. "Surely you are mistaken. Lady Jane is but eleven years."

Nan nodded. "Aye, but the Lord Admiral has already approached Princess Elizabeth, and she is but my age. Fifteen! She would not have him, by the way."

My spoon hung suspended in air. "The admiral has approached Princess Elizabeth? Already?"

"She had to leave us because he fancied her. Did you know that? Even before the poor Queen died, he fancied the Princess. Now that the Queen is dead, the admiral has no one. And his brother, the Protector, whom he loathes, has the young King's ear. If the admiral can't have the Princess Elizabeth, of course he would look to his ward. That's how he is. He must have power. Trust me. I have seen much in the three years I have sewn his clothes."

She took a sip of wine and opened her mouth to continue, but a shadow crossed the doorway. Alice stood framed between the posts.

"Didn't I tell you to finish, lass? The coach leaves in ten minutes!"

Nan stood, fingering a crumb at the corner of her mouth. Alice made no move to leave. Nan looked down at me.

"Farewell, Lucy. Perhaps I will see you at Chelsea. If you are to stay with the Lady Jane, that is."

"Come on, then!" Alice barked.

"Farewell," I said.

Nan left the room and Alice followed. I was now alone, and the fire in the grate had reduced to embers. I sipped the broth. It had grown cold.

I climbed the stairs to the wardrobe room and the sleeping quarters that adjoined it, eager to pen a letter home to my parents to let them know where I was. As I stepped onto the landing, a man about my father's age rounded a corner for the main stairs, and I stepped back into a curtsy.

He was tall, handsome, and dressed in traveling clothes. I knew without being told this man was Thomas Seymour, the Lord Admiral. I waited for him to continue on his way. When he did not, I raised my head.

"You are the seamstress from Bradgate?" His voice was not unkind, but his tone was much opposed to casual interest.

"Yes, my lord."

"You brought this letter?" He waved a piece of parchment in front of me. I had not seen the letter before. I did not know what to say.

" 'Twas inside the Lady Jane's trunk," he said.

I fumbled for words. "I…I did not pack the lady's trunk, my lord."

He regarded me silently, and it was obvious, even in the darkness of the candlelit landing, that he was deciding if I was telling him the truth.

"You did not place this letter in the Lady Jane's trunk?" He extended the open letter toward me. I could make out the last line and one name.
Edward.

"No, my lord."

"Do you know who did?"

"No, my lord."

He fell silent. I wished to continue on my way, but yet he stood there.

"What is your name?" he finally said.

"Lucy Day, my lord."

"Have there been guests of late at Bradgate? My brother, the Lord Protector?" He sounded angry, as if the words cut his lips as they left his mouth.

"No, my lord."

He waved the letter. "But his son?"

I nodded. "Aye…and his mother, the duchess."

"How long were they there?"

I sensed my face growing warm and red. When I did not answer right away, he took a step toward me. He reached out his other arm, and I involuntarily stepped back.

When he spoke again, his voice was tender and smooth. He gently took hold of my chin to raise my head. No man had ever touched me like that. The heat in my face deepened. He tipped his head in a gesture of kindness. "My concern is for my ward, the Lady Jane. She has suffered a great loss. We all have. This letter troubled her. I ask only to ascertain the motivation behind it."

The Lord Admiral dropped his hand, but he had taken a step closer to me. I could smell scent on him. Spicy and lingering, like Christmas wine. "How long were the duchess and my nephew there? Why did they come?"

I wanted to look away, but he sought my gaze. "They came to hunt, my lord."

His eyes widened. "To hunt?"

I detected a layer of hostility in his question, but not toward me.

"Yes, my lord."

"And were they successful?"

Surely the admiral knew a wardrobe seamstress would have little reason to hear of the successes of hunting parties in Bradgate's woods. But I
had the distinct feeling we were not talking about stags.

"I do not know, my lord."

He stood there, studying my face, contemplating, I think, if I would
be an ally or an obstacle in the days and weeks to come with regard to his
plans for Lady Jane's future. Then he smiled at me. Thoughtful and
serene. His countenance was disarming.

"It was my pleasure to meet you, Lucy. Perhaps I shall see you again
on a happier day."

"I am dreadfully sorry for my lord's loss." I curtsied.

"Yes. It was a great loss indeed," he said, and then he swept past me.
I watched him take the stairs. At the turn in the stairs, he looked up at me
and smiled. Then he disappeared into the wide entry.

When I turned to make my way to the wardrobe and my cot, I saw
that Lady Jane was standing on the stair that led to her rooms. I had no
idea how long she had been standing there. Perhaps she had been there
the entire time the Lord Admiral spoke to me. She looked so sad, and I
could nearly hear her mourning dress whispering, "She weeps, she weeps."

"Does my lady have need of anything?" I said as I curtsied to her.

She closed the distance between us. When she was near to me, she
nodded toward the staircase the Lord Admiral had flown down.

"Did you see who that letter was from?"

"My lady?" It hadn't occurred to me that she had not read the letter
before the admiral took it from her.

"The letter in the Lord Admiral's hands. Did you see who it was
from?"

I had not intended to read anything not addressed to me, but I had, indeed, seen the name Edward and the line he had written just before he signed it. I hesitated.

"I will not be angry," she said in earnest. "The Lord Admiral was there in my sitting room when my trunk was opened. He saw the letter before I did. Was it from my mother?"

Was it dread or hope in her voice? I could not tell.

"Please, tell me," she whispered.

"It was not from my lady's mother."

Her shoulders seemed to relax. Or fall. "Who was it from, Lucy?"

"From…from young Edward Seymour, my lady. He and his mother, the duchess, were visiting Bradgate when I left."

"Edward…," she breathed.

"Yes."

She looked past me toward the darkness of the windows that stretched the height of the corridor. Toward home, no doubt. "Edward," she said. Her reverie seemed a private matter. I could not guess what she knew about the Protector's son being at Bradgate. Talk below stairs was just talk. And I could not guess how she might feel about a betrothal to the Lord Admiral's nephew. Or to anyone.

"If you will excuse me, my lady." I curtsied and took a step away, but she reached out a thin arm and touched my elbow.

"Wait. Did you read it?"

"No, certainly not, my lady!"

"I do not mean while you traveled here. I mean when he stood there with it. Could you read any part of it?"

I swallowed hard. Unease lay in her young voice. "Please?"

"Edward Seymour offered you his heartfelt condolences, my lady."

She nodded. "That is what you saw? That is all that you saw?"

"Yes, my lady."

Jane let go of my arm and exhaled. "Thank you, Lucy." She turned away from me and made her way back to her room.

And I, to mine.

It only occurred to me as I climbed into my bed, after writing a note to my parents, that the admiral had lied to me. He told me the letter from Edward had troubled Lady Jane, but she had not even seen it.

Nine

The funeral for Katherine Parr, the Queen Dowager, took place on Friday, the eighth of September, at the chapel at Sudeley Castle. The Lady Jane, dressed in the gown I had fitted for her, walked behind the Queen's casket, which was borne by six men in black hooded gowns. I carried my lady's train.

It was the first funeral I had been to under the Church of England, which King Henry created in 1534 so that he could set aside his first wife, Catherine of Aragon, and marry Anne Boleyn. Dr. Miles Coverdale, of the Reformist religious teaching, was the almoner. There was no mention of Rome, nor was a word spoken in Latin. There was singing and psalms, but in truth, I could only look on my lady, whose sadness seemed bigger than her tiny frame in that great tent of a dress. When the Queen's body was lowered into the ground, the choir sang *Te Deum* in English. I had never heard the words in English before. The song was beautiful, but my lady shuddered so when the casket disappeared from our sight. I do not know if she even heard the words.

It seemed the funeral had no more begun than it was over. The mourners got into their carriages and sped away before the sun was high in the late summer sky. I accompanied my lady back to her rooms and helped her take off the whispering mourner's gown. She asked me to please put it in a place where she would not have to look at it.

Nan Hargrave had left with the Lord Admiral the night before, and the Queen's attendants had begun to pack their things as soon as the mid-day meal was over. So that left only myself and the scowling Miss Alice in the wardrobe room as the sun veered west. She sat on a stool and mended a farthingale for Lady Margery Seymour, the Lord Admiral's mother, who was to stay as a chaperone for Lady Jane in a house that was suddenly bereft of female company.

"You are staying, then? With the Lady Jane?" Alice asked me as I hung the black dress as far back on the rung as I could.

"Yes, madam."

"Even if she stays on with my lord?"

It was apparently no secret that the admiral fully intended to keep Jane in his household. But no one at Bradgate had given me instructions regarding this. The last word I had from the Lady Jane's mother, the mar-chioness, was that I was to accompany Lady Jane back to Bradgate after the Queen's funeral. Yet no one had announced the arrival of a carriage to take us there.

"I do not know, madam," I answered.

"What am I supposed to do with you?" she mumbled, but certainly loud enough for me to hear. I was at Sudeley for the express purpose of tending to Jane's wardrobe needs. An eleven-year-old child only had so many.

"Well, if you ask me—," she began, but then she abruptly fell silent. I looked up from the dresses in front of me. Lady Jane stood in the door-way. I fell to a curtsy and Alice, frowning and struggling to her feet, bowed with the unwieldy farthingale hoop in her arms.

Jane had changed into a gown of tawny taffeta, the bodice of which was embroidered with gold-thread butterflies. A gold girdle circled her waist, studded with Indian pearls at the intersections. Along the under-side of her french hood was a cloudlike ruching of white lawn. She looked lovely and strangely serene in light of the activities earlier in the day.

"Can I do anything for you, my lady?" I asked.

She hesitated a moment, as if she suddenly had misgivings about coming to me. "Would you like to see the baby?" An undercurrent of uncertainty laced her voice.

Alice, who had huffed back down onto her footstool, jerked her head up. Surprised, no doubt, at Jane's invitation. Jealous, perhaps.

"Of course, my lady," I replied.

Jane's smile was measured but immediate. She turned out of the doorway, and I followed her, leaving Alice to her ponderings.

"Your gown is beautiful, my lady," I said as I followed her down a long hallway that I had not to that point set foot on.

"The Queen gave this one to me. It was her favorite."

We took a few steps in silence.

"You were very brave today, my lady," I said. "I can see how much you loved the Queen."

"She was like a mother to me." Jane looked off down the carpeted corridor as we walked, but her gaze seemed unfocused. "More a mother to me than my own."

Jane stopped suddenly and swiveled to face me. Her dress rustled in protest. "I misspoke! I meant the Queen was very kind to me!"

Jane's eyes were bright with fear. My dealings with the marchioness had been few to that point, but it had been obvious, even to me, that she had lofty expectations for and of Jane that were unmet. Bridget told me that the marchioness had no patience with her eldest daughter, especially when Jane spoke her mind, and she did not hesitate to strike Jane if her anger was roused. Bridget also reminded me that this was of no concern to me. She must surely have thought that when Jane and I returned to Bradgate, there could likely be harsh words from the marchioness—or worse. And I was to mind my own business.

Jane blinked back tears of dread. I could see she was already picturing me relaying to her mother what I had just heard her say. The thought appalled me.

"You have nothing to fear from me, my lady. Nothing," I assured her.

She seemed to need a few moments to test her confidence that I would keep my word.

"I misspoke," she said again, flatly.

"The Queen was indeed kind to you," I said. "Surely you are only grieving her loss." I held her gaze, intent on her knowing I was no spy for her mother.

This satisfied her. We resumed our progress to the nursery.

"My mother was one of the Queen's attendants when the King was still alive," Jane said, her voice contemplative. "She brought me to court with her. That's when I met the Queen Katherine."

It still seemed absurd to me that a child should be at court, but I kept this to myself. "And how did my lady like being at court?" I said instead.

She seemed to have heard a different question. "I was so happy when Mama chose to have me accompany her. My little sister Kate was so jealous. If I had known how difficult it was going to be to please Mama, I might have suggested she take Kate instead. You've no doubt dressed my little sister. You know what she is like. She would have loved it."

I had met young Katherine Grey. Even at nine, Kate loved being the apex of everyone's attention. I nodded.

We neared the nursery door, and Jane stopped as she placed her hand on the door to open it. "Mama didn't bring me to court to have me near her. She brought me so that I would be noticed."

"By the admiral?"

"By His Majesty. The King." She turned from me and opened the door.

Inside the spacious room, the woman I had seen in the staff dining room paced a Persian rug with a shining bundle in her arms. All around her was lace and silk and gold and velvet. The nursery had been prepared at great expense. The woman appeared puzzled that I was there. But she smiled at Jane, and her eyes shimmered with compassion.

"My lady."

"Hello, Beatrice. Have you met Lucy Day? My mother sent her here for me from Bradgate." Jane moved toward the woman and the babe in her arms.

Beatrice nodded to me, but I detected she assumed I might be a copy of Nan Hargrave whom she clearly had no affection for. I could only guess it had something to do with Nan's loose tongue, especially regarding the admiral.

"How do you do?"

"Very nice to meet you," Beatrice said evenly. She turned to Jane. "Have you come to visit Miss Mary?"

Jane nodded and extended her arms, and Beatrice transferred the bundle to her. I saw in Jane's arms a tiny human face surrounded by lace and white lawn—the babe's sapphire eyes were open and alert. Her rosebud lips were bunched into a wee red bloom, and a sheen of golden silk crowned the babe's head. Jane bent down and kissed the infant, whispering a greeting.

"You can leave us," Jane said to Beatrice, not looking up from the child's cherubic face.

"My lady?" Beatrice's eyes were wide.

"My parents are coming. I fear I shall be leaving here soon and I won't see Mary again." Jane raised her head, and I could that her eyes had turned glossy. "I would like to be alone with her."

Beatrice looked to me, her eyes questioning.

"Lucy will stay with me and fetch you if I need assistance." Jane's attention turned again to the babe.

Beatrice hesitated and then curtsied. "As you wish, my lady."

I felt Beatrice's eyes on me as she left, but I did not look at her. When she was gone, Jane cooed to the child and laughed as the child cooed back. Jane walked over to the fireplace where a pleasant flame kept the vast room warm. I followed her.

"Here. Take the child while I settle." Jane handed me the babe and then knelt down on the thick carpet in front of the hearth, arranging her skirts around her. Then she reached for the child, and I handed the little Lady Mary to her.

"Sit with me?" she said as she took the child.

I knelt down across from Jane. "She is beautiful." The child raised a tiny hand from within the folds of the lacy coverings and nearly waved at us.

Jane nodded and smiled.

I had not heard the marquess and marchioness were coming, so I chanced a question.

"Did a message arrive today from your parents?" I asked.

"Yes. They wrote that they are coming to fetch me home. They… they think my interests are better served at home now that the Queen is gone. They are not convinced the admiral's plans to ensure a royal betrothal for me will proceed without…without the Queen's influence."

She looked up at me, and I sensed she was inviting me to conversation, the kind of conversation two friends might have when they are our age and imagining what it might be like to be held and kissed and loved by a man. In that moment, I felt the distance between us begin to fade.

"Would you be happy with a betrothal to His Majesty?" I whispered, a bit cowardly, I admit.

But she visibly relaxed as soon as the words left my mouth, as though she'd been longing to talk openly about this for many days.

"Ellen has told me if I am ever asked such a question, the answer is always yes." Jane bent and kissed the child's fist. "I am His Majesty's humble servant, and I am ready to fulfill my duty to God, the King, and England." She turned her head to look at me, welcoming me to question her.

"Is that what Mrs. Ellen thinks?"

Jane smiled. "Ellen does not want me to say anything that would anger my parents. This is the answer they would have me give. And Ellen counsels me to answer thus so that they will have no reason to be unhappy with me."

"I see."

"I enjoy the King's company," she went on. "He is…different than his father was. Quieter. Thoughtful. I imagine I could learn to be fond of him."

We were both quiet as we contemplated the notion that love between two of noble birth often follows long after the vows are spoken and the marriage consummated. Neither one of us voiced the obvious, that fondness might not bloom at all.

Again, she leaned down and kissed the babe's tiny fingers. "Are you betrothed?"

I shook my head. "No, my lady."

"Is there someone you wish to be betrothed to?"

Again, I shook my head. Marriage still seemed a long distance off for me, and that thought did not trouble me. There had been a young man in my village, during my growing-up years, who made my heart flutter whenever he was near. He married someone else the summer I turned thirteen. There had been no one since then who made my heart flutter. I did not wish to marry anyone who did not.

"Will your parents choose for you?" she asked.

I stumbled over my response. "I… Of course any young man who wishes to marry me will have to ask my father for permission." This was not the same, and we both knew it.

But she simply nodded. Her eyes communicated a glimmer of envy, and it occurred to me there was a reason behind her asking.

"If I could choose for myself, do you know who I would pick?" Her cheeks grew crimson, and she smiled as she looked away from me.

My own cheeks warmed a bit as I considered the awkwardness of our conversation. "I am sure I do not, my lady."

She peeked up at me and laughed lightly. "Guess."

I fumbled for an answer. "Someone at court?"

Her grin widened, and I saw such hope and expectation there.

"Edward Seymour," she whispered. "The Lord Protector's son. The one who sent the letter."

For a moment, neither one of us spoke. I could see she felt a kinship for me for other reasons besides my holding her the day before while she cried and the closeness in our age. I had seen Edward Seymour's letter. I hadn't read it, but I had seen it. I had seen the flowing script, the shape of his letters, the flourish of his pen as he wrote her a note of condolence.

The restlessness I had witnessed the night previous wasn't because she feared the note's contents but because the young man whose attention made her blush had sent her a note, and she had been denied the pleasure of reading it. And reading it again. And again.

"I did not think he even remembered me," she said softly. "I've only met him once. But I remember him. I remember how he made me feel. You probably think I am too young to know that feeling."

I shook my head. "No, my lady. I don't think that."

"Did you see him when he was at Bradgate?"

"Aye, my lady."

"What do you think of him, Lucy?" Her voice was hopeful.

"He...he seems a kind soul. He was polite to your parents and kind to your sisters. He has a winsome smile."

She grinned and her eyes spoke elation, and then, just as quickly, she turned apprehensive. "You mustn't speak of this to the admiral, Lucy. It would vex him if he knew I had affection for his brother's son. He and his brother, the Protector, they do not…they…" But she could say no more, for the door opened behind us, and Mrs. Ellen swept into the room.

"There you are!" Mrs. Ellen said cheerfully as she made her way to us.

And as she did, Jane and I returned to our normal places—she, the second cousin to the King of England, and I, the humble daughter of a gentleman tailor.

Ten

The Lord Admiral returned to Sudeley not long after Queen Katherine was laid to rest. He did not announce where he had been while away, but there were whispers among the house staff that he had spent time with Princess Elizabeth, and such whispers were always followed by tittering and smirking. He promptly pronounced to the household the evening of his return that we would be relocating to Hanworth. The reason was not given, but Mrs. Ellen told me the admiral was intent on convincing Jane's parents to allow her to remain his ward and that his prospects to secure a marriage between my lady and His Majesty were still favorable. Hanworth was easier to reach by carriage. It would be that much easier to fetch Jane back from Bradgate.

Jane was melancholy as we prepared to leave and spoke little as I worked to gather her gowns, hoods, and capes. Later, when I asked Mrs. Ellen if my lady was ill, she said, "Lady Jane was happy here at Sudeley. 'Tis difficult to leave, even with the Queen in her grave. And the babe will not be joining us."

This surprised me. "Why not?"

She shrugged. "The admiral has no need of the child."

"Need?"

Mrs. Ellen tipped her head and leaned in toward me. "If you are to be staying with us, the sooner you know this, the better, though if you repeat this to anyone, especially to the Lady Jane, I shall deny I said it."

She waited for me to acknowledge her and I nodded. But the nod was not enough.

"You are to say nothing of this to Jane," Mrs. Ellen went on. "She dotes on the admiral. And I'll not have you spoiling that for her. Do I have your word?"

"Yes, madam."

She leaned closer. "The admiral only troubles himself with that which will advance his own prospects. Do you hear what I am saying, lass? He is kind to her for a reason. She does not need to know what it is. She deserves such kindness."

I nodded. Jane's being here in the admiral's household was a scheme to secure himself an admirable future, not just her. "What will happen to the babe?" I asked.

Mrs. Ellen pulled back from me. "I hear she's being sent away to family in the north."

"Whose family?"

She huffed and crooked her hands on her hips. "You ask the same questions as the Lady Jane. I do not know. And it is of no concern to us."

She stepped away. The conversation was over. I finished packing the Lady Jane's wardrobe and saw to its loading on one of the many carriages we were taking to Hanworth. I was not called for again that day.

The next morning we were on our way.

As soon as we were situated at Hanworth, the admiral dispatched a messenger with a letter to Jane's parents, advising them of our new location and appealing to them to allow Jane to stay on as his ward. He invited the marquess and the marchioness to join him at Hanworth, instead of Sudeley, to secure Jane's situation.

To Jane's relief, they agreed to come and discuss the matter.

A fortnight later, on the morning they arrived, Jane paced the rugs in her rooms, reciting Latin verses to keep herself calm. She waited to dress until she was summoned, so as not to wrinkle her skirt. I thought perhaps she would choose the tawny gown she had worn the afternoon of the Queen's funeral, but she told me to bring the crimson one with the black trim. I found the gown quickly in the wardrobe room. The gown was deep red velvet with false sleeves of gold damask, turned back with miniver. The skirt boasted a long oval train and a pomander for the waist of gold filigree with a dense perfumed ball inside. The matching gabled headdress looked too big for Jane's head.

When I brought her the gown and headdress, Jane stood, saying not a word. She did not appear to be fond of the dress I had brought her.

"This is the right dress, my lady?" I asked, suddenly unsure.

Mrs. Ellen had followed me in with a necklace of rubies in her hand. "'Tis the right dress," she mumbled.

I looked to Jane and smiled. "I thought perhaps you might wear the dress with the gold butterflies."

"My mother prefers this dress," Jane said simply, and she held out her arms for the bodice.

I was not called for until late in the afternoon, but I was certain Jane had been allowed to stay with the Lord Admiral. No one summoned me to pack Lady Jane's wardrobe. From my garret window in the wardrobe room, I saw the marquess and marchioness step into their carriage as the sun began to dip. Jane was not with them. The marchioness was speaking to the marquess as they climbed inside, and her face was pinched with anger. I could not hear what she was saying, but she did not appear to be content. I was surprised they were not at least staying the night.

They sped away, and I listened for voices on the stairs—any kind of voices—that would let me know what had been decided. Finally, I was called for. I found Jane in her sitting room looking happy but weary. Mrs. Ellen was helping her remove the headdress.

"I should like to get out of this dress, Lucy," she said to me as I entered the room and curtsied.

"Certainly, my lady." I went to her. "It went well with your parents?" I ventured.

"They have decided I shall stay."

From behind her, Mrs. Ellen undid the clasp on her heavy necklace. She was frowning.

I began to detach the sleeves. "You are happy, then?"

"Yes. I miss Bradgate, but I...I should like to be near the Lord Admiral just now. He still grieves for the Queen. And Mama and Papa would have me near London. To be at court."

Mrs. Ellen caught my eye and gave her head a tiny shake, as one does when one is exasperated.

I removed the second sleeve and began to unhook the bodice. "And shall I be staying with you, my lady?"

Jane turned slightly to look at me. "Mama wanted to send you back, but I asked her if you could stay. Since I will be at court." She smiled slightly at me.

"I am most happy to stay with my lady," I said.

She turned back around. "I think she was vexed that I saw the wisdom in your staying before she did."

I could sense that Jane's satisfaction in my staying had more to do with what lay in her heart than what hung in her wardrobe. She had found a friend in me, and that both unnerved and warmed me. I had only worked for one other nobleman before and had not found friendship in that household. I had not expected to. "Would you like me to make a new gown for you, my lady?" I said. "Something for the holidays, perhaps?"

Jane half turned again. "That would be lovely." Her voice was light and happy.

Mrs. Ellen had the necklace and the pomander in her hands and seemed pleased that I had moved the conversation away from what had transpired during Jane's meeting with her parents. She beamed at me. "I'll just put these away."

"And how are your parents, my lady?" I asked as I loosened the skirt from around her waist.

"They are well. They…they couldn't stay."

I pretended I did not already know this. "Oh. A pity."

"They had to get back. Edward Seymour and his mother are again at Bradgate." Jane stepped out of the skirt.

"Did…did you wish to go back with them, my lady?" The moment I said it, I wished I had not. It was far too personal a question. But Jane answered me before I could ask her forgiveness.

"I did. I should like to have seen Edward again. To see if he is as I remember him. I even asked if they would like me to come home with them for a visit, but Mama asked what purpose there would be in that."

Jane looked small and young standing there in her undergarments. The headdress had pulled at the plaits in her hair, giving her a lost look.

"It doesn't matter," she continued, in a voice that sounded much older than she looked. "The Lord Admiral thinks he can have me betrothed to the King by this time next year. Hand me that gown."

I lifted a pale pink gown of soft silk off the foot of her bed and helped her slip inside it. She tied the satin bow and sighed quietly.

Mrs. Ellen came back into the room, and Lady Jane announced that she would like to lie down and rest before supper. Mrs. Ellen helped her climb atop her bed, and I made sure I had all the sections of her gown in my arms.

"Rest well, my lady," Mrs. Ellen said, and we both turned to go.

Outside her room, Mrs. Ellen told me to ask one of the maids for a tisane for Jane. I said I would be happy to.

"Is she pleased she's staying with the admiral?" I asked.

Mrs. Ellen nodded. "'Tis what she wanted. But I wish she had not been privy to all the details. She does not need to know how much the Lord Admiral is being paid."

I did not know what she meant. "Pardon?"

"The marquess is paying the Lord Admiral to keep Jane on as his ward."

"Paying him?"

Mrs. Ellen frowned. "Two thousand pounds."

The autumn months brought us to London, to Seymour Place. We saw little of the admiral. Lady Jane's tutor kept her busy in lessons, far busier than I would've guessed a young woman of her station would be. I spent the weeks mending tears, letting down hems, reattaching buttons and hooks, and in my spare time, I worked on a Christmas dress for Jane, a creamy white gown embroidered with swans and lilies and lined with ermine. I was alone in the wardrobe room most days.

I wrote to my parents that I did not think I would be home for the holidays, that it appeared Jane and I were to stay at Seymour Place in London for the festivities. It would be the second year that I would be away from home at Christmas. My mother had sensed my melancholy, and in her return letter, told me perhaps 'twas the Lord's design that I spend Christmas with the young Lady Jane, who clearly was fond of me and no doubt needed my friendship. My mother enclosed a kerchief that my father had stitched as he sat in his chair by the fire. I tucked it into my sleeve at once to have it with me always. It smelled of him. Of home.

I endeavored to pay no mind to the below-stairs gossip, but it proved difficult, since so much of it had to do with the Lord Admiral.

There was talk that he had poisoned the Queen, which I refused to believe; there would have been no point in that whatsoever. I was relieved that Jane was spared hearing this outlandish rumor. But there were others that were harder to discount or prevent her from hearing.

One of the kitchen maids told me it was at Hanworth the past spring that the admiral would sneak before sunrise into Princess Elizabeth's bedroom to tickle her while she still lay abed. All while being newly wed to the Queen Dowager.

Then, when the admiral declined to attend Parliament in November, there was talk that he was spending too much time up north, apparently amassing a small army for a reason no one knew, and that he was consorting with pirates, also for reasons unknown.

He was with us at Christmas, but his thoughts were elsewhere. I saw less of him than Lady Jane did, yet she asked me—of all people—what the admiral could be occupied with that demanded so much of his time.

I did not know, of course, but I did overhear a conversation he had with his mother, Lady Margery, who was Jane's chaperone whenever the admiral was away. I heard only a snippet of the conversation as I sat beneath a window in the library, writing to my parents, two days before Christmas.

Lady Margery and the admiral were in hushed conversation as they walked past the open doors of the library and then stopped just past them. They had not seen me.

Lady Margery said, "But he's your brother!"

The admiral replied with something I could not hear.

"What you are doing is treasonous, Thomas! I beg you to reconsider! You cannot do this without the sanction of the Privy Council. You know this!"

"And you should know that I have friends on the Council. Alliances. Mother, you worry too much."

They began to walk away, but not before I heard Lady Margery again remind the admiral, in an agonized voice, that the Protector was his brother.

January arrived with a vengeful chill, and the household seemed to be holding its breath as we waited for warmth to return to us. Jane immersed herself in her studies to pass the hours, and I offered to make Lady Margery a new dress so that I, too, would have something to take my mind off the tension in the household.

On a stormy day that flung ice on every window, a messenger came to Seymour Place and asked to speak to Lady Margery. She met with the messenger inside the drawing room, and we heard her cry out within seconds of meeting with him. Those of us on the stairs who heard her, rushed to the room.

Lady Margery's face was ashen, and she clutched a missive to her throat as if it were a dagger. Unable to speak, she thrust the letter toward the lot of us. I was the closest, and I took it from her, glad my father had seen to it that Cecily and I both knew our letters. I read aloud.

The admiral had been arrested for plotting to depose his brother the Protector, and for planning to abduct his nephew the King, and for planning to marry the Princess Elizabeth without the approval of the Privy Council, which alone was considered an act of treason.

Gasps of shock filled the room. As I recited the impossible charges, Lady Margery sank down onto a couch and began to weep.

Convicted traitors had but one sentence in England, and we all knew it. If the admiral was found guilty, he would lose his head. It was that simple.

The thought repulsed me, and I immediately thought of Jane upstairs in her classroom, studying Cicero; unaware that at that moment her guardian sat in the Tower, that the father of the young man she fancied would have to pass sentence on him, and that everything was about to change for her.

Everything.

Jane

Massapequa, Long Island

Eleven

As my train rumbled toward Massapequa, sunlight filtered through the window and glinted off the ring's ancient stones as I toyed with it on my pinkie. It didn't quite fit my ring finger—too tight—and spun easily on my littlest finger. My practical side reminded me I should've been carrying the ring to Long Island in the velvet-lined case Stacy found for me at the shop. Wilson had been insistent I transport the ring in the box. But as I'd settled into my seat on the train that morning, the ring seemed to call to me from inside my purse. I had slipped it on before even leaving Grand Central.

It'd been a while since I'd taken the train to my parents'. Brad had kept a Jeep garaged with some New Jersey friends for the last four years. We let them use it, and they housed it for us. On the rare weekend when Brad wasn't on call, he liked to take his canoe out to Harriman State Park or the Tivoli Marshes. It was the only reason, really, that he bought the Jeep. When we made the trip out to my parents' or when I made it alone, I usually took it. But I didn't have the Jeep; Brad did. Molly and Jeff would've let me use their car to go to my sister's birthday party, but they needed it to attend their niece's wedding in Danbury.

I didn't mind, though. The train's gentle rocking was soothing to me. As was the ring's touch on my finger.

At first the thought of the ring's actually being three or four hundred years old had unnerved me, so I had casually suggested to Wilson that maybe the ring had been placed in the lining of the book a mere twenty or thirty years ago.

"Is that what you think?" he had said, a gentle challenge in every word, and I had answered that I did not.

Wilson was able to read the inscription, without any trouble, within seconds of my handing the ring to him along with a magnifying glass. He'd taught Latin back in the 1980s to high schoolers who, as he said it, hadn't a modicum of respect for anyone or anything.

He'd held the ring up to the gooseneck lamp on my desk and squinted as he read the words. Stacy and I stood next to him and waited.

"Vulnerasti cor meum, soror mea, sponsa," he said. "I believe this is a verse from the Canticle of Canticles."

"The what?"

"Song of Solomon," Stacy said. "The love poem in the Old Testament."

" 'You have captured my heart, my sister, my bride,' " Wilson recited.

"It's like an engagement ring!" Stacy exclaimed. "I think it's so fabulous that your name is on it, Jane. I mean, how cool is that?"

Wilson handed the ring back to me. "The band is exceptionally small. The lady who wore that must've had exceedingly slender fingers."

"Or she could have been young," Stacy said. "Didn't they marry young hundreds of years ago?"

"Nobility certainly did," Wilson replied. "You really should have that appraised and insured. If it's as old as I think it is, well, I can't even imagine how much it is worth." Then he frowned. "It's dangerous for you to carry it around like you found it in a box of Cracker Jack."

"I know. I promise I will take care of that, Wilson," I said. "But I'm not…I'm not sure I should keep it." I put the ring on my pinkie and stared at it.

"What do you mean?" Stacy asked.

"Whoever Emma bought these boxes from couldn't have known

about the existence of the book or the ring. What if it has been in the seller's family the last three centuries? It would be like stealing if I kept it."

"It most certainly would not," Wilson said. "And if it had been in their family decade upon decade, what possessed them to stow the prayer book and the ring in a rusty old box and maroon them in the rafters of a machine shed or whatever it was? I'll bet it's been a couple hundred years since anyone has known about the book or the ring. Besides, you bought the ring fair and square. When you paid for the boxes, you paid for the books. And when you paid for the books, you paid for the ring."

"I know it's not technically stealing, but I feel like I need to at least inquire about the ring."

Stacy nodded. "I think I would too."

"I wouldn't," Wilson said, switching off the lamp. "I'd have it properly appraised and insured, and then, after I'd admired it for a little while, I'd donate it to a British museum. That's where a ring like that belongs. And the prayer book for that matter. Not in the hands of people who've no respect for their own history."

"Well, one thing at a time, I think. I'm taking it home with me this weekend to Long Island. The man I worked for in high school specializes in antique jewelry."

Wilson had sniffed. "I seriously doubt a Long Island jeweler has ever seen a ring like this one. You'd be better off taking it to the Metropolitan and having a curator look at it."

"I suppose," I murmured.

"What's to suppose?"

"I don't know, Wilson," I said, the reason formulating, even as I told him I didn't know what the reason was. "I just want it to be mine for a little bit longer, I guess. If I take it to a museum, they will want to keep it."

"Well, of course they will. That's the best place for it."

"Perhaps."

"Well…," Wilson began, but he didn't finish. The door to the store jangled, and he looked relieved to have a reason to excuse himself.

Stacy turned to me. "Such a pretty ring." She reached out her hand. "May I?"

I handed it to her. She placed it on the top half of her ring finger. She could nearly slip it over her knuckle.

"I wonder if they ended up happy," she mused. "The Jane who wore this and the man who gave it to her. Want me to find a ring box for you?"

"Sure." I slipped the ring back on my pinkie. The right one this time.

My phone had beeped at me as I slipped the ring back on, reminding me I had an appointment with Dr. Kirtland. I'd gotten lucky. A cancellation in his schedule had allowed me to see him three days after I'd nervously called his office to make an appointment.

Half an hour later, I found myself in a sea of chairs upholstered in navy blue, inside Jonah Kirtland's counseling group office in Midtown. I'd given the woman at the front desk my name and taken a seat amid half a dozen other people who also waited. No one looked up at me as I settled into a chair, and I appreciated that. I decided I would remember that for the future; to respect the anonymity of those who'd found their way to that office like I had.

I set my purse down by my feet and looked about the room. A nautical theme permeated the décor. Brass fixtures. Wide-beamed wood paneling on the walls. Framed pictures of seascapes with easy coastal tides—the kind that bring shells and seaweed to the shore, not broken timbers of wrecked ships. An antique skylight binnacle stood in one corner with a gleaming compass atop it, and I itched to go look at it but didn't want to draw attention to myself. I also wasn't quite ready to stand up. The room gave me the distinct impression I was aboard a swaying ship.

Instead, I leafed through a *Smithsonian* as I waited, wondering with every page-turn if it was possible to get seasick while seated in a doctor's office. My foot bounced up and down intermittently, and I worked to keep it still as the minutes ticked by. My phone trilled, and I fumbled to silence it, noticing that it was my mother who was calling me. I turned the power off and dropped the phone back in my purse.

A few minutes later, my name was called. I followed a young woman down a carpeted hall to one of several tall doors of polished wood, grateful that as soon I'd stood, the dizziness ebbed. She knocked once and then opened it.

The woman entered the office, and at first I couldn't see the person behind the desk. All I could see was the woman's back, the edges of a desk, more blue upholstery, more seascapes, more nautical antiques, and a glass-topped table by a window with a little wooden bowl at its center.

"Dr. Kirtland, your three o'clock is here."

A man moved from behind the desk and came into view. I flinched.

Dr. Kirtland didn't look a day over thirty. He wore jeans, a red-striped button-down shirt, and russet Birkenstocks. Curly hair cut short, wide eyes gray as steel, a full nose, and the youthful, tanned skin of a man who perhaps still got acne from time to time.

He walked over to me, extended his hand, and the woman stepped back so that I could clasp it. "Nice to meet you, Mrs. Lindsay. I'm Jonah Kirtland."

I wordlessly shook his hand.

The woman slipped past us and left the room, closing the door behind her.

Jonah Kirtland smiled at me. "Please. Have a seat."

He motioned me not to the chairs opposite his massive and neat desk, but to the small, glass-topped table by the window. I folded myself into a chair, still unable to say a word. I knew then what it was Molly had started to say about Dr. Kirtland but then hadn't.

He's young.

Dr. Kirtland sat down in the chair across from me. He didn't have a tablet or a folder or even a piece of paper with him, even though I had filled out paperwork and e-mailed it the day before. He crossed one leg over another, grabbed a handful of shelled pistachios from the wooden bowl, and then leaned back.

"Pistachios?" He nodded to the bowl.

"No. No, thank you."

"Don't like pistachios?"

"Uh. No. I mean, yes, I like them. I just… No, no thanks."

"So how's your day been so far?"

He tossed a few nuts into his mouth, crunched them and waited for me to answer.

"Fine, I guess. They're all pretty much the same right now." I was staring at the bowl of pistachios, not even aware that I was.

"Sure you don't want some?" he asked lightly.

I shook my head. I wanted to run. Tears were springing to my eyes for absolutely no reason.

"You must like the ocean," I sputtered, casting my gaze about the room, desperate to ease the tension inside me. There was a catch in my voice. I knew he'd heard it.

"Actually, a decorator was paid to come in here and make our offices look friendly and inviting."

I bit my lip to quell the tears that had no business showing up at that moment. I nodded.

"So did it work?" he asked.

I jerked my head back to face him. "What?"

"Does it feel warm and inviting here, Mrs. Lindsay?"

I swallowed hard. "Actually, I…I am not a fan of the ocean. I don't like open water. You can't see the bottom. You can't see where it ends." I looked away from him to the window, where below us a busy world went about a reckless routine.

"Have you always felt that way about open water?"

I didn't look away from the unyielding concrete below us. "Yes." But then I turned back to face him, suddenly nervous about him knowing my oldest fear so early in the conversation and misunderstanding it. I wasn't afraid of water. I was afraid of what lay beyond the water. Deep, dark nothingness. My childhood fears had nothing to do with what I was experiencing now.

"Look, I'm not afraid of drowning. I can swim fine. I just like being able to see the bottom. I like being able to see where it ends. I don't like not knowing. I don't..." My voice fell away as images of dark seas and deep lakes filled my mind; bottomless places without any handholds or even a hint of where the unknown ended and safety began.

It hadn't struck me until that moment that my longstanding aversion to open water was in any way related to the reason why I now sat in the counselor's office.

Dr. Kirtland leaned forward in his chair. "Mrs. Lindsay, you're not the first person to sit in that chair and wonder why they're here. I know it took courage for you to come here. Let me put your mind at rest. You don't have to worry about giving me any wrong answers. There aren't any. I am not going to solve your troubles. You are. But I am going to help you. I promise you that."

He folded his hands in front of him and waited for me to say something. Framed documents hung on the wall behind him; rectangular evidences of his many accomplishments. A soft glare hovering on the glass covering his doctorate from Columbia University outlined his curly head like a pale halo.

"Would you like to tell me what brought you here today?" His tone was patient. Several long, unhurried seconds floated by. He waited for me.

"But you already know why I'm here," I murmured.

"I know what Molly told me. And I know what your file says. But you've told me nothing." Still the patient tone. His eyes were locked onto mine. Soothing. Calming. Young. My gaze fell to his left hand. A gold band on his ring finger. Shiny. New.

"I...I don't think I can do this," I finally said.

"You don't think you can tell me why you're here?"

"I... You...you seem very... I mean, I can see that you've got a PhD from Columbia, and there are half a dozen other documents on that wall giving me reasons why I should be able to talk to you, but you seem... Look. My husband left me after twenty-two years of marriage. And you seem very...young."

"I am thirty-four, Mrs. Lindsay." He said it neither defensively or agreeably. He just said it.

Only ten years younger. Ten years. When I was getting married, he was twelve. Did that matter? Perhaps not. I really didn't know.

But I knew I didn't want to lie alone and awake anymore in the bed Brad and I had shared.

His eyes never left mine. I eased back in my chair. "Can you please call me Jane?"

"If you'd like."

I nodded.

"All right, Jane. How about if we just start at the beginning?"

"The beginning? You mean when Brad left?"

"No. I mean the beginning. Tell me about you. I want to hear about you. Shall we start there? Can you do that?"

"About me?" My eyes still shimmered with tears that threatened to slip over the edge. I felt them.

"Yes." His smile was gentle. He reached for a box of tissues on the windowsill between us and pushed it toward me. "Sometimes things get a little worse before they get better, Jane. But they will get better. I'm thinking you want that. Right?"

Again, he waited—his breathing even and unhurried and his crossed legs still. I pulled a tissue out, and the fluffy sound of fragile paper scraping against stiff cardboard seemed to whisper the answer for me.

Yes.

Twelve

My father called as my train pulled into Massapequa Park Station. He was stuck in traffic on Broadway. I told him not to worry; that I'd grab a cup of coffee and wait for him. I injected as much of a confident tone as I could as I told him good-bye, hoping he would pick up on it. My parents were going to want to talk about why Brad was really in New Hampshire, and I was not ready to have that conversation yet. My mother already hinted on the phone the night before that she and my father were getting the distinct impression something was up with Brad and me, and they'd rather not be in the dark about it—as if my marriage was a prized possession of theirs, on loan to me, and they needed to know the true reasons for Brad's absence. Not his absence at Leslie's party—I had a great excuse for that: Connor had a track meet that weekend at UMass, and Brad was going to cheer him on. That's also why he had the car and I was taking the train.

Only my parents and Leslie and her husband, Todd, knew about the job in Manchester. The rest of the extended family would think Brad was just gone for the day, being the supportive father that, of course, he was.

It wasn't the awkward moments at the party that I was half dreading as I settled onto a bench with a cup of coffee. It was the hour or two Sunday morning when I would be alone with my parents that I wasn't looking forward to.

As I sat in the late morning sunshine, I silently practiced the responses

Dr. Kirtland encouraged me to use if my parents asked questions about Brad that I didn't feel ready to answer. It hadn't taken long in that first counseling session for the conversation to swing to my parents. Dr. Kirtland said sometimes that's where the beginning of the journey is.

I had said, "But I don't want to talk about my parents. This is not my parents' problem, it's mine."

To which he said, "Yes, but we're not talking about ownership of a problem right now. We're not even talking about the problem itself. The problem of you not being able to sleep is actually not what we're dealing with right now. It's not even your husband's leaving you."

"Well, what is it then?"

"We're going to focus on you. Not your marriage. Not your parents. We're going to focus on how you see you."

"But you just said sometimes the journey starts with the parents."

"I think for you, it might. I think we're going to need to understand to what extent you rely on your parents for part of your validation. When we've figured that out, we'll spend some time figuring out why you've relied on your marriage for the rest of it."

Validation. The word didn't sit well with me. I immediately thought of a parking stub. I wanted to tell him I didn't like that word, but that just sounded childish in my head.

Our session had been nearly over at that point anyway, and Dr. Kirtland had quickly moved on to coach me on how to handle my parents' questions. Before I left, he told me gently that I could eliminate this particular stressor in my life by just telling them the truth. Because then they would know. I mentally practiced his answers on the way home:

> *Mom and Dad, I appreciate your concern about Brad and me, and when there's something you should know, I'll be the first to tell you.*

This is not something we need to discuss this weekend. This weekend is about Leslie. Let's just keep it about her, okay?

Brad's checking out a job in New Hampshire. It's a big move to make if he doesn't like the job. We're not rushing into anything.

On the phone, the night before I left, Molly told me she thought the responses were perfect. And that I should practice saying them out loud.

"What if they ask why I haven't gone up to New Hampshire to see Brad?" I asked her. "Or why he's only been down once to see me?"

"That's when you politely tell them that really isn't any of their business."

"I could never say something like that, and you know it."

"Well, Janie, that's why they keep intruding on your private life. You let them."

It had hurt a little, hearing that from her, even though I knew after just an hour with Dr. Kirtland it was partly true.

"Do you think I rely on my parents for validation?" I asked.

She'd laughed, but it was light and quick. She hadn't been laughing at me. "Did Jonah tell you that?"

"Dr. Kirtland thinks I find my validation in my parents and in my marriage. And since both of those relationships are kind of messed up right now, I'm messed up. It's why I can't sleep."

"Did he say that's why you can't sleep?"

I ignored her. "I just don't like that word. Validation. It sounds so…impersonal."

"So call it something else. Affirmation or self-worth. Whatever. Call it whatever you want."

The ease with which these other words fell from her lips had silenced me for a moment. She had known exactly what Dr. Kirtland was talking about. And she agreed with him. A tremor of frustration rippled through me as I formulated a response.

"Jane?"

"Hey. I happen to appreciate hearing what other people think. I always have. I think it's good to listen to the advice of other people before you make an important decision." My voice sounded a little shaky, as if I almost didn't believe my own words.

She had paused just for a moment. "Jane, I really don't think Dr. Kirtland was talking about you feeling compelled to get advice from other people before you make important decisions."

"Yes, he was."

"I think he was probably talking about you feeling compelled to let other people *make* the important decisions."

"What are you talking about?" The words flew out of my mouth. "How do you know that's what he meant?"

One of her daughters had needed her at that moment, and we had to cut our conversation short. She told me to call her on Sunday when I got home from Long Island. We said good-bye on a weird note, disconnected.

As I waited for my father, it occurred to me that just before we hung up, she'd quickly apologized if those words had hurt me. But she hadn't apologized for saying them.

I was happy to see that my sister was in the car with my dad when his relatively new Volvo pulled into the train station. Dad wouldn't begin any interviews on the true nature of Brad's whereabouts with Leslie in the car. At least my parents were discreet when they butted into my private life.

I tossed my empty coffee cup into the trash as he and Leslie got out of the car and walked toward me. Dad, wearing the striped short-sleeved shirt I gave him for Father's Day last year, gave me his customary peck on the cheek. The steel gray in the fabric of his shirt matched his slicked, silver hair. He smelled of Lava soap, as always. Leslie had on a bright pink, fitted T-shirt and stonewashed jeans. Hoop earrings the size of tea saucers hung from her ears. Her short-cropped hair was streaked with shades of bronze, copper, and gold.

We embraced and I wished her a happy birthday.

"This is all you've got?" My dad had my overnight bag in his hands and was looking about my feet for, I assume, a suitcase.

"I'm just staying overnight, Dad." I laughed.

"Your mother said you were staying Sunday night too."

I never told my mother any such thing. "Um. No, I need to get back to Manhattan tomorrow."

"She's a working girl now, Dad. Remember?" Leslie said as we began to make our way to Dad's car. "The antique shop?"

Dad ignored her sarcasm. "Your mother said you hired a new girl. She said you could stay until Monday."

"Well, yes, I've hired someone, but she's only part-time, Dad. And I never said I was staying Sunday night too."

We arrived at the car. As I put out my hand to open the passenger door, Leslie pointed to the ring on my pinkie. Sunbeams were stroking the gems.

"Hey. Is that a new ring?"

"Actually, it's a rather old ring. I just got it in a shipment from Emma this past week. I want to take it to David Longmont and see if he can appraise it for me." As my dad tossed my overnight bag into the trunk, I leaned toward my sister.

"It has my first name engraved inside," I said softly.

Her eyes were wide as Dad slammed the trunk shut and announced that David Longmont was retired.

I called over my shoulder. "I hear he still hangs out there now that his son has taken over the business."

"Can I see it?" Leslie said as we both slid into the car.

I took off the ring and handed it over the seat to Leslie. She immediately held it up to the window, squinting to read the inscription.

My dad got inside the car, and his brow furrowed as he watched Leslie. "What's she doing?"

"The ring has an inscription," I answered.

"Vul...vil...," Leslie attempted as she stared at the ring's underside. "What *is* that? I can barely read it."

"*Vulnerasti cor meum, soror mea, sponsa.* It's Latin. It means 'You have captured my heart, my sister, my bride.'"

"Holy cow," Leslie breathed. "How old is this thing?"

"I found it hidden inside the lining of a three-hundred-year-old prayer book, so—"

"What's three hundred years old?" My dad had started the car and shifted into reverse to back out of his parking space.

"Wow...," Leslie murmured. She was reading my name.

Jane.

I turned to face my dad. "The ring might be."

"And you're walking around with it? You're *wearing* it?"

I reached over the seat, and Leslie handed the ring back to me. "If it has survived the last three hundred years stuck in a book in someone's barn, I think it will survive a trip to Long Island."

"David Longmont is going to flip!" Leslie exclaimed. "Especially when he sees your name in it."

"Your name's in what?" Dad said, easing his way out of the parking lot.

"The name 'Jane' is inscribed inside too," I replied.

"How much did you pay for it?" Dad turned onto the main avenue out of the station.

"How much did you pay for this car?" Leslie quipped.

"I'm just saying a ring that old must've cost a fair sum, that's all. You might want to be careful how you handle it." He sounded miffed.

"If it makes you feel better, I have a case for it, Dad. I am wearing it because I like knowing where it is."

"I don't need to feel better. You just need—"

But Leslie interrupted him. "I'll take you down to David's shop today, Jane. Todd wants to play baseball this afternoon with some old high school friends, and he's taking Bryce and Paige with him. I don't want to go for the whole thing. We can go shopping and then to the jewelry store and then we can get ice cream and then maybe catch the last inning."

"Your mother's going to be too busy to do all that," Dad said, concern in every word. "She has to get everything ready for the party tonight."

Behind him, Leslie crossed her eyes. "We won't pull her away from the preparations."

Before Dad could say anything else, Leslie began to describe to me how her friends at work celebrated her fortieth the night before in Atlantic City and how she didn't get home until three in the morning. She described the evening as well as the afternoon leading up to it in vivid detail, allowing me to relax as we made our way into the neighborhood where she and I grew up.

The streets were peaceful. Men in plaid shorts were mowing their lawns, women in straw hats were putting down impatiens and alyssum in their flower beds, and children were shooting hoops in their driveways. The colors of April—always shining and vibrant after a monochromatic winter—were alive at every glance, down every side street.

I had always pictured my life looking something like this, living in a house like my parents' with its gray dormer windows trimmed in white, wide cements steps to the painted wood porch, on a street named after a tree, in a cozy suburb that could be anywhere.

I'd imagined I'd have daughters and sons, at least one or two of each, and that we'd take long family vacations in the summer and play board games on stormy nights, and that we'd have a million inside jokes that were funny only to us. I'd pictured big family dinners, fun secrets between my daughters, laughter and wrestling among my sons, and a kinship with my husband that my friends would marvel at, and that our house would be the one all the teenagers would flock to.

But we'd spent our only child's teenage years in a Manhattan town house, watching old James Bond movies on rainy nights, and eating out more than we ate in. When we lived in Connecticut, during the years I wished for another child and was kept wishing despite many years of trying, our home had been a stylish rambler in a new Stanford subdivision, one of several models that repeated itself every fourth house. Connor was usually ready for bed by the time Brad finally got home from work. He and I ate dinner at eight or eight-thirty, sometimes in front of the television where Brad often fell asleep with his fork in his hand.

Free weekends were spent canoeing or fishing, neither of which I enjoyed. I had been happy to let Connor and Brad take off at dawn on weekend mornings to seek out the water, leaving me to scout out antique stores with friends. At the time it seemed like we were both getting to do what we wanted. From the perspective of the front seat of my father's Volvo, it didn't seem that way now.

As we closed the distance to my childhood home, I was keenly aware that my life had turned out differently than what I'd imagined when these streets were my streets, when nothing had been decided yet, when I was young and the world seemed spacious and inviting.

My parents' house came into view as Leslie rambled on, and my nostalgic thoughts were yanked away. My mother was on the porch watering her hanging baskets. She turned toward us as if surprised we were already home, when in actuality, I saw her rise from the swing as we made the turn onto the street—a blur of blue sweat suit and silver gray hair—and reach for the watering can at her feet.

Thirteen

My parents had lived in that house since I was three. They bought it before they even knew my mother was pregnant with Leslie, back when Dad was head custodian at the local hospital and going to school at night to get a degree in mechanical engineering.

The floors were hardwood, and the rooms were spacious and square, just the right shape and size for my mother to reinvent every time a new home fashion made headlines.

The house was built in 1950, with the charm—like all the houses on my parents' street—that architecturally defined the years of hope and renewal following World War II.

Inside, past its quaint exterior features, my mother had groomed her flair for interior creativity. She had toyed with English country garden quaintness, Scandinavian sparseness, Oriental mystical, and now the current—Moorish kaleidoscope—all of which have had as their foundational furniture my mother's three white sofas with their square cushions. On that day the walls were a blend of apricot and amber hues. Crimson, mauve, and chocolate brown pillows were scattered about the trio of white couches. Sconces and mirrors framed in brass lined the walls. Ebony-stained pine accent tables and bookcases stood in contrast to the brilliant whiteness of the sofas and window trims. Honey and cedar scented the air. Gossamer curtains hung from the windows, flung easily over wooden blinds that my mother kept from genre to genre for nighttime privacy.

As I stepped inside, past the Moroccan landscape that dominated the living room, I saw that my mother had draped the dining room in swaths of coral fabric. Silver and sea-foam green helium balloons were anchored to chair backs and table legs. Bouquets of purple larkspur, iris, and Bombay dendrobium orchids in tall vases were everywhere. The décor extended past the dining room onto the back patio where the profusion of purple, coral, and sea foam continued.

Leslie leaned into me and whispered that if it weren't for the balloons, she'd think it was a perfect setup for a rather elegant wake.

My mother had her hands on her hips as she watched me take in the birthday decorations. My father had taken my overnight bag up to my old room.

"Well?" she said. "What does it need?"

"It looks…great, Mom. I don't think it needs anything else. Really. It looks fabulous," I told her.

"I don't know," she replied, as if pining for a second opinion.

"Hey, Mom. Jane and I are going to do a little shopping and then take in the last half of Todd's baseball game." Leslie grabbed my arm.

Mom turned to us, crinkling one eyebrow.

"Can we pick up anything for the party?" Leslie added quickly.

"You're going shopping? For what? It's your birthday, Leslie. People will be bringing you presents. What could you need to shop for today?"

"I might want a different blouse to wear to the party tonight. Something that will match the, uh, color scheme."

"I thought you were wearing white. You told me you were wearing white."

"Oh, and we're also going to stop and see David Longmont. Jane has a new ring!" Leslie thrust my hand toward our mother. I tensed without meaning to.

Mom peered down at the ring. "Did Brad get that for you?" She raised her head and our eyes met.

"I bought this for the store."

"Hmm. Looks kind of fussy. Where'd you find it?"

"Well, actually it was hidden in some books Emma sent me for inventory. I think it might be really old."

"Her name is in it." My dad had appeared from the hallway, and my bag was no longer in his hands.

"Her *name* is in it?"

"The name 'Jane' is engraved inside." I took the ring off and handed it to her. She squinted as she tried to read the inscription.

"Isn't that the coolest thing?" Leslie said.

"I can't read it. It's too small. What are all those other words? They look strange."

"It's Latin." I reached for the ring. I didn't feel like telling her the translation.

"So can we pick up anything for the party while we're out?" Leslie sensed my unease.

My mother slowly handed the ring back to me. "Why do you think it's so old?"

I placed the ring back on my right pinkie. "Because I found it hidden inside the binding of a seventeenth-century prayer book."

"Seventeenth century… Good Lord! Why on earth are you *wearing* it, Jane!" she exclaimed.

"Ice? Napkins? A fifth of gin?" Leslie continued.

Mom turned to my sister. "I am just asking a simple question, Leslie. And, no, I already have everything."

"She likes knowing where it is." My dad started to walk past us to go into the kitchen. Leslie reached for him.

"Dad, Todd has the Camry. Can Jane and I have the Volvo?"

He hesitated and then reached in his pocket for the keys and handed them to her. "Park in the shade, if you can."

Leslie took the keys, and we headed for the front door.

"Just make sure you are back by five, so you can freshen up," Mom called as she followed us. "And take sunscreen for the kids!"

Mom was just behind us as Leslie opened the front door. She touched me on my elbow.

"Jane, why can't you stay Sunday night too? Brad's not even here. And your father and I want to talk to you."

Leslie mumbled something and stepped out onto the porch and headed to the car in the driveway.

I turned to Mom and delivered the line that came easiest to me. "Let's just keep this weekend about Leslie, okay? It's her birthday."

"It's not her birthday tomorrow."

I practiced the next line in my head before I said it. "If it's Brad you want to talk about, there's really nothing new I can tell you. He's still try- ing out the new job in New Hampshire."

She frowned. "Something is wrong. We know it. We want to help you. It's not normal for two married people to live in two different states in two different apartments."

"It's not normal for a forty-four-year-old to have to talk about private matters with her parents," Leslie yelled from across the hood of the car. Then she yanked open the driver's side door and slid inside.

My mother tossed Leslie an exasperated look and swiveled her head to face me. "We know something is wrong, Jane. Isn't it about time you admitted it to yourself? You can't fix something unless you admit it's broken."

I searched my brain for one of Dr. Kirtland's gems, but my mind was suddenly blank of any other practiced response.

"It's Leslie's birthday," I murmured. "And we're going shopping." I took a couple of steps toward the car. Mom followed me down the steps.

"You shouldn't just give up on your marriage, Jane. Think of Connor and what this will do to him. You and Brad should see a professional instead of just throwing in the towel like this. I can't believe you are just giving up on your marriage."

Inside the car I saw Leslie shaking her head. *Let's go,* she mouthed.

I turned toward my mother as a new thought, one that I hadn't exactly practiced with Dr. Kirtland, crawled out of my throat. "Well, I am glad we at least agree on that. It's *my* marriage, Mom. Mine. And you've really no idea what you are talking about."

I walked to the car and got in. Leslie started the engine, and I waved to Mom—a gentle salute—as she stood there, staring at me.

We were out of the driveway before Leslie turned to high-five me. But I didn't raise my hand to meet hers. I wondered instead if Dr. Kirtland would have congratulated me or merely offered me a pistachio.

For my sister's birthday present, I had chosen an Edwardian *sautoir* necklace with colors that mimicked the odd beauty of gasoline in a wet gutter. I wasn't a fan of the Edwardian look myself—too much lace and feathers and far too many pearls, bows, and tassels. But I knew Leslie would like it. It had an elongated art deco look that matched her flair for the unconventional.

I had found the necklace at a dealership in Philadelphia on a buying trip I had taken three weeks before Brad told me he was leaving. Brad had that weekend off, and I had invited him to come with me. He had declined, telling me he was going sailing with a bunch of guys from the hospital. I didn't think anything of it at the time. Brad loved to sail. I didn't. I remember being happy that he was getting out with friends to do something he really enjoyed. But I'd wondered since then if he declined because he knew then he was planning his escape. He hadn't interviewed for the New Hampshire job, but he surely knew about it already. And I, likewise, wondered if any conversation with any of those guys on that sailboat began with, "I'm thinking of leaving Jane."

Leslie was the one who told me later to waste no time trying to imagine what Brad might have said to anyone that day. Chances are he said nothing.

"Brad's a quiet egghead who contemplates far more than he speaks. He always has been. That's why you fell for him," she told me. I'd called her two days after Brad left to tell her what had happened.

"Don't obsess about why he needs some time away, Jane," she'd continued. "It's not attractive, and it's not why he fell for you."

"And how would you know why he fell for me?" In daring her to tell me, I realized, perhaps for the first time, that I'd wanted to know that since the day Brad proposed.

She hadn't even hesitated. "Because you were safe and demure and you had that elegant Audrey Hepburn look going on."

"Safe?" I didn't know whether to feel insulted or complimented. "You're saying he fell in love with me because I was safe?"

"Yes, safe. Of course, safe. He was probably under the same pressure you were to find a good marriage partner before he left college. Where else would a nice-looking nerd like him and a demure woman like you meet a future spouse?"

"I wasn't under any pressure to marry anybody," I'd exclaimed, but my face had already warmed with color. My parents told me the day I graduated from high school that college would be the best place for a shy girl like me to find a good husband. Pressure from my parents always felt like care before it felt like anything else.

"Yes, you were," she said.

"Like you weren't?" But I'd said it without conviction. My parents' expectations for Leslie had been as heavy as the ones they had for me. But Leslie didn't bend to pressure. And it was clear to me as we drove away in my father's car that she also didn't rely on my parents or anyone else to validate her choices. Or make them for her.

And she never had.

Leslie decided to reverse our plans and get ice cream first before going to see David Longmont. As we spooned ice cream into our mouths, she congratulated me for reminding our mother the only life she had the right to orchestrate was her own.

I felt no sense of victory. I wanted instead to pull my cell phone out of my purse and call Mom and at least apologize.

"Apologize for what?" Leslie was indignant.

"I think I hurt her feelings."

"Well, she hurts yours all the time. Don't you think she needs to know what that's like from time to time?"

"Yes, but she doesn't mean to."

"What she *means* to do is call all the shots for you. You want her to keep doing that, by all means, call her up."

I poked at my ice cream.

"Look. I'm sorry, Jane. The way she... It just makes me mad. It's like they are still worried about how we make them look. It's ridiculous. Drives me crazy."

I held my spoon in midair as Leslie's words—words that I'd actually not considered before—fell about my ears. My parents were worried how the future of my marriage would reflect on them.

On their choice for me.

Brad.

❦

David Longmont peered at the ring through the thick lens of a magnifying glass strapped to his head like motorcycle goggles. Curly tufts of hair as white as cotton caressed the sides of the magnifier by his ears. His goatee moved up and down as he chewed a piece of spearmint gum.

"Where again did your buyer find this?" His voice was soft like an FM disc jockey at 3 a.m.

"She bought some boxes of books and dishes at a jumble sale in Wales. In Cardiff. The ring was hidden inside a 1662 prayer book."

"What's a jumble sale?" Leslie asked.

"It's like a flea market or swap meet."

"But this isn't a Welsh design," David continued. "It looks English to me. And pre-Elizabethan." David looked up at me. "It's at least a hundred years older than 1662."

"Wow!" Leslie crowed, smiling wide.

"Of course, you will want to have it dated by someone with more experience than me. But as near as I can tell, it's an authentic mid-sixteenth-century piece."

"Cool!" Leslie said. "So how much is it worth?"

David pushed the magnifier up on his head and handed the ring back to me. "Well, the gems are quality cuts, the sapphire is clear, the rubies are uniform in color, and the diamonds, though small, are uniformly faceted. I have a man's signet ring from the same time period here in the shop that I wouldn't let go for anything less than thirty-five hundred dollars. With yours, you have the age of the ring and the stones contributing to its value, so I am thinking at least six thousand. More, depending on whether you can find out who it belonged to."

"Holy cow…," Leslie breathed.

"What do you mean by 'who it belonged to'?" I asked.

David shrugged. "Well, if my signet ring belonged to someone like Oliver Cromwell, it would be worth more. I'm sure if this ring belonged to someone of titled nobility, that fact could increase its value."

"Do you think it might have belonged to someone of nobility?" I was afraid for some reason to put the ring back on my finger, and not just because of its monetary value. I reached into my purse for the black ring box.

"Maybe," David replied. "I'd say with that inscription, it's most likely a betrothal or wedding gift. And it certainly is more ring than a commoner could have afforded. Commoners didn't use Latin, so it would make sense that a highly educated man gave this to a highly educated woman."

"But how could a nobleman's family lose track of it?" I asked. "I mean, I found it in a box of books that apparently had been forgotten for decades."

"Well, any number of things could have happened over the years. It could've been stolen or the family's heirs could have fallen on hard times and sold it at some point. Hard to say."

"How would I begin to even figure out who it belonged to?"

"Well, you could start with where your buyer friend found these boxes. And then start inquiring of experts in that time period."

"And maybe research aristocratic couples who were wed that year, where the bride's name was Jane?" Leslie offered.

David crossed his arms across his chest. "Well, I'm afraid that might be a dead end, going about it that way."

Something in the way he said these words pricked me. "How come?"

"I wouldn't assume the woman who was given this ring actually married the man who gave it to her."

Again, I sensed a deepening sadness, a thrusting into my soul.

"Why not?" Leslie asked.

"There are no signs that this ring has been worn. No signs at all on its underside. The engraving shows no evidence that flesh rubbed up against it."

"They never married?" Leslie sounded disappointed.

"I'm just saying it looks like the woman who was given this ring didn't wear it. And if she didn't wear it, then something likely happened to her betrothal. Something came between her and the man who gave it to her. Maybe she refused him. Maybe he died before they could marry. Or maybe she did. Who knows?"

The ring with my name on it felt warm in my hand after David's handling and assessment.

I slipped the ring into the tiny black velvet cloud and clasped the box shut.

Fourteen

I t wasn't until we arrived at my old high school that I found out the
baseball game was more than just a pickup game between old friends.
The class that graduated the year after me was having their twenty-fifth
reunion that night, and it was their unofficial alumni game Todd was
playing in. Todd's cousin was in that class, and Todd played because they
begged him to. Todd was the star pitcher back when they were all seniors
and Todd was a junior.

So instead of the spectators consisting of half a dozen wives and kids,
the bleachers were full of people, young and old. There must have been
close to a hundred people sitting in the stands and lined up in the shade
in collapsible canvas chairs.

"Crud. I guess we should've brought chairs," Leslie said as we arrived
at the field at the bottom of the sixth.

My niece, Paige, stood up from the top row of the bleachers and
waved to us, and Leslie and I made our way up, excusing our way past
people. I gave my niece a quick hug and then said hello to my nephew.
Bryce smiled in relief. No hugs from aunts in public when you are thirteen.

"Lot of people here," Leslie remarked, scanning the crowd.

"There were more before," Paige said. "Some people left already to
get ready for their party tonight. I heard them talking about it."

Just then Todd was going up to bat. Leslie began to shout encouragement. Others cheering for the men on Todd's team joined her.

I leaned back against the bleacher rails behind me, and I felt my body mentally slide backward in time, back to when this school was my school, and I was on the brink of my adult life. I was dating Kyle then, and life was fairly simple. Kyle didn't play baseball, but we had mutual friends who did. The last time I was at this field had been when Kyle and I were days away from graduating, and dating other people was far from either one of our thoughts. The bleachers were wooden back then; I was wearing a yellow eyelet sundress, and he and I shared a rainbow snow cone.

Kyle was the first boy I ever kissed. The first boy whose last name I practiced writing during study hall; the first boy whose presence in a room made me feel anxious and alive.

My parents liked Kyle, but I had the impression, even then, that they assumed my relationship with Kyle was a flimsy high school romance that would evaporate in time. It alarmed them when it didn't, though I didn't see it as alarm back then. Kyle was over to my house often, and I to his. His sister, Jenny, younger than us by just a year, became a good friend, and his mom taught me how to sew. His dad was just like Kyle, kind, but fun to be around, spontaneous, and always in the mood for adventure. They took me on their family vacation to Maine the summer between Kyle's and my junior and senior year.

When I came home from that trip, my parents sat me down in my bedroom and told me that I would soon be starting my last year of high school, applying to colleges, and charting a course for the rest of my life. My life choices were going to start to matter in ways they never had before. It was time to start thinking about what lay beyond high school.

I remember thinking that I wasn't too familiar with making life choices and that I just wanted to enjoy being a senior.

They asked me then if I thought I would marry and have kids one day. I had blushed and said, "Well, sure."

"Then you might want to rethink your idea to go into hotel management," Mom had said.

That had been my dream job when I was seventeen, on the cusp of my last year at home. I wanted to own a fancy inn on Martha's Vineyard and live like I was on vacation. I had already pictured Kyle at my side, taking care of all the physical aspects of the place. He was a whiz at building things and had already won ribbons at the state fair for construction projects he did in wood shop.

"Why?" I'd asked.

"Because you would never have any time off. That is the nature of hotel management. And the busiest time of the year for you would be in the summer, when your kids are out of school. You would never see them. They would basically have to grow up without you. You would regret it in the end, Jane."

"You really should consider majoring in education," Dad had said. "You have excellent grades in every subject. You could easily become a teacher, Jane. A good one. And then you'd have your summers off. You could take those trips to the Vineyard and enjoy your family instead of being isolated from them."

"I guess," I had said.

"And don't make any hasty decisions about marriage, Jane. You are so young. Who you marry will determine so much about how and where you spend the rest of your life. There is so much to consider. More than you know."

"I'm not... I...," but I hadn't been able to finish the sentence.

"Think about where you want to be in five years. In ten years," Dad had said. "The decisions you make today are going to determine where you will be. Trust me on this."

They never said Kyle's name in that conversation. Not once. But my suitcase from Maine was still lying open and unpacked at my feet. I still had mosquito bites on my ankles from the trip.

They knew Kyle was planning on going to vocational school, not college, and that he wanted to spend some time doing relief work in Africa and Asia before settling down to a construction job in the States. They were all for acts of benevolence. They were even supportive of Kyle's wanting to go overseas to be a part of something grand.

But they saw no place for me in that picture. At all.

Later, after I had met Brad, I began to understand that they were actually happy Kyle had his eyes on Kenya a month before we graduated.

They wanted Kyle as far away from me as possible.

All during the last year of high school and especially the lazy summer weeks after graduation—before I left for Boston, and Kyle to Virginia—my parents subtly encouraged me to allow Kyle to follow his dreams. Not to make demands of him. And to consider my own future and study load.

The week before we were to part, after Kyle picked me up from my last day at David Longmont's store, I asked Kyle if he thought we should give ourselves the freedom to date other people.

"Is that what you want?" he had said.

"My parents think it's a good idea. They said I need to let you follow your dreams. And that I need to follow mine."

Several long moments passed before he told me that maybe they were right.

We didn't call it breaking up. We called it letting go.

And we had parted as friends. We called and wrote to each other off and on the first year. But Kyle's letters became infrequent after he left for Africa.

And then, of course, in my sophomore year at Boston, I met Brad, whom my parents welcomed with open arms.

I lost touch with Kyle after that.

He was still in Kenya the following summer when I married Brad. At my ten-year high-school reunion, I heard Kyle was in Nepal. At our twenty-year reunion, no one knew where Kyle was. I could barely remember what his voice sounded like...

Todd hit a rocket into left field, and I was yanked out of my reverie. All around me people rose to their feet and began to yell. I stood also, but my cheering voice sounded fake in my ears.

It suddenly seemed absurd to me that all the men on the field, and all of us in the bleachers, were acting as if time had reversed itself and we were all back in high school. It was as if no time had passed, as if we all hadn't lived a quarter of a century since high school in the folds of our many choices.

We could just pull out a baseball bat and a ball and make the past and everything about it simply evaporate. And pick up somehow where we left off.

As if it were that simple. As if that's what we really wanted.

Fifteen

Leslie was ecstatic about the necklace. She convinced me to let her open the gift before the other guests arrived. She and Todd and the kids were staying at Todd's parents' house across town, but she came back to our parents' house to get ready for the party after the baseball game. We were in my old bedroom when she opened my present to her.

"I totally love it," she gushed. She floated over to the full-length mirror in her gauzy white strapless dress and pulled the necklace on over her head. It hung past her navel, just like I thought it would. She doubled the length, and the tassel-like pendant hung halfway down her chest. "It's perfect. Where did you find it? Is it an antique?"

"I got it in Philly a couple months ago. It's Edwardian."

"Okay. What does that mean?"

"King Edward was the son of Queen Victoria, so we're talking turn of the century."

"So, that's like, a hundred years old!" Her eyes widened. "Does that mean I have to keep it in a box?"

"No. I want you to wear it."

She grinned, cinched the second loop around her neck, and grabbed the pendant, swinging it around like a flapper in the roaring twenties. "I love it, doll!"

"I thought you would."

Leslie struck a pose in front of the mirror. "You should wear that ring at the party tonight. People will ask about it, and then you can tell them it's from the Dark Ages, and all of Mom and Dad's friends will start gasping for air and peppering them with questions about why on earth you are wearing it."

I laughed. "Not exactly the Dark Ages, Les. And I really don't know if I should keep wearing it. I don't even know if I should keep it."

"Of course you should keep it! It has your name on it!"

"That doesn't make it mine."

She walked over and stretched out on the bed next to me. "You bought it, Jane. That makes it yours."

"Well, I bought some books, and it just happened to be hidden inside one of them."

"So?"

"I paid one hundred pounds for the books and dishes, and the ring is worth seven *thousand* dollars."

"Six. David said six."

"I think if the person whom Emma bought it from had the prayer book in their family, then—"

Leslie sat up on the bed. "No, Jane. Don't even go there. They sold that book fair and square. The book is obviously ancient, and they sold it anyway. That's how much they care about old things. Don't you even think of offering that ring back to them. I'll never speak to you again if you do."

"Such nasty words from a birthday girl."

"I'm serious!" But she was smiling.

I took the black box out of my purse and opened it. The ring glinted a hello to me. "I would like to try to find out whose it was, though."

"That is something I will let you do. But you can't just give it back. To anybody. I think you should keep it anyway. For heaven's sake, your name is in it! Don't you think that's just a bit more than coincidental?"

"Maybe," I murmured. "I wonder…I wonder what happened to this Jane. I wonder why she never wore the ring. I wonder if she didn't love the man who gave it to her."

Leslie hesitated for a moment. Then she took the ring from out of the box and slipped it on her little finger. "I bet she loved him madly, whoever he was. But he died of the plague the day before they were to wed. And she was so brokenhearted she became a nun and sealed the ring in the prayer book and never loved again!"

"It's a Protestant prayer book, Les."

"Yeah. So?"

"So what's the likelihood she became a nun?"

"Whatever. She loved him. And he loved her."

"Think so?"

"Yes. I think they loved each other. Something they couldn't control came between them. If they had had their way, they would've been married and the inscription would have been worn to unintelligible gobbledygook by now. And actually, you wouldn't even know about this ring because this Jane died with it on her finger, having never taken it off. And she was old and arthritic after being married for sixty years, and no one could get it past the first knuckle." She handed the ring back to me. "They loved each other."

I held the ring in my palm for a few seconds before I put it back on my finger. We were both quiet. "Why do you think Brad left me, Les?" I asked a moment later.

She slid an arm around me. "Jane. The only reasons that matter are Brad's reasons. It doesn't matter why I think he left. It doesn't even matter why you think he left. You may not like his reasons, but you're going to have to make sense of them if the two of you are going to figure this out."

I leaned into her. "I…I just feel so…lost. Like I'm disconnected from everything that matters to me. I can't believe he's gone, Les. I miss the way his hospital clothes smell. I miss reading the Sunday paper with him. I miss making him dinner. I miss his stupid worms in the fridge. I miss… his nearness."

Leslie squeezed my arm. "I know you do."

"And I can't help thinking that…it just feels like…" A tear slipped down my cheek. I wiped it away with the back of my hand. "Like there's another woman. Like there *should* be another woman. But there isn't. He says there isn't. Sometimes I wish there was."

"No, you don't," Leslie said quickly, rubbing my shoulder. "You don't wish that."

"I would understand it then."

"No. You would have someone to hate then. And wouldn't it be nice to heap all this negative energy onto someone you'd find easy to hate? C'mon, Jane. You don't want that."

The angry seed of a headache was forming at my temples. "Mom and Dad wouldn't adore him so much if he were having an affair, you know. It would sure bring him down a couple pegs… They think it's my fault Brad's in New Hampshire. That I kicked him out or something. Or maybe they think I'm the one having an affair."

"This is none of their business unless you let them have at it. And why are we even talking about this? All this serious talk is messing up my birthday. Let's go poke our fingers into the roses on my cake."

She stood.

I reached over to turn off the light on the bedside table, and a strange sensation of loss and loneliness fell over me as the rings on my hand sparkled under the glow of the lamp: long-ago Jane's betrothal ring and my own wedding band and engagement ring.

"You go ahead. I'll just be a minute," I said.

Leslie hesitated. "All right. Don't be long. Mom will ask about you. And then she will come up."

She turned and left me, closing the door behind her.

I sat there for several long moments massaging an infant headache away. I wanted to talk to Brad. I wanted to hear his voice, hear him say my name. I wanted him to offer me a strand of hope, however thin, that I was someone he still loved.

I reached into my purse and pulled out my cell phone. It was a little after six thirty in the evening, and the track meet should've been over. Perhaps Brad and Connor were grabbing a bite to eat. Maybe Brad was already on his way back to Manchester. My fingers trembled as I clicked through the contacts and landed on Brad's name. I pressed the button to dial, my heart thumping in my chest. I had no idea what I was going say to him. I just wanted to hear his voice.

The call went to his voice mail. In a tangled, distant way, I got my wish. I heard his voice. *"Hi. You've reached Brad Lindsay. I can't take your call at the moment, but please leave a message for me, and I'll get back to you as soon as I can."*

My mind stumbled over the words, "I'll get back to you as soon as I can," which I had heard dozens of times before when I'd left voice messages for my husband, but it meant something different that day. I could barely form words. For the first few seconds after the beep, I said nothing. Then I launched into a rambling message.

"Hey, it's me. I just wanted to… Well, I was thinking the track meet might be over, and um, I was just getting ready to go downstairs and help Mom with the last preparations for the party, and I just…"

My voice broke away, and a thick, hot lump swelled inside my throat. I struggled to continue. "I'm…I'm… I have no idea what I am trying to say. I just…I just really miss you today, Brad. I'm sorry if that's not something you want to hear. I just had to say it. Um. Okay. I guess we'll talk later. Bye."

I pressed the button to end the call, and my face was hot with embarrassment. I wished there was a way to erase what I had said. I was about to call him back and apologize when I decided to call Connor instead. Maybe Brad was with him, and I could just tell Brad about the message I left and convince him to erase it.

Connor answered on the third ring.

"Hey, Mom." He sounded tired.

"Hey!" I faked a happy greeting. "How did it go today?"

"Not bad. I broke my personal record on the four hundred. Wasn't enough to win it. But I was happy. Coach was happy."

"That's great, honey. I am really happy for you. I wish I could've been there."

"Maybe you can come up next weekend. It's a home meet."

I sensed the anticipation in his voice. He wanted me to come. "I'd really like that. I'll see if I can make that work."

"Good."

"Is...is Dad still with you?"

"He left about fifteen minutes ago."

"Is he headed back to Manchester, then?"

"Well, I guess. That's where he's living, right?"

There was a slight sarcastic edge to Connor's voice.

"Well, I'll just wait until he calls me back. I've already left a voice mail for him."

"Why? What for?"

Now Connor's tone was clipped.

"I beg your pardon?"

"What did you want to talk to him about?"

"Well, Connor, that's kind of between Dad and me." Connor had never spoken to me like that before. He sounded perturbed.

"So you guys are finally going to talk?"

"What?"

"I said, so you guys are finally going to talk?"

"I heard what you said. I really don't know, Connor. I am taking my cues from your dad right now. He wanted space. That's what I am trying to give him."

Connor was quiet. I wanted to see his face. I wanted to know what he was thinking. I had always been able to tell before. When he was little, when he was still at home, I knew how to read him. Always. When he was hurt or angry or frustrated or afraid, I could always tell. He wouldn't say anything, but I could tell, and I would ask him what was bothering him, and he would tell me, and there'd be quiet relief in his voice that I had asked. But he was silent now and two hundred miles away from me. I didn't know what he was thinking.

"What is it you want me to do, Connor?" I asked. "What am I supposed to do?"

It scared me how much I wanted my college-age son to tell me what to do. Realization washed over me like a rogue wave. Molly was right. Jonah Kirtland was right. I didn't want to make my own decisions. Or I didn't know how. Or I simply didn't have the courage to try.

My son said nothing for several seconds. When he finally spoke, he sounded older than his twenty years, like he knew the answer to my question but would not share it with me. "The team bus is ready to leave, Mom. I need to go."

Regret enveloped me.

"I'm sorry! I didn't mean to dump that question on you, Connor. Really, I'm sorry."

"Okay."

"I really will try to come next weekend. I promise."

"All right."

We said good-bye, and I reminded him that I loved him. I ended the call and stared at my phone, willing the screen to light up with an incoming call from Brad. I was still holding the silent phone in my hand when my mother opened the bedroom door and told me the party had begun and people were wondering where I was.

Lucy

Bradgate Hall, Leicestershire,
England, 1551

Sixteen

Our coach pulled into the quiet serenity of Bradgate just as the sun slipped into a hedgerow of summer clouds and approaching mist.

As we exited the coaches, the lot of us—from the marquess himself to the footman, whose name I did not know—breathed in great gulps of air, expelling the disease-tainted air of London lingering in our lungs. There was the unspoken hope among us all that we had not waited too long to leave the city where the sweating sickness was snatching souls left and right.

Were the decision mine, I would have retired with my family to the country long before then. The sickness had but one indiscriminate mercy. Sometimes it was quick. There were those who awoke with it in the morning and were dead of it by evening, burned by fever, run through with nausea and so pained with agonies in the head that they wished for death and were granted it.

My parents wrote that I should come home, no employment was worth such risk, but my father's illness lingered, and the cost of his medicine was too much for him and my mother to bear alone. I knew the money I had sent home every season had kept him alive. To leave my post surely would've hastened his death.

Plus, I had grown fond of my lady.

I had worried daily for the Lady Jane spending so much time in the company of so many at parties and balls, all at her parents' insistence. She risked contamination every time she ventured outside her rooms at Richmond Palace.

The marquess and marchioness had relentlessly sought to advance Jane's social position. As soon as the furor over the Lord Admiral's execution had abated, and people began to forget that there had ever been a tie between Lady Jane and Lord Admiral Thomas Seymour, I was tasked every fortnight with making a new dress for Jane so that she could be paraded about court as a most suitable match.

There was no longer any talk of a betrothal between His Majesty and my employer's daughter; it seemed an idea doomed in any case, since it had been the Lord Admiral's quest—among so many other ruined schemes. Talk above stairs and below as we returned to Bradgate was that King Edward had been betrothed to a French princess in a bid to placate our cantankerous neighbors across the channel.

This was, in fact, not just idle gossip among the house staff. The Privy Council, of which the marquess was now a member, had indeed orchestrated such an arrangement to be carried out when His Majesty reached his majority. He was not quite fourteen. Jane had learned of these plans from the King himself when she was his guest earlier in the summer.

The morning of that particular event, the marchioness was all aflutter in Jane's rooms as I helped her dress, berating Jane one moment as she readied to meet the King and advising her the next, as if her mother believed there was still a glimmer of hope that the King might marry Jane after all.

Even I could see that would never happen.

Jane did that morning what she always did: tried her best to please her mother. She said, "Yes, madam," to every instruction, except for when the marchioness instructed her to report back everything the King said regarding anything. The moment the marchioness said this, I felt Jane stiffen as I cinched her corset. Her indignation rippled beneath my finger-tips and I shuddered. I had now been her dressmaker for nearly three years. I knew Jane would not let the appalling request slip by without a comment.

"Madam, I could not possibly dishonor the King by spying on him," Jane had said, earning such a quick and terrible slap across her cheek, it nearly knocked her and me both off our feet.

"How dare you accuse me of asking such a thing!" The marchioness seethed.

Jane's back tensed under my fingers as I steadied my own feet and returned to hooking her bodice. I rubbed the small of her back with my thumb as I believed it was on the tip of my lady's tongue to ask her mother what it was she called that kind of surveillance if not spying. I did not want her to ask it. To my utter relief, she did not.

"Beg her pardon," I whispered through my teeth.

Jane inhaled and swallowed. "Please forgive me, madam. I misspoke."

The marchioness closed the remaining distance between us. Her eyes glittered with anger. "Leave us, Lucy," she said.

What could I do but curtsy and make my leave?

When I was summoned to the coaches later to accompany Lady Jane to court, I rode with the other attendants. I did not see Jane again until that afternoon when I was called to her waiting room to straighten her sleeves, smooth the wrinkles in her train, and straighten the edge of her french hood. We did not speak. Other attendants were with us as Jane waited the King's summons. A tiny bloom of ashy red lay across the line of Jane's chin where one of the marchioness's rings had dug into her flesh. Someone had filled the wound with peach-colored talc.

It was many hours later, after the evening meal, that Lady Jane returned to the guest bedchamber. Mrs. Ellen helped her undress and spoke gently to her. I stood at Mrs. Ellen's elbow and took the yellow satin gown, one that I had made from a French pattern, to place it in the wardrobe in the next room. Jane looked both exhausted and animated, older than her fourteen years; I don't think Mrs. Ellen noticed that underneath the obvious fatigue was a veiled layer of perplexed delight. Something had happened in the hours that Jane had been with the King. Something Jane wished to hide because she didn't know what to make of it. She caught my eye in the mirror in front of us and then quickly looked away.

I knew in that moment someone else had also been at court that day. Young Edward Seymour.

In the early days after the Lord Admiral's execution, Jane had grieved Thomas Seymour's death as one who had little knowledge of all that he'd been accused and suspected of. She knew he had wanted to overthrow his brother, the elder Edward Seymour, Protector of the King. She knew he had plans to snatch the King away in the middle of the night to free him from what he called the Privy Council's prisonlike hold on His Majesty. She didn't know he had been planning to secretly marry the Princess Elizabeth nor that there was talk that the Princess had been with child— his child—as his wife, the Queen Dowager, lay dying. Jane didn't know that he had even toyed with making her his bride when it seemed he could not get the Princess, so desperate was he to regain power at court.

And when the admiral was arrested, Jane expected her parents to rise to his defense, which they did not. She expected the Protector to seek a pardon for his brother, which he did not.

For many months, Jane did not know what to do with the attraction she felt for the Protector's son. Young Edward's father had signed off on the execution of the admiral, the man who had taken her into his care, lavished gifts on her, and brought happiness to her beloved Queen Katherine. Jane spoke of her conflicted thoughts once in a while to me, though I think only to me. For the most part, she poured her being into her studies to quell her fears that she would never know happiness again.

She wrote many letters to learned friends of her tutor, Mr. Aylmer, a passionate Reformer who encouraged such endeavors.

The letters and the learning kept my lady occupied. It seemed to me that the new religion had seeped into her very bones and soul, and her grieving the Lord Admiral's death was a separate spiritual pursuit altogether. My father told me on one of my visits home that the marquess and dozens of other noblemen had embraced the new religion because King Henry's court was favorable toward it. He and my mother had adopted the practices of the new religion when I was but a child, initially for the same reasons. But for Lady Jane, political posturing had nothing to do with her devotion to the church of Christ that had no pope. She truly believed in it.

It was also no doubt encouraging to Lady Jane that the house of Seymour was also opposed to Rome. In the months that preceded the admiral's execution, and when young Edward Seymour was present at public events, Jane would confide in me afterward that she could not seem to stem the admiration she felt for him, despite his father's role in the admiral's death. And though she tried to avoid young Edward's company, her parents saw to it that she was often at the same events he attended. This, even though the Protector had been removed from his post after disagreements between him and John Dudley, Earl of Warwick. According to conversations I overheard between Jane's parents, John Dudley was a powerful voice on the Council, who apparently had his eye on the elder Seymour's enviable position as guardian of the King's interests.

Jane seemed to want affirmation from me that it was no sin to admire young Edward Seymour. I told her you cannot help whom your heart is drawn to. Redirecting your heart's inclinations by sheer will is like trying to tease an eastern wind to change its course by holding up your arms and pointing west.

On that evening of her reception with the King, as I took her gown to stow in the wardrobe, I heard Lady Jane dismiss Mrs. Ellen to her room, as she wanted to retire. It had been an exhausting day. I lingered at the wardrobe, ready to head to my own cot in the adjoining sleeping quarters, but listening for movement on the other side of the door.

Jane opened the door into the wardrobe room and asked if I might bring her a different chemise to wear to bed. The one she had on made her itch. I followed her back into her room with a soft gown, very much like the one she already had on, and helped her change.

"I saw him today." She did not look at me.

"I know."

She swiveled her head around. "Who has spoken to you?" Her voice was urgent.

"No one, my lady. I have spoken to no one, and no one has spoken to me. I can see it in your eyes. That is all. I daresay no one else can, my lady. Not even Mrs. Ellen. And I shall say nothing to anyone."

Jane relaxed and then handed me a brush. She sat on a couch, and I began to pull the soft bristles through her long, brown hair.

"I saw him looking at me from across the banquet hall. I was at the King's table. All through the meal, Edward Seymour stared at me. I tried to be attentive to the King, but my eyes kept turning to Edward across the room."

"Did Edward Seymour look…angry, my lady?"

"No. I should say he looked…vexed."

"Were you able to speak to him?" My strokes were long and gentle.

"There was a moment during the dancing that I spoke to him."

I leaned over her and smiled. "Did he ask you to dance?"

She smiled back. "He did. Just the one dance."

I waited for her to tell me more. I could not ask her outright.

"Edward asked how it was that I had secured the King's attention. He said it as if…as if he were jealous, Lucy."

"Perhaps he was."

She grinned. And the little red bloom at her chin widened. She touched it but didn't seem to be aware that she had.

"So?" I asked.

"I reminded him that the King and I are second cousins. Surely he wouldn't begrudge the King time with his cousin."

"Well done!" I said cheerfully.

Jane turned her head toward me. "Then he said to me, 'Perhaps you and your second cousin spoke of his impending marriage to Princess Elisabeth of Valois?'"

"He did?"

"Indeed! And I said I was not at liberty to divulge the details of my private conversations with the King!"

I laughed. "My lady! How clever you are!"

She turned her head away from me, smiling, and I resumed my brushing. "'Tis true," she said. After a moment of silence. "'Tis true the King is to marry the princess from France. He told me himself."

It was impossible to guess how this knowledge met with her. "And is my lady at peace with that arrangement?"

"I like my cousin, I mean, the King. But I do not think I would marry him were the choice mine alone to make. I have no wish to be a queen. And he is…impatient. I do not think he cares for books and learning as I do. He does not avail himself of the new religion's many writings. We scarce had anything to talk about."

"Perhaps the affairs of the throne keep him too busy to read all the books you read?"

She was thoughtful for a moment. "I suppose."

Again, there was silence.

"It was not that way with Edward Seymour," she finally said.

"My lady?"

"We had much to talk about. I was sad when the music ended and the dance was over. I went back to the King and searched my mind for topics to discuss."

"I see. So you and the King had few words?" I asked.

She nodded.

I leaned over and whispered, "Then you shall have little to report back to the marchioness!"

Jane erupted into a fit of laughter, sweet and childlike, such that tears began to roll down her cheek and rest on the crimson remnant of her mother's scorn.

It was less than a fortnight later that the sickness began to plague the streets and halls of London, sweeping its way into palaces and crofts with equal vigor.

Jane did not see the King again, nor Edward Seymour, before the marquess was finally persuaded to see his family safely back to Bradgate.

My lady had said nothing to me, but I knew she wondered when she would see young Seymour again. At Bradgate, London and all that attended it seemed very far away.

But not long after our arrival, we received news that would change everything for the Grey household.

The marchioness's two half brothers, young lads of her late father, the Duke of Suffolk, and his second wife, had died of the sweating sickness, both of them within hours of each other. The marchioness's stepmother, the Duchess Katherine Willoughby, was a nobleman's widow without an heir, a mother without titled sons.

Overnight the Marquess and Marchioness of Dorset became Duke and Duchess of Suffolk.

Seventeen

Jane seemed happy to be back at Bradgate, away from the endless parties, sporting events, and ceremonies that kept her in the public eye and me forever with a needle and thread in my hand.

I, too, was content to be in the pastoral countryside, closer to home and only a mile from where my sister, Cecily, had taken a position at the manor home of a wealthy merchant and his wife.

I was no longer Bridget's apprentice; she had finally retired to her daughter's humble home in Leeds when she could no longer conceal her failing sight. But the duchess certainly would not trust the household's wardrobe to an eighteen-year-old seamstress such as me, and in truth I did not wish to be responsible for the duchess's garments. She brought in two seasoned dressmakers to take Bridget's place as well as half a dozen new and accomplished attendants as befitting her new title. And while I feared I might be relegated to mending tears in riding breeches and farthingales in some back turret, the duchess let me be. Mrs. Ellen told me Jane asked her mother if she might keep me. Everyone at court always commented on the dresses I made for her—so Jane told her mother—and that comment alone was enough to keep me at Jane's side.

With no court appearances to make that summer, Jane's parents had the time and inclination to employ themselves with the matter of Jane's betrothal.

Jane was never privy to any of these conversations, nor was I. But there was always an attendant or server or maid pouring wine or opening a window or lighting a lamp to hear snippets of these dialogues. When the day cooled and the household staff took their evening meal, these overheard conversations would be discussed and dissected, I suppose because we, too, had time on our hands those long summer evenings far away from London's frantic pace.

I did not take part in the conversations, though I was often subtly invited to do so. Surely I, who spent so much time in the dressing rooms of the duchess and her daughters, could shed light on matters that would affect the household staff. But no one asked me outright to confirm or deny anything. Even among the staff, there was a sense of class and privilege. It would have been unseemly to ask me, because of my proximity to the family. Yet often the room turned to me for a comment, and I usually would not give it. Sometimes I could tune out the conversation, which was not an unwise thing to do; often the talk turned to topics no one had enough information to adequately discuss.

But the evening when the after-meal talk turned to Jane's marital prospects, I lingered at the board, poking at a dish of baked apples and listening to every word.

According to one of the duke's valets, there was much talk between the duke and duchess that afternoon on the immediacy to secure a suitable match for Jane.

"If she didn't always have her fair nose in a book all the time, she might be easier to pair up," said one of the pages. "She's not altogether unpleasant to look upon. But a man likes a lass who can laugh at a yarn, sing a fair tune, strike a coquettish pose, eh?"

"It dinna matter what the man who marries the Lady Jane thinks of her," a maid said. "That man will marry whomever his parents say he will marry. That's the way it always is."

"Nay. She will probably be stuck with some old lord who's outlived three wives already and hasn't an heir," another maid said. "He'll need a cane to walk down the wedding aisle."

"And a potion to climb into the wedding bed!" the page quipped.

The room erupted in laughter. I was a second away from leaving the board when the valet cleared his throat. "The duke and duchess have not chosen an old man for Lady Jane," he said.

All eyes turned to him, including my own.

"Pray, tell us!" said the first maid.

"They have dispatched a messenger to the Duke of Somerset."

My spoon trembled a bit in my hand. Somerset was the very same elder Edward Seymour, the former Lord Protector.

Father to young Edward Seymour.

"Somerset?" the page said. "But 'e is married!"

" 'E's got a son, you dolt!" the second maid exclaimed.

"Aye, the young Edward Seymour," the valet continued.

I could not help myself. I spoke.

"What kind of dispatch did they send?" I asked.

Heads swiveled to look at me.

"Do you not know, Lucy?" the valet answered, genuinely surprised that I did not.

"What kind of dispatch?" I repeated my question, with no hint of anything but mild curiosity.

"The duke has asked Somerset to come to Bradgate forthwith to discuss the marriage arrangement of Lady Jane to his son." The valet stared at me.

"But Somerset is no longer the King's Protector," said one of the older housekeepers. "Pushed out by… What's his name?"

"John Dudley," said another.

"Yes. Dudley. I am much surprised the duke would consider a betrothal between Somerset's son and his eldest daughter. Think on it! Somerset was imprisoned in the Tower not so long ago."

"Ah, but he is there no longer," the valet said. "Fortunes turn on a moment at court."

"Yes, but he *was* in the Tower. If you were the duke, would you marry your daughter, who is what, fourth in line to the throne of England, to the son of a man who'd been overthrown and imprisoned? I do not see the wisdom in it."

"Fortunes turn on a *moment,*" the valet said again. "You spend too much time fluffing pillows at the duke's country estate. I've seen how fortunes can change at court. One moment you are disgraced, and the next you are exalted."

"Aye, and the exact opposite can 'appen, quick as you can blink!" the housekeeper said. "Exalted one moment, and kneeling before the executioner the next."

"Think what you will. The dispatch was sent." The valet then turned to me. "And it is expected Somerset will make his way with all haste to Bradgate, accompanied by young Edward."

He continued to stare at me, inviting me to comment on his conversation with the housekeeper. All eyes were on me, as the room waited to hear what I would say about a match between a young girl whose frame I knew as well as my own and the son of a fallen leader. I spent more time with Jane than any of them.

"We would be wise to prepare to welcome Somerset and his family with the grace and dignity the duke expects of us." I rose and took my leave.

There was snickering as I walked away. I heard someone mimic my words, tossing them at my back with derision. And then there was laughter. I did not turn as I made my way out of the staff dining room.

My heart longed to share the news with Jane that Edward was coming to Bradgate and that her father was seeing to her betrothal to him. But I could not trust in hearsay. I could not know beyond doubt that the valet's words were true—that a letter had been dispatched and that he knew its contents. I also could not bring below-stairs chatter into the chamber of my employer's daughter. Mrs. Ellen would have my head. And so would my own mother, if she were to learn of it. I was the daughter of a gentleman tailor, not a milkman.

Plus, I was troubled by what the old housekeeper had said. Jane's previous betrothal hopes had been pinned on the ruler of England. And now her father was considering the son of a duke whose political downfall had recently sent him to the Tower?

How much did Jane know of these things? How much did she need to know?

I did not wish to return to my chamber, just yet, with these thoughts tumbling in my head. The evening twilight, always long and unhurried in an English summer, bid me to come out to the garden. And I obeyed.

The heat of the day had dissipated, and evening birdsong filled the purple-blue haze of approaching nightfall. I breathed deeply the lavender- and rose-scented air, and the beauty of the coming night calmed me. I made my way down a set of stone steps to the edge of one of the reflecting pools. An infant moon was starting to shimmer on its surface, and I began to sing softly a Welsh lullaby my mother used to sing to me.

I missed my parents and my village home of Haversfield, especially on lovely summer nights like this one. I had been to visit my parents after the last Christmas, and then only for a few days, as those in noble circles made the cold winter months bearable by giving parties. And parties required the making of dresses. My parents, especially my father, had always been careful in their praise for me, measuring it out so that I should not grow proud or ungrateful and instilled in me a desire to be found worthy of whatever gifts and abilities the Lord God had bestowed on me. They also reminded me, whenever I saw them, that Providence had secured for me a most important post as dressmaker to the Lady Jane, and that I should, at all times, be thankful, loyal, and gracious, not only to the Lady Jane but to her parents. And to seek God's favor in every dealing I had with this family.

The lullaby on my lips and the longing in my heart to see my mother and father brought tears to my eyes, and I found I could no longer keep singing. The tune fell away from my lips, and there was silence for just a moment, and then a man's voice.

"I would that you should continue."

I stumbled sideways as I snapped my head around. A young man sat on a bench behind me, overlooking the reflecting pool. He had a book in his lap, but it was closed. In the fading light, I saw that he wore a dark suit coat and a ruffled white shirt. He wasn't nobility, but neither was he a groundskeeper. He sprang from the bench to steady my footing.

"I beg your pardon!" he exclaimed. "I truly had no wish to startle you, miss."

"I d-did not see you there!" I stammered as his arm on mine steadied me.

"Please forgive me. Are you quite all right?"

"Yes. Yes, of course." My eyes were drawn to his hand on my elbow. He dropped it.

"Again, I do beg your pardon. I was simply taken with your little tune. I have not heard it since I was a child. My grandmother used to sing that lullaby to me."

His voice was kind, and he seemed genuinely remorseful for having startled me. He looked about twenty years, with dark brown hair, dark eyes, and educated speech.

"Yes. I..." I found myself unable to take my eyes away from his. I felt my cheeks color. I was glad he could not see them. "Good evening." I took one step away from him, ready to curtsy and escape.

"Wait! Please!" he said quickly, again touching my elbow. "Are you a guest here as well?"

"Pardon?" I whispered, looking at his hand, which again he dropped. "Are you a guest here at Bradgate?"

I stiffened with embarrassment and shame. Only another guest would ask that. "No," I said quickly, curtsying and turning to leave.

"My name is Nicholas Staverton," he said quickly, stepping in front of me. "I am here as a guest of John Aylmer, the tutor."

"Welcome to Bradgate, sir," I said and again attempted to make my leave.

But he stood there in front of me as the moon continued to rise, and his face changed to one of concern. "Are you troubled?"

I could not form a suitable answer to such a question. I just stood there staring at him, amazed and astonished at such a strange and personal inquiry.

He pointed to my cheek with his finger, just inches from my jaw line. "You...you have been crying."

Instinctively I drew my hand to my cheek. I had stopped singing moments earlier because emotion had overcome me as I thought about my parents. Those unchecked tears had slid down my cheeks. And there they rested, sparkling, no doubt, in the pearled moonlight.

"I am quite well. Thank you very much for your concern," I whispered, anxious to be away from him, but also strangely frozen to where I stood.

"You are not a guest?" he asked again.

"I am dressmaker to the Lady Jane, daughter of the Duke of Suffolk."

His eyes brightened. "You are Lucy! Lady Jane has told me all about you!"

Again, I started to totter on my feet, but this time I managed to keep my footing without Nicholas Staverton's assistance. "I beg your pardon?"

"I sat in the classes today with Lady Jane and Lady Katherine and their tutor, Mr. Aylmer. I am a student at Oxford. I am here as Mr. Aylmer's guest. Lady Jane spoke of you!"

"She...she spoke of me?" My voice sounded mousy and thin to my ears.

He laughed. "Oh! Not to worry. The Lady Jane spoke most highly of you. She said you are one of the few in the household who will listen to her thoughts on the writings of the Reformers, save for Mr. Aylmer, of course. She thinks you are very wise."

"I... That is very kind of her, of course."

We stood there, looking at each other. I was flummoxed to my core. He, on the other hand, looked serene and in no hurry to end our exchange. My heart began to pound in my chest.

"That song you were singing, do you know all the words?" he said.

"I... Yes, I know the words."

"I haven't heard it in such a long time. Perhaps you could dictate them to me, before I return to Oxford. I should like to have a record of the words. My grandmother died when I was little. I have missed her. So perhaps I might...see you again?"

The pounding intensified.

"Perhaps," I said.

Mr. Staverton smiled. "Perhaps you would recite them to me?"

"Yes," I answered, unable to keep from smiling myself. Darkness was falling all around us. I curtsied hastily. "Good night, Mr. Staverton."

I sped away on the steps that had brought me to the pool.

"So I will see you tomorrow, then, Miss...Lucy?"

"Day!" I called out and continued my brisk pace.

"Day?"

I turned around. "My name is Miss Day. Lucy Day."

I continued up the steps, the pounding in my chest now a different rhythm.

I turned back once to look at him. He still stood at the pool, watching me go.

It was many hours before sleep came to me that night.

Eighteen

The day following my meeting with Nicholas Staverton at the reflecting pool, Jane was summoned to her parents' reception room. Wondering if perhaps they would be advising her of the imminent arrival of Edward Seymour, I encouraged her to choose a happy gown, one that her mother especially would find attractive. Jane allowed me to bring to her a dress of crimson damask with turned-back sleeves lined with silvery white satin that shone like the moon. Tiny pearls lined the seams.

As I dressed her, she stared at me, brows furrowed. "What is it that you know, Lucy Day?" she asked me. "Why do you have me wear this dress, when a plain black velvet frock would suffice for my parents?"

I paused. "This gown is exceptionally lovely on you, my lady," I said a moment later.

"Why should I need to appear lovely to my parents? What do you know?"

"My lady, please don't ask me," I murmured, feeling the heat of embarrassment that she could so easily tell I was keeping something from her.

She reached for my arm. "Are they sending me away? Are they sending me back to court?"

"No, my lady. Not at all."

"What is it then? I can see in your eyes that something is disquieting you. What is it? I order you to tell me."

"My lady, please."

"Tell me."

"What I know is only what I have heard below stairs, my lady. It might not be true."

"What have you heard? Have they chosen someone for me? Is that what it is? Do you know whom they have chosen?" Her voice trembled.

I came around to face her and took her hands in mine. "I know nothing for certain, my lady. Do you understand? I have only heard talk. And I am not to share gossip from below stairs with you. Please don't ask me."

I started to pull my hands away, but she kept them firm in her grasp.

"Lucy, please. Have they chosen someone?"

"My lady…"

"Do I know him? Is he very old? Has he already had a wife? Was he kind to her?"

Her questions flew off her lips like seedpods off a thistle. I saw dread in her eyes, and a slim line of sweat had broken on her brow. Compassion for her overcame me.

I leaned forward so no one could hear me if her panicked questions had brought anyone running to the closed door.

"You mustn't repeat this to anyone, my lady," I whispered.

She nodded frantically, eyes wide.

"The man they have chosen is no one that you should fear," I said.

"How do you know this?" she implored. "How do you know I should not fear him?"

"Because you know him. You are fond of him."

Her eyes never left mine. "Fond?" she whispered.

"Yes. Especially fond, my lady."

A second slipped by. "Edward," she breathed.

I nodded and stepped back.

She closed her eyes and inhaled, as if she wanted to hold that moment in her lungs and hide it away somewhere. "How do you know this?" she said, her eyes still shut.

"One of your father's valets said he saw a letter that your father sent to the Duke of Somerset, asking him to come to Bradgate to discuss the betrothal between you and Edward."

Jane's eyes flew open. "Edward is coming here?"

"This is what the valet said, my lady. I do not know if it is true. I do not know if any of this is true."

Jane reached for the couch behind her and sat down on it. "I never dreamed they would choose someone I cared for. I did not think it was possible. I still cannot believe it."

I knelt beside her. "And it would be prudent to wait to believe it until your parents speak of it. Please, say nothing until they do!"

Jane laid a hand on my shoulder. "Do not fret, Lucy. I shall say nothing."

Despite her assurances, I was the one now trembling. If I was wrong, Jane would have to bear a double disappointment. If her parents were to choose someone other than Edward Seymour, she would not only have to accept that loss but submit to a marriage with someone she did not love; a predicament she had long resigned herself to, and which I had just swept away with a word.

"If I am mistaken… If the valet is mistaken—," I began, but she cut me off.

"The valet has no reason to spread a lie such as this. I daresay he has nothing to gain by it."

I sat back on my folded legs, wishing I could pull the minutes back. She must've sensed my regret. She put both hands on my shoulders.

"I am forever grateful that you told me, Lucy. When they tell me—"

"If."

"I shall have the dignified and proper response of a refined young lady prepared to do her parents' bidding." Then she began to laugh. "Exceptionally prepared!"

I laughed too, albeit nervously. "My lady, you are only fourteen! Surely you will not marry so soon!"

"Perhaps in the spring!" she said happily. She stood, pulling me to my feet as well. "Can you just imagine, Lucy! Can you imagine it! Edward!" She giggled.

"You must stop giggling!" I whispered.

"I shall try!" But she erupted into more laughter.

"My lady!"

"I am trying!" She spun around the room once and then caught my hands to spin with her.

"You are not trying in the least!" I said.

"Oh, Lucy. I am so happy."

"My lady, *please.*"

A knock sounded at her door and Jane stopped spinning. We fell into each other and she laughed. "Yes?" she said.

Mrs. Ellen opened the door, gave us both a cursory look, and then nodded to Jane.

"Your parents will receive you now."

Jane spun around to me. "Come with me!" she said.

"I cannot!"

"Walk with me to the room, then. Bear my train."

Mrs. Ellen was frowning, pondering what secret Jane and I had between us. I agreed to walk with Jane merely to silence her.

"As you wish." I pulled up her train in my arms and followed her to the door. At the threshold Mrs. Ellen reached out a steady hand and smoothed an errant curl that had sprung from Jane's hood.

"Jumping about in your chamber in this fine dress, were you?" Mrs. Ellen said to Jane, but she cast a critical eye toward me.

"Oh, don't chastise Lucy, Ellen. I am the one who felt like spinning."

"Now don't be giving the duke and duchess any reason to be cross with you, lass," Mrs. Ellen said as Jane and I stepped into the hall. "Mind your tongue."

"Yes, yes," Jane said hastily, and I heard a suppressed laugh in her tone. Mrs. Ellen continued to look after us with questioning eyes. But she asked us nothing and I was grateful.

We made our way into the main corridor and were soon passing the classroom where Jane and her sister performed their studies. My eyes, of their own will, peered into the room as we walked past. Nicholas Staverton was leaning over a writing desk. He raised his head and smiled. He began to move quickly to the door, but I was obliged to keep walking. Though I could not see him, I sensed him behind me at the door of the classroom, watching me follow Lady Jane down the long hallway.

"You met Nicholas Staverton," Jane said softly when we were several steps away.

"P-pardon?" I stuttered, though I had heard her.

"You met Nicholas Staverton," she said again, and she looked over her shoulder in the direction of the classroom. I did the same without thinking, and there he was. Mr. Staverton, leaning on the door frame, watching us. Jane's tutor, Mr. Aylmer, stood next to him. Mr. Aylmer looked vexed. Mr. Staverton was smiling.

I jerked my head back to face forward as my cheeks bloomed with heat.

"Mr. Aylmer looks pained," I said quickly, anxious to move away from any conversation about the young student visiting from Oxford.

"He surely doesn't approve of this scarlet dress. Princess Elizabeth wears only black and gray, like a dutiful Reformed girl should. I *shouldn't* be wearing it. And I know you met Mr. Staverton because he told me this morning while Mr. Aylmer read my Latin translation."

She peeked over her shoulder at me. A hint of a smile rested on her lips.

"Oh…yes, I did," I managed. "Quite by accident. I was out for some air after supper last night. He… I…I was at the reflecting pool. I didn't see him."

"Yes. He told me that. He told me you were singing. He thought it was lovely."

"I am sure he was only being kind." I nearly dropped the train of her gown.

"No. He said it was lovely. Angelic. You were singing a lullaby his grandmother used to sing to him."

"I doubt it was angelic," I said, attempting to laugh and failing.

"He was quite taken with you, Lucy. Quite taken. Earlier this morning, I was jealous of you."

"My lady, I—"

"He wants to see you before he leaves tomorrow. So you can tell him the words to the lullaby. Though I daresay that it is just an excuse to see you."

"But I—"

"Maybe you should see him now, while I am with my parents."

"I do not know, my lady, I am not—"

But Jane stopped, turned, and held up her hand. From far down the hallway, I heard footsteps. I hadn't the courage to turn. Several moments later, Mr. Staverton stood beside us.

"My lady," he said, bowing. "Miss Day."

I curtsied but could not raise my eyes to his.

"Mr. Staverton, perhaps you and Lucy, I mean, Miss Day, might wait for me in the music room while my parents receive me?"

"It would be my pleasure!" Mr. Staverton replied quickly.

"Miss Day shall be along shortly, then. You might wish to bring your quill and tablet."

Jane politely nodded a wordless dismissal, turned quickly, and took a step forward.

I looked back for just a second before joining her, and Nicholas Staverton was bowing to me.

I arrived at the music room before Mr. Staverton, for which I was grateful. My heart was skipping about underneath my corset and nearly causing me to belch. I stood at a window overlooking the vast park at Bradgate and counted slowly in Latin, as Jane had taught me, to steady my thundering heart. It had been a very long time since a man had so captured my attention. A very long time. I had forgotten how confounding it was.

I did not hear him step into the room.

"Quindecim," I whispered.

"Fifteen?"

I whirled around.

"I seem to excel at startling you, Miss Day. I assure you, my intentions are far from it."

"I was counting," I said, somewhat dazed.

"What were you counting?"

"What?"

Nicholas came to the window beside me and looked out on the park, convinced, no doubt, that I'd been tallying stags or geese or puffy clouds in the sky. "What were you counting?" he asked again.

His nearness was mesmerizing, and I knew it was fruitless to pretend any longer that it wasn't. I was not a skilled liar. I never had been.

"Absolutely nothing," I whispered.

Nicholas turned to me, a puzzled look on his face. Quite endearing, that.

"Why were you counting nothing? In Latin?" His voice was soft, inviting.

"To calm myself."

"Calm yourself? Are you restless?" He laughed.

"Something like that." I knew my face would turn as crimson as Jane's dress. I felt the shade spring to my cheeks, and I just let it. What else could I do? I could not look at him.

He placed his hands on the windowsill, and our fingertips almost touched. "Then perhaps I shall have to start counting as well. I am also somewhat restless."

"You are mocking me," I murmured.

"Indeed I am not. Have you tried counting in Greek?"

"Lady Jane has not taught me Greek," I said.

"Ah, so she taught you the Latin, did she? Perhaps you would allow someone else to teach you how to count in Greek?"

The thundering in my chest resumed its frenzied pace. "Whatever for?"

"For counting absolutely nothing in Greek."

I couldn't keep a smile from spreading across my face.

"Miss Day, might I write to you after I return to Oxford? And perhaps you might do me the honor of writing back to me? You are not betrothed, are you? Does someone have your heart?"

"No," I replied, blushing anew.

"I should like to know everything about you, Miss Day."

"I do not imagine there is much to tell you, Mr. Staverton," I said, moving my hand away from the window and the dizzying proximity of his fingers. "I am the daughter of a gentleman tailor. I make dresses for the daughter of the Duke of Suffolk."

"You sing lullabies," Mr. Staverton said.

"One lullaby."

He went on. "You care for the people God places in your path. You are polite to strangers. Gracious to people who do not deserve grace. Curious about the deep things of God. You listen when others do not. You do not spread gossip or speak ill of those who have made poor choices. You are patient. Intelligent. Kind."

"Who...? What...?" but I couldn't form a full sentence, so surprised was I.

"The Lady Jane speaks very highly of you," Nicholas said. "I told you that last night after I unfortunately interrupted a very beautiful lullaby."

At that moment I remembered Jane had instructed him to bring his quill and tablet so that I might dictate to him the words of the lullaby.

"You forgot your quill and tablet," I said.

He looked down at his empty hands. "Indeed."

"But you went back to the classroom to get them."

"So I did."

"And?"

He laughed. "And I had my quill and tablet in my hands, and I was about to bring them here to the music room, but I thought that if I forgot them, I would have to arrange for another meeting with you before I leave Bradgate."

Nicholas was about to say something else when Jane swept into the room, her face radiant.

"My lady!" I said, instantly afraid she had heard everything, when I knew that was impossible. "You are back so soon!"

"Lucy! 'Tis true. 'Tis true!"

She came to me, then grabbed my hand and pulled me toward the door. "Mama says you are to see to my wardrobe at once. He is coming tomorrow. Hello, Mr. Staverton."

"My lady," Nicholas said, bowing, his brow crinkled with amusement.

"Tomorrow?" I said.

"Yes, yes!" She dropped my hand. "We are to prepare my gowns!" Jane flew out of the room, the train I had carried wafting up about the door frame like a wave on a tossed sea.

I turned toward Nicholas and curtsied. "Until another time, Mr. Staverton."

He took a step toward me. "I will see you tomorrow, before I leave?" I nodded.

He inclined his head toward the doorway and Jane's retreating foot-falls. "What is true?"

I wanted to tell him. I wanted to tell him sometimes Providence shines down on you and you are allowed to marry the one your heart beats for.

"I am unfortunately not at liberty to tell you, Mr. Staverton," I said instead. But I smiled at him, and I held his gaze, before I turned and left to follow Jane.

I think he knew I wished I could.

Nineteen

J ane was awake at dawn's light. I had no sooner dressed when a maid
was sent to fetch me. I followed the young girl to Jane's bedchamber,
down hallways that were bathed in silence. No one else was awake.

I found her standing in front of the gown her mother had asked her
to wear—a lovely garment of midnight blue, trimmed in ermine and Flo-
rentine gold filigree, with a matching reticulated and jeweled caul for
Jane's long brown hair.

Jane was frowning. When she saw me, I fell to a curtsy, and she motioned me forward. "I think I should wear green," she said, poking at the
deep blue fabric.

"Oh…but the duchess—," I began.

"Yes, I know. But Edward likes green. I heard him say it once."

I looked about the room for Mrs. Ellen, whom I knew would direct
Jane's attention back to the directive from the duchess. The dress in front
of us was the dress Jane was to wear. I had been awake past midnight
making sure every jewel, bit of lace, and trim was securely fastened. Mrs.
Ellen was not in the room.

"This dress is quite spectacular, my lady. I daresay your young lord
will not notice it is not green."

"Do you think Edward will be happy I've been chosen for him?" Jane
said absently, stroking the dress but seeming not to be aware of her hand
on the fabric.

"Of course, my lady."

"You say that because you must."

I took a step toward her. "But remember when you were with His Majesty earlier this summer? Remember how you told me Edward stared at you from across the table? Remember how he wished to remind you the King would be marrying a French princess?"

The corners of Jane's mouth drew upward slightly. "He did stare at me, did he not?"

"Yes," I said, though I had been in my garret room at Richmond Palace the evening Jane was with the King. "He was vexed that you had the King's attention and not his."

"Indeed," Jane said, sliding her finger down the dress's jeweled bodice. "What if my father and Edward's father do not agree on the terms? What if—"

"I wouldn't think on things that may never require thought, my lady."

"It is not official, you know. My father told me he is in *discussions* with the Duke of Somerset regarding my betrothal." Jane looked up at me and smiled. "My mother told me I was to behave civilly and graciously to young Edward Seymour, no matter what I thought of him as a future husband, or she'd make life miserable for me. I had to pinch myself not to burst out laughing!"

Jane chanced a giggle, though I could see she was still nervous.

Mrs. Ellen came into the room, saw us both, and clucked her tongue loudly. "What is this?" She turned to me. "You will not be dressing her this early. The dress will wrinkle!"

"I have not asked her to dress me, Ellen."

"Then why is Lucy here? The sun is just now breaking over the park!"

"Because I asked her here. I thought perhaps I should wear my green gown, the one Lucy made for the King's birthday party last October."

Mrs. Ellen pointed to the blue dress. "The duchess will have both my head and Lucy's if you are not in this gown at noon!"

"Edward likes green."

"The young earl will not be betrothed to your dress, lass," Mrs. Ellen said. "Come now. I have a nice bath prepared for you. Let Lucy downstairs to eat before the house awakes."

Jane turned to me. "You will come when it is time for me to dress?"

"Most certainly," I assured her.

The morning passed quickly because I was summoned to Jane's younger sister Lady Katherine after breakfast to mend a tear in the dress she would be wearing to receive the Duke of Somerset and his family later that afternoon. I could not help but wince when I saw that Katherine's dress was a calming shade of sea green.

I could only hope that Jane would be too preoccupied with the proceedings of the day to notice.

When I was finally free to return to Lady Jane's rooms, I found her to be strangely calm and serene.

"Are you quite all right, my lady?" I closed the door behind me so she could dress.

"I am, Lucy. Don't fret over me, or I shall lose my composure, and I've spent all morning praying it into existence. Fetch that nightmare of a gown."

I lifted the midnight blue gown from where it hung and brought it to her. "'Tis not a nightmare of a gown, my lady. 'Tis a dream upon a midnight sea."

"You really think so?" she said as she stepped into the skirt.

"I do."

As I continued to dress her with the bodice, sleeves, sash, and caul, Jane practiced greetings under her breath.

"My lord, how wonderful it is to see you. I trust your travel to Bradgate was pleasant. My lord, how wonderful it is to see you. I trust your travel to Bradgate was pleasant," she whispered.

When her outfit was complete, I turned her to the looking glass in her room so she could see how elegant she looked.

"There now. You look like a princess," I said.

She fingered the sapphire necklace that hung at her throat and cocked her head to look at the caul as it hung down her back, glittering with gold filigree rosettes and tiny pearls.

A knock sounded at the door. Mrs. Ellen came in at Jane's bidding. "Why, you are a vision, my sweet lass!" she cooed.

Jane smiled at her but said nothing.

There was a moment of silence, and then Mrs. Ellen gently asked Jane if she was ready to go. Her parents were asking for her.

Jane turned to me. "Did you say your prayers this morning, Lucy?"

"Of course, my lady."

"Did you pray for me?"

I reached for her hand and squeezed it. "I pray for you every morning, my lady."

She squeezed mine back and then inhaled deeply, raised her chin, and asked me to kindly bear her train.

Our walk to the duke's reception room, with Mrs. Ellen at our side, was nothing like the one the day before, when she wasn't with us. Jane didn't speak and neither did I.

Once, I did hear Jane whisper, "My lord, how wonderful it is to see you. I trust your travel to Bradgate was pleasant."

At the door to the reception room, she turned to me. "I shall see you in my chamber when I return, Lucy." And with that, Mrs. Ellen opened the door, Jane stepped inside, and all I saw was the back of a young man with thick hair the color of wheat.

I made my way back to Jane's rooms to tidy up the wardrobe after dressing her. On my way I met Mr. Staverton on the stairs. He was dressed in clothes to travel and carried a cape over his arms. I curtsied.

"Oh, Miss Day!" His tone was joyous and hopeful. "I was much afraid I would not see you again before I returned to Oxford."

"You are leaving Bradgate, Mr. Staverton?" He was not supposed to return to Oxford until nightfall. It was just past noon. A strange and tiny ribbon of sadness wound its way through me in an instant.

"With the Duke of Somerset and his family here, Mr. Aylmer thought it best I take my leave at midday so as not to trouble Lady Jane's parents. I hear today is a most important day for young Jane."

"Yes. Yes it is."

He paused for a moment. "Would you care to walk with me to the carriage, Miss Day?"

"It would be my pleasure."

We began to descend the stairs. An awkward silence fell about us. "And how is Lady Jane this morning?" he finally asked.

"She is well," I answered. "She is nervous."

"Of course. Mr. Aylmer tells me she is to be betrothed to the young Edward Seymour."

I nodded.

"Are they acquainted?"

"Yes. Jane's guardian was Edward's uncle."

"Ah, yes. The unfortunate Lord Admiral."

I stiffened involuntarily. "Lady Jane was very fond of her guardian. There was much about him she was not aware of."

"I meant no disrespect," Nicholas said quickly. "What happened to him was indeed unfortunate."

"True. But he brought much of it on himself, I'm afraid."

"I…I worry for his brother, the elder Edward Seymour. He hasn't the same selfish arrogance as Thomas Seymour. And he is quite popular among the people. But he seems to have wound up in the same predicament as his brother. He has fallen out of favor with His Majesty's Council."

"But he was released from the Tower months ago," I said.

"Indeed. But not reinstated as Protector. The elder Seymour's position is a bit tenuous, I think. John Dudley is not overfond of him."

"John Dudley?"

"He is a very powerful man at the moment, Miss Day. He has the King's ear."

We reached the bottom of the stairs and turned to make our way to the entrance to Bradgate Hall.

"What is it that John Dudley wants?" I asked. "If he has the King's ear, what more could he want?"

"To have the King's muscle, I suppose. He is desperate to have His Majesty marry a Reformer. He doesn't want Rome to interfere ever again with the government of the Crown. With Princess Mary, in theory, next in line to the throne, John Dudley would have King Edward married and producing Reformed heirs posthaste. Mary would bring Catholicism back to the realm were she to rule. John Dudley won't have it."

"The King is but fourteen this October, and already he is rushed to produce an heir!"

"All in due time, I am sure. But still. This is the talk at Oxford. His

Majesty has always been prone to illness. It is disconcerting to those opposed to Rome. Dudley worries about the throne reverting back to Catholic rule."

"Would that be so terrible, Mr. Staverton? 'Tis the same God that is worshiped."

"Ah, but it is not the part about God that has men at odds over this. It is the part about men. And power. And practice."

We stepped outside into the glory of a late summer noon. Birds sang in nearby trees. Horses at the waiting carriage shuffled their feet. A warm breeze tugged at my hair. A coachman opened the carriage door for Nicholas and waited.

"I did not dictate the words to the lullaby," I said.

Nicholas held out his hand. A second later, I stretched out my own hand. He pressed into it a slip of parchment.

"'Tis my address at Oxford. Perhaps you would send the words to me, Miss Day?"

As I took the bit of parchment, our fingertips brushed, sending a tremor through my body. He took my hand, bowed, and kissed it.

"I shall be waiting every day to hear from you, Miss Day."

He turned, then stepped into the carriage and took his seat. His eyes were on mine as the door closed and the carriage began to move. He held my gaze until the carriage was well past the steps.

The carriage had turned to follow the curve in the drive before I realized I had not curtsied a farewell or even bid him Godspeed. My hand still tingled where he had kissed it.

I was not summoned to Lady Jane's rooms until long after the evening meal. I was not part of the day's developments at all, which allowed me many hours to ponder the pull I felt toward Nicholas Staverton. My sole duties after tending to Jane's wardrobe were to mend a bit of torn lace on Lady Katherine's gown and then assist Jane's youngest sister, Mary—who only made an appearance in the afternoon—dress in a gown of sunny yellow, which made the little girl look like a bouncing daffodil. After this I was dismissed to the wardrobe room by the duchess's attendants to spend the afternoon as I wished. I spent it contemplating the strange set of feelings Mr. Staverton had awakened in me. It annoyed me some that he knew so much about me, via Jane's kind but liberal tongue, and that I knew so very little about him. And his admiration for me was unsettling. The young man whom I had pined for all those years ago when I was but a child had not even known I pined. I found myself sad that Mr. Staverton had left so soon, even though his presence in the house had been disconcerting, albeit to no one save me. I missed his presence the moment he left.

I only saw the Duke of Somerset, his wife, and his son Edward, from the third-story windows as the two families partook of afternoon ices in the rose garden. From my limited vantage point, it appeared that the two families were having a lovely late summer afternoon, but the two dukes appeared to be cautious and pensive. Neither one laughed or smiled.

Young Edward and Lady Jane did remove themselves to a bench in the garden, but in the full view of their parents and several attendants, of course. At one point I saw Edward hand something to Jane, but it seemed a stolen moment that I was not meant to see, nor anyone else. I looked away until my peripheral vision suggested the two were rejoining the others underneath a striped canopy where a trio of musicians began to play happy tunes.

When at last I was called for, I found Jane sitting in the cushions of one of the windowsills in her bedchamber, looking out onto an indigo sky and its sprinkling of stars. She had dismissed her other attendants. Even Mrs. Ellen was gone. We were alone.

"Lucy!" she said, when I stepped into the room.

I curtsied and came to her. She patted the pillows next to her. Instinctively, I looked to see who might see me take a seat on the sill with her, even though I knew there was no one else in the room.

"Do not worry. I sent the others away. And Mrs. Ellen is off to fetch me something from the kitchen. I was too excited to eat before now."

I wordlessly took a seat, arranging my legs for a speedy change in position should the door open and Mrs. Ellen step in. Jane seemed content, but on edge, as well. I waited for her to speak.

"You were right," she said softly.

"My lady?"

"Edward is quite happy to be in a marriage contract with me!" Her smile widened, and she looked away from me, toward the vast, slow-moving summer twilight outside her window.

"You spoke with him, then?"

"Oh yes. We spoke!"

"So it is official? You are betrothed to him?" I could not help but lean toward her in excitement for her.

Jane cocked her head so that her forehead rested on a diamond-shaped pane. A line of worry appeared on her forehead. "There is nothing in writing. Not yet anyway."

"Perhaps that will come later?" I suggested.

"Maybe. I think Papa is waiting until the duke's affairs are settled. I heard them talking, my father and Edward's father, about John Dudley and the Privy Council and the mess Edward's father was in. The Duke of Somerset has had a falling out with John Dudley, you know. I don't care for him."

"Pardon?" Though I had heard her.

"I don't care for John Dudley. I don't trust him."

I said nothing.

"But the people love Edward's father," she went on. "They call him the good duke."

Again, I merely listened.

"But I do not want to trouble my mind with any of that." Jane leaned toward me. "Lucy, Edward wants to marry me. He does! He told me his heart has stirred for me since his uncle became my guardian! And I laughed and told him it has been the same for me."

"I am so glad for you, my lady," I said.

She leaned even closer. "He gave me a gift, Lucy!" Jane stretched out her hand. On her ring finger on her left hand, a lovely sapphire, set about with rubies and tiny diamonds, glittered on a gold band.

"It is beautiful," I said.

"Look inside." Jane took the ring off her finger and handed it to me. I turned the ring toward the opalescent moon on the other side of the glass. I could make out Jane's name in beautiful script. But there were other words, tiny and foreign to me.

Jane sensed my inability to read what Edward had inscribed there.

"It's Latin," she said. "From the Song of Solomon. It reads, 'You have captured my heart, my sister, my bride.' "

Twenty

With the frosts of October, the sweating sickness waned, and the noblemen and women who had retired to the countryside began to return to London. Jane's parents, as the newly named Duke and Duchess of Suffolk, were eager to be back at court to display their new titles. They made plans to return—and bring Jane with them—at the first opportunity.

I was given leave to return home before we headed south.

Nicholas had written me the moment he had returned to Oxford, and I had quickly returned a letter to him with the words to the lullaby. His next letter arrived only days after. We found a kinship in each other's thoughts and even in matters of faith that surprised us both, perhaps me more so than him. By the turning of the leaves, we had exchanged a dozen notes. I began to dread the thought of our friendship ending, or worse, of its never blooming past friendship. I was to learn he felt the same way. He asked if he might ask permission of my father to court me, even if only by letters, and I admit this was the primary reason I entreated the duchess to allow me a visit home to Haversfield before the household returned to London.

My father spent his days seated by the fire, wrapped in blankets, even in the summer, where he could mend seams and stitch pockets in between his frequent naps. Within an hour of my arriving home, I knelt by him at this chair and told him there was something I needed to ask him.

"I've met a young man, Papa. A student at Oxford. He is a friend of Lady Jane's tutor, Mr. Aylmer. His name is Nicholas Staverton. He wishes to court me, albeit through letters."

My papa's long illness had robbed him of strength and vigor. But he smiled and laid a hand on my cheek. "Tell me about him."

I shared what I knew of Nicholas, how we met, his kind heart and genteel manner.

"And what are Mr. Staverton's plans after Oxford, Lucy?"

I told Papa that Nicholas wished to teach, that his uncle was headmaster of the King's School in Worcester and that perhaps he might join him there upon graduation.

"And where does this young man stand on matters of faith, child?" Papa asked.

It was against the King's law to practice the Catholic mass; such had been the case since Henry the Eighth broke away from Rome. There were those, including the banished Princess Mary, who defied this mandate and quietly went about finding priests to bless their communion bread and wine. It was dangerous business. But Nicholas had no bonds with Rome, and not just because it was against the King's law. This mattered to me, that Nicholas believed what he did because he was convinced of it, not because it was the safe or popular choice. And I knew it would matter to my father.

"Mr. Staverton is a follower of His Majesty's faith—and yours, Papa."

My father touched my face. "Would it please you if Mr. Staverton were to court you? Would this make you happy?"

I nodded. It surprised me how much I believed it would.

"Tell Mr. Staverton he may write to me," my father said. "I should like it very much if he would write to me."

In the next room, I heard my mother exclaim a celebration was in order and that she would bake a ginger tart. It was then I realized how much my parents had prayed for my future. Cecily was already betrothed. My father's illness showed no signs of leaving him. They had worried about me. My announcement—my request—had been an answer to their prayers. I wrote to Nicholas that hour.

Leaving Haversfield to return to Lady Jane was bittersweet. I prayed God would spare my father's life long enough to see me married.

In the weeks after Edward Seymour and his family left Bradgate, both Jane and I waited upon coaches that brought us news from the men who'd won our affections. There were many evenings that Jane and I would find a quiet corner to share the news of the letters we'd received. And sometimes we'd write our letters at the same hour, Jane in her bedchamber and I in mine, and in the morning as I readied her wardrobe for the day, we'd share what we had written.

Jane's parents did not discourage her many letters to Edward, nor did they encourage them. Some days Jane would wear the ring Edward had given her, but most days she would place it in the Turkish jewel box on her dressing table. I think the duchess's moods dictated Jane's confidence in whether or not she'd wear the ring. On the days the ring was placed in the box, she did not confide in me the reason why. She seemed sad and withdrawn on those days, spending long hours translating passages of Italian or Arabic, for no reason—it seemed to me—than to pass the time.

When the duchess announced that the family was returning to court, Jane's spirits brightened. If the lords and ladies were returning to London, it would follow that Edward Seymour and his family would be also. I packed Jane's wardrobe with care, as commanded by the duchess, and we set out for London on a chilly autumn morn.

In my letters to Nicholas, I admitted I had learned to care deeply for young Jane but that she would likely be married within a year's time, and I did not know if I wished to stay in the duke's employ without Jane to sew for. I enjoyed her sister Lady Katherine's company, but we shared no bond. It was quite likely that when Jane married, I would be dismissed. The duchess had plenty of dressmakers and tailors on her staff. I believe she had kept me on her staff because Jane had begged her to.

There was no reason to assume that Jane would have the freedom to employ me when she became a young earl's wife. Seymour, no doubt, had his own household staff.

Though Nicholas had compassion for the loss I would feel at leaving the Grey household, I could tell he was relieved that I could envision a future that didn't include working for the Duke of Suffolk. Knowing that the road ahead of me was to be far different than the one I had traveled thus far, I began to bit by bit ease myself away mentally from Jane. She would be leaving for Seymour's home, I would be leaving for my own, back in Haversfield, and then upon Nicholas's future graduation, to Nicholas's home, God be willing. I needed to help her prepare for her new life as Edward Seymour's wife. And I needed to think about my own preparations.

In a year's time, it seemed, everything would be different.

We had been in London for near a month, and still there had been no visit from young Edward Seymour. Jane still received letters from him, but he spoke only of the distant future and never of the worrisome present. His father continued to wage a political battle with John Dudley, now the new Duke of Northumberland, and Dudley's many supporters. The elder Seymour's problems were far from over; he had been arrested a second time and deposited in the Tower. It was difficult for Jane to maintain a pleasant countenance at the many parties and events her parents pulled her to, as John Dudley was often at such events.

One evening I was summoned to Jane's chambers to help her dress for a dinner engagement. The duchess had chosen the gown for that evening, and it was particularly elegant—nasturtium red velvet with turned-back sleeves of peacock blue, worked with a cornflower design of gold. Spanish embellishments decorated the inside of the open collar and the wrist-frills. A second collar of white gauze had been embroidered with red silk. Jane took one look at the dress and announced she wished to wear black.

"Please, my lady," I urged. "The duchess—"

"Princess Elizabeth would never wear such a brazen garment. I should be wearing black." She stared at the dress in my hands as if it were a loathsome snake.

"But you will look beautiful in this dress," I said.

She turned from me. "I don't want to be beautiful."

"But why ever not?" I asked.

She choked back a sob. "I don't want to be beautiful."

"What troubles you tonight, my lady?" I asked her.

For a moment she said nothing. "I am afraid," she finally whispered. Her gaze rested unblinking on the dress and its shouting colors.

"Afraid of what, my lady?"

But she would not answer me.

I said nothing and waited for wisdom. I did not know what to say to her. To my gratitude, a moment later, she turned back around and stretched out her arms for the bodice. I saw that Edward's ring was on her finger, but the stones were turned inward toward her palm.

Half an hour later, the dress was on her. I walked with her, bearing her train, to the barge that would take her on the Thames to a party I was sure Edward would not be attending.

When she returned at midnight, I helped her disengage from the dress she had not wanted to wear. Mrs. Ellen was there too, fussing over her and asking who was the handsome young lord who had been after Jane's attention all evening?

Jane shrugged. "It does not matter."

"Handsome young lord?" I asked, directing the question to Mrs. Ellen.

"Och. Yes, 'tis all Lady Katherine spoke of on the barge coming home. That a handsome gentleman had eyes only for Jane."

Jane moved away from us to her bed, her white chemise falling about her body like the cloak of an angel.

"But…but my lady is betrothed," I whispered.

"Perhaps this will speed things along," Mrs. Ellen whispered back. "'Tis not official, the agreement with Somerset. Perhaps this will speed things along."

I learned the next morning the handsome young lord was John Dudley's son, Guildford.

As Christmas neared, I was most anxious to be dismissed for the holidays to be with my family. Nicholas was coming to meet my parents, and I could scarce think of anything else. I knew our time of betrothal would be lengthy. Nicholas had yet another year at Oxford. But still I was oft imagining myself the lady of my own house, wife to Nicholas Staverton, sewing infant smocks instead of ball gowns.

In late November a package arrived for Jane from the Princess Mary, who was living in virtual exile in Hertfordshire. There were plans in place for Jane and her mother to spend Christmas with the Princess Mary, and the package was an early present so that Jane would have something lovely to wear when Mary of Guise came to visit London the following week. Inside the box was an exquisite gown of French design. The cone-shaped bodice included a partlet of embroidered gauze with an upstanding collar finished in tiny, bright pleats. The sleeves, with puffs at the shoulders, were embellished with ribbons of gold, tiny pearls, and jeweled buttons.

The skirt was a creamy satin and the mantle was of blue velvet embroidered with lilies. Jewels glittered everywhere, at every seam and gather. It seemed to shout, as a champion might, "At last. We are victorious!"

Lady Jane gasped when she saw it. "Whatever would I do with such a dress!" she exclaimed.

"Why, wear it, my wee lass!" Mrs. Ellen answered. " 'Tis a dress finer than any queen's!"

"I…I couldn't." The color in Jane's face had drained, and she looked at the dress with something akin to fear. "No upstanding Reformed girl would wear it! Elizabeth wouldn't. I won't."

"Elizabeth is not going to Princess Mary's home for Christmas either. You are!"

"Why would she send this to me? Is she mocking me?" Jane turned to me. "Is the Princess Mary mocking me?"

Mrs. Ellen spoke before I could answer that I'd no idea why Princess Mary would send such an expensive gown. "She is fond of you, my lady!" Mrs. Ellen put her hands on her ample hips. "Does she need more reason than that?"

But Jane turned away from the gown.

"You will be writing the Princess Mary this very afternoon to thank her or the duchess will hear of it, and you don't want that, my lady," Mrs. Ellen said, lifting the dress from within the box.

"When do you leave, Lucy?" Jane said absently. Mrs. Ellen clucked her tongue and whispered something under her breath. She swept out of the room, carrying the glistening dress in her arms.

"Not for several weeks, my lady."

"I wish you were coming with us to the Princess Mary's."

"I shall only be gone for a few days."

"Is Mr. Staverton coming to see you?" She fingered the ring Edward had given her.

"God be willing," I answered.

"God be willing," she said, though not to me.

A week later, as I assisted Jane down the stairs to supper, a messenger burst into the hall with dreadful news. The Duke of Somerset, Edward Seymour's father, had just been tried at Westminster Hall on an exaggerated charge of treason, convicted, and condemned to death.

Jane flew to her chambers, begging Mrs. Ellen over and over to tell her what this meant for her and Edward. Jane's parents had not summoned her, nor were they even at home when the news came.

But Mrs. Ellen didn't know.

None of us knew.

All Jane could do was sit at the window, spinning Edward's ring on her finger as she waited for her parents to return home.

Jane

Upper West Side, Manhattan

Twenty-One

꧁❦꧂

Molly sat across from me, stroking the stem of her coffee mug. Jeff and their girls were in Central Park enjoying the April brilliance of a Sunday afternoon. I had been back in Manhattan for less than an hour, having left my parents' house that morning a little after noon, much to their dismay. Leslie had come over early to have breakfast with us and then stayed until I left. My parents never had the long talk alone with me they'd wanted to have. I had come to Molly's straight from the train station.

I took a sip from my water glass.

"We're still friends, right?" Molly said.

I smiled at her. "I'm not mad at you, if that's what you mean."

"I felt really bad about what I said about you letting everybody make your decisions. And I didn't like it that you were gone and I couldn't tell you in person that I felt bad about it."

"It's all right, Molly. I suppose I've known all along what you said was true." A breeze blew up onto her patio and fluttered the flowered tablecloth on the table between us. The flattened rose petals seemed to applaud. "I let my parents choose my college major; I let them decide Kyle wasn't the right guy for me. I let Brad choose where we'd live. I let my mother choose the job I have now. I even let my parents choose Brad. And now I am letting Brad choose whether we've a marriage worth saving or not."

Silence stretched across the table for a few moments. The breeze wafted away. Then Molly spoke.

"Did you and Brad talk at all this weekend?"

I'd kept my phone close to me all during Leslie's party, ready to excuse myself if Brad called. When he didn't, I reasoned that he got my voice mail too late to call back and would call me in the morning.

When he didn't do that, I thought perhaps he wanted to wait until I was back in Manhattan, or at least on the train, away from my mother's listening ears before he returned my call.

"I called him last night, before Leslie's party started. Left a ridiculous message."

"A ridiculous message?"

"I stammered and stuttered, and I told him I missed him. He didn't call me back."

Molly looked down at her lap, as if struggling to know what to say next. Something niggled at me.

"Why did you ask me if Brad and I had talked this weekend?" I asked.

And then suddenly I knew.

She had seen him. He had been here. In Manhattan.

Not the day before. The day before, he was at UMass with Connor. If he came, he came that day. And it's a four-hour drive from Manchester to Manhattan.

"Is Brad still here?" I whispered. "Is he with Jeff and the girls?"

Molly blinked slowly. "Probably not." She looked up at me.

I willed my voice to stay calm. "Probably not still here, or probably not with Jeff and the girls?"

"Jane—," she began, but I cut her off.

"Just tell me."

"He was going to leave to drive back around two today. That's when you were getting off the subway to come here."

"Two? He left at two? He drove four hours to spend an hour here, and then he turned around and left?"

"He drove down last night. He said he got to your apartment around eleven."

"*My* apartment?"

"Geez, yours collectively, Jane!"

I didn't want to take out my anger and frustration on Molly. But I couldn't seem to rein in the hurt. "Sorry."

"For what it's worth, he looks pathetic."

"You're just saying that."

"No, I'm not. Jeff thought so too."

It irked me that Molly and Jeff saw Brad, talked to Brad, observed Brad, and I hadn't. It didn't seem fair.

"Did he come over here? Did he just show up on your doorstep?"

"He came over to talk to Jeff for a little bit. He did ask about you, Jane. He asked how we thought you were getting along. And he asked if we knew when you were getting back today."

"Why couldn't he just have called me himself?" I exploded. "I had my phone in my lap on the train ride home! The whole way!"

"Well, why didn't you just call him?"

"I did call him! Last night! I told you that. This whole thing about space and distance was *his* idea. He wanted it and I've tried very hard to give it to him!"

"Maybe you shouldn't try so hard."

"What's that supposed to mean?" I shot back.

"I think you're giving him more space than he deserves. Or needs. I don't think you should try so hard."

"It's what he said he wanted."

"Well, people don't always know exactly what they want."

"Why are you telling me this? Did he say something to you?"

"It's what he didn't say, Jane. I don't know how to explain it. He seems kind of restless. I just think you should begin to reclaim the space you lent him."

"Easy for you to say." I lifted my glass and swallowed the last of the mineral water. It had warmed in the sunny alcove of her balcony and tasted metallic.

"You should call him tonight."

"Right."

"You should. He said Connor wants you to come up to Dartmouth next Saturday for his next track meet."

"He said that? Did he say how I was supposed to get there? He has the car."

"I think that's why he came over here. He asked us if we could give you a lift to Newark next Saturday morning so you could catch a commuter flight. We said yes."

"A commuter flight."

"He said he feels bad that he has the car and you can't get to any of Connor's meets. I think he means to pay for your plane ticket."

"My plane ticket." My voice was flat.

"I think he wants to see you. I think maybe he has missed you."

I stood up. Too much information was sliding into me. The possibility of Brad missing me tingled inside my head, like the pins-and-needles sensation that brings a sleepy limb back to awareness. It was both intensely welcome and bracing.

"I haven't been home yet. I need to call Emma before it gets too late. It's already after eight in England."

"Did you hear what I said?"

"I heard you. I just need to go."

"And you're not mad at me."

"I'm not mad at you." I leaned down to grab my purse.

"And you'll call Brad tonight. Right?" she asked.

"Emma first."

Molly stood as well, and we headed back inside her apartment carrying our cups. "You calling her about the ring?"

"Yes. My jeweler friend says it's the real deal, pre-Elizabethan near as he can tell. He says it could be worth six thousand dollars."

"Wow. That's amazing."

"I guess. I don't know. I wish I knew where it came from. I really don't think the previous owner had any inkling what was in that box where I found the prayer book. Someone, at some point, hid the ring inside it. I'd like to find out why, if I can."

"Just to satisfy your curiosity, then?"

"Yes. No. I mean, yes, I am curious. But there's something else about the ring that draws me."

"Your name is in it," Molly said.

Yes.

My name.

Jane.

I grabbed my overnight bag at her front door, and she hugged me good-bye.

When my hand was on her doorknob, I turned back to face her. "Did you talk to Brad about anything else? Did Jeff talk to him?"

She hesitated only a minute. "He really didn't say anything more to me. And I don't know what he and Jeff talked about. Jeff didn't want to say. They didn't talk long. Brad's not a talker. But I am telling you. He looked different to me."

A sigh escaped me. "Okay. See you later."

I used the time during my seven-block trek to my apartment to call Emma and ask where in Cardiff she found the boxes. If she asked why, I'd decided to tell her I found a ring crammed inside one of the books and was wondering how old it might be. If she pressed me, I would probably end up telling her everything. She answered on the fourth ring.

"Emma, it's Jane. Have I called too late?"

"Jane! Not at all. Just in from a very bad dress rehearsal of *Twelfth Night*. Dreadful, really. Didn't think I'd hear from you until next month, love. What's up?"

"I didn't think I would be calling either, and I'll keep it short. I just need to talk to you about those boxes you sent—"

"But I told you last week those boxes were in dreadful shape. Remember? I couldn't help it this go-around."

"No, that's not why I called. I just... I was wondering if you could tell me where you found the boxes. The books, especially."

"They all came from the same jumble sale, Jane. I told you that, love. In Cardiff. In Wales."

"Yes, but did you buy them from an estate dealer or a merchant who has a shop in town?"

"Is something amiss, then?" The casual lift in her voice was replaced with concern.

"Not amiss, really. I just... I found something shoved up inside the binding of one of the books. It was a very old book, actually."

"What did you find?"

I hesitated, just for a second. "A ring."

"A ring? A nice one? Did you find another bloody Hope Diamond, Jane?"

"No, no, nothing like that. I mean it's quite pretty, but—"

"How old?"

I stepped into a busy crosswalk. "Old."

"Jane, how old?" I could tell she was smiling.

When I hesitated she laughed. "Really, Jane. What kind of person do you think I am? It's yours, love. I am not going to fetch my solicitor to get it back from you. Besides I've already cashed your check. How old?"

"Maybe the mid–fifteen hundreds."

Emma pulled the phone away from her mouth, and I heard a few choice words. She came back to me, almost breathless with astonishment. "You cheeky little girl! Inside the binding of a book! Do you always go looking for four-hundred-year-old rings in the bindings of books?"

"Very funny. And it's not official. I just had a friend of mine look at it. He says I need to take it to an expert to know for sure."

"I can't believe you found a four-hundred-year-old ring in a box of dirt and junk! Can't believe it!"

"Maybe four hundred years old. And, Emma, it has my name etched inside."

"No…," she whispered. "Truly?"

"There's a few Latin words, and then my name. Jane."

"You're giving me the willies, Janie."

"Interesting, isn't it?"

"So you're wonderin' how much it's worth?"

"Yes. Well, sort of."

"What do you mean, sort of?"

"I just…" But I didn't finish the thought. I didn't think Emma would understand the growing notion I had that the ring came to me in some quirky bend of Providence. Now. At this point in my life, when the wheels of my routine existence were grinding to a halt, leaving me to wonder what the heck I was supposed to do and if there really were choices that were mine to make.

"I'd like to know as much as possible about it," I finished. "My jeweler friend says it was likely given as a betrothal gift. I'd like to know who gave to whom."

Emma clucked her tongue. "That's not the kind of answer you're likely to find at a jumble sale, love. They call it a jumble for a reason."

"I know. But I have to start somewhere. Will you be heading back to Cardiff any time soon?"

"I could maybe sneak in a trip. There's a clothing consignment shop in Bristol I've been wanting to get to. Could maybe swing by Cardiff and see if I can find the man who sold it to me. He was just a scraggly old man, Jane. Maybe one tooth left in his mouth. He wasn't a dealer, I can tell you that much."

"But you'll try to find out who he is?"

"I'll go back to the empty lot. There's a jumble sale there every Saturday in the spring and summer, I hear. Maybe he's a regular. What do you want me to ask him if I find him?"

"Ask him if I can call him. Tell him I just have a couple questions about where the boxes of books came from."

"All right, love. Don't get your hopes up, though. Like as not, you'll probably have to be content with just wondering."

"Maybe."

"So. Anything new on Brad?"

"No. Nothing new."

"He's still in New Hampshire?"

I kept a sigh from escaping. "Yes."

"She probably lives up there, you know."

"What?"

"The other woman. She probably lives up there."

Heat spread across my face. "There is no other woman."

"Oh, Jane, don't be daft. Of course there is."

"He promised me there isn't."

She paused. "Right. Have it your way, then. Hey. You should come see me, Jane. I'll take you to my favorite singles' pub."

"I'm not single."

"Right."

"Good-bye, Emma."

We hung up, and for the fourth time that day, I checked to see if Brad actually had tried to call me back and I missed it. But there was no missed call.

I hadn't missed anything.

I rounded the corner to my street and headed up the cement steps to my apartment building, my thoughts in a tumble over Brad's having been at Molly and Jeff's this morning, and Brad asking them to get me to the airport to catch a flight he intended to pay for. Brad making sure I could get to New Hampshire next weekend. It almost seemed like Brad was orchestrating a meeting.

I turned the key in the front door to my apartment and stepped inside, tossing my overnight bag onto the floor as I pushed the door closed behind me.

Movement ahead of me on the couch startled me, and the back of my head bumped against the front door.

Brad was standing there, waiting for me.

Twenty-Two

"Hi, Jane." Brad wore a soft pair of chinos and a creamy yellow polo shirt. In one hand he held a half-empty bottle of water. The other was tucked in his pants pocket. His face was tanned—from canoeing and track meets most likely—and his hair was longer than he'd ever worn it before.

"Brad." My voice sounded almost childlike. "Molly said you were heading back to New Hampshire."

"Oh. So you've been to Molly and Jeff's already?"

"I stopped off at their place on my way home from Long Island. She said you'd been by earlier today. That you were going to leave at two."

He hesitated, just for a moment. "I changed my mind. I decided to wait until after you got back, but I was beginning to think you'd decided to stay in Long Island another day." He set the bottle down on the coffee table.

"Sorry you had to wait," I muttered, not knowing what else to say.

"No, it's okay. Did Molly tell you I'd like to help you get to Connor's track meet next weekend? There's a flight that gets into Manchester at ten thirty in the morning. I can…I can pick you up, if you want. We'll be able to catch the first event if your plane's on time. I know Connor would love to have you there."

"Yes. I mean, I've missed being there."

"So it's okay with you if I make those arrangements?"

"I guess so."

We stood there, in our living room, staring at each other as a couple of awkward seconds hung between us. Then he moved toward me and stretched out his hand. "Can I talk to you?"

I tentatively reached out my own hand, and he wrapped his hand around it. His hand was warm. Brad folded his fingers around mine and pulled me toward the couch. He set me down, released my hand, and then took the armchair next to me, leaning forward on it like doctors do when they must deliver troubling news.

I wanted to get up and run.

He looked down at his shoes and then raised his head to look at me. "I'm really sorry I didn't call you back last night."

"I'm sorry you didn't too." I barely whispered it, but I knew he heard me.

"I honestly didn't know how to respond, Jane. I didn't want to get into it on the phone, especially since you were at your parents'."

Something snapped—or maybe bent—inside me. He sounded so calm and confident, and I had felt so anxious and insecure. It made me angry. And afraid.

"Get into what?"

"You know what I mean."

The frustration, fueled by fear, mounted. "The fact that I miss you? That I don't know how I am supposed to be working out the problems you think we have in our marriage when you aren't even here? You didn't want to get into that?"

"Jane."

"I mean, really, Brad. I spend my days waiting to hear from you, waiting to see what it is you want, waiting to see if you still want to be married to me. Is that what you didn't want to get into on the phone?"

He looked away, toward the hallway and our bedroom. "I didn't know what you wanted me to say."

"You didn't call me back last night because you didn't know what I wanted you to say?"

"You said you felt lonely. What was I supposed to say to that, Jane? 'Sorry for making you feel lonely'? Is that what you wanted me to say?"

The mix of disappointment and fear swirled inside me, gaining density like egg whites becoming meringue. A tiny part of me wanted to hurt him. "I wanted you to say you miss me too. Don't you? Don't you miss me at all?"

Brad turned back to me. "Sometimes. Yes."

I flinched as if he'd poked me with a stick. "Sometimes?"

"I don't miss the way things were between us, Jane. I don't miss that."

I could feel my eyes growing warm and moist. Brad's brutal honesty after weeks of polite silence stung. "Why didn't you say anything? If you were unhappy, why didn't you say anything? We could've gone in for counseling."

"I didn't…I didn't know I was unhappy. And to tell you the truth, I didn't want to go in for counseling."

His answer stunned me. "Why?"

"Because I just didn't know if I wanted to fix it."

He said it like he saw shattered bones in an x-ray and had absolutely no desire to see them mended. None.

"How can you just give up?" It was out of my mouth before I realized this is exactly what my mother said to me the morning before, when Leslie and I left to go shopping and I told her she had no idea what she was talking about.

"I never said I was giving up. I said we needed some space. When I left, I didn't have the energy or motivation to try to fix anything. I'm not saying I never will."

Hurt welled up within me. I lowered my head into my hands. "What makes you think I have the energy to live alone here, to come home every night to an empty apartment? What makes you think I have the motivation to keep hoping and praying and waiting to see if you will come back to me?"

Brad said nothing.

"What about what I want? What about how I feel about all this?" I lifted my head to face him. "I gave you your space. I've let you alone. I've not been on your case. I did everything you asked of me!"

My chest was heaving, and the tears were falling freely.

"I know this isn't just about me." His voice was a whisper.

Brad looked away again, toward the gauzy curtains quivering at our open patio doors. He didn't answer.

I came to him and dropped to my knees. "Do you still love me?"

He took his time answering me. "I love the idea of us. I love the idea of marriage, of growing old with someone who completes me, of sharing my life with someone who is my soul mate. I love the idea of that."

"But you don't love me?"

He turned back from gazing at the curtains. "Do you love me?"

"Of course I do!"

"I know you think you do, Jane. But what if maybe you also just love the idea of marriage, just like I do? You love the idea of growing old with someone who completes you. You love the idea."

"I love you, Brad."

He looked into my eyes as if waiting to catch me in a lie.

I told him again that I loved him.

He inhaled deeply, looked away for a second, and then turned back. "I heard you, Jane. I heard you and Leslie talking at your parents' anniversary party last year. I heard what you said."

"What?"

"I heard you. In the kitchen. When you thought you two were alone. I heard you."

The air around us seemed to stiffen and pucker. Color rose to my cheeks as mentally I placed myself back at my parents' fiftieth anniversary party. Leslie and I were making punch in the kitchen. She was teasing me for wishing I had married Kyle instead of Brad, reminding me that at my bridal shower I confessed I thought I might be marrying the wrong man.

Oh, God.

Perhaps I said God's name out loud. It was as much a prayer for divine assistance as I have ever prayed.

"I heard you."

"It was nothing!" I whispered. "Just silly talk!"

"Was it? Was it really? After all our years together, don't we deserve to be honest with each other?"

"I didn't mean it," I whimpered.

"Think about it, Jane. We married each other because it made sense. Your parents, my mother, they were the ones who pushed us to get engaged. I let them because I didn't like dating, and you let them because you didn't like being alone. And we wanted the same things. A loyal spouse, a good home, children, security, friendship, companionship, physical intimacy. We got what we wanted. We got what other people wanted for us."

"You have never loved me?" I could barely eke out the words. They fell off my tongue like splinters.

He paused before answering. "That's not what I said. And I care for you very much. You are a wonderful mother and a kind, compassionate person. But I'm just not sure about anything else. And I think you have the same doubts I do. You always have."

I slumped down onto the couch, dizzy. "How long have you had doubts?" I asked him.

"How long have you?"

He said it gently. He had said everything gently.

"It started before your parents' party, didn't it?" he continued. "Long before then. Jane, I've been struggling with the same questions."

I was drained of energy, of reason. As much as I wanted him to stay, I wanted him to go.

"Look, I didn't come here to tell you all this," he said. "Really, I didn't. I waited for you to get back from your parents' because I felt I owed you an apology for not calling you last night. And I wanted to make sure that you can come to Connor's meet next weekend. You were right. Our separation has affected him. He needs to see us together. He needs to see that when it comes to him, we aren't divided. You...you will still let me pick you up at the airport on Saturday morning, right?"

I nodded, numb.

Brad stood, hesitated, and then reached for his water bottle. "I need to head back."

Again, I nodded.

He leaned over me and kissed my forehead. I wanted to hit him. I wanted to hold him. I shut my eyes as his lips touched my skin. The sensation was tender. And brutal.

He stepped back, and though my eyes were still closed, I could tell he was staring at me.

"Will you be all right?"

"A little late for compassion," I whispered, but this time he did not hear me.

"Jane?"

"I'm fine."

Again, Brad paused. "You'll think about what I said?"

I opened my eyes. "Does it matter what I think?"

"It has always mattered." He turned then, walked to our front door, and opened it. Brad was gone with a quiet click.

His water bottle had left a ring of condensation on the coffee table. I ran my fingers gently through the wetness, marring the perfect, glistening circle.

Twenty-Three

A light rain was falling Monday morning as I walked down Amsterdam. My raincoat flapped open every time a car drove past me, inviting a spattering shower to christen my ankles. I held my umbrella with my right hand, and in the curl of my fist, Jane's ring glimmered in the falling wetness on my pinkie. Even in the drizzle of a late April shower, the ring begged to be noticed, sparkling, even though there was no sun. In my other hand, I carried an insulated mug of Kona coffee. I made it extra strong that morning.

I stayed up late talking to Leslie, and then, of course, slept poorly.

Leslie said there had to be some truth in what Brad said. About me. About me having doubts about the reasons Brad and I married in the first place.

"If he really did hear the whole punch-bowl conversation, then he heard enough to know you can't possibly be as surprised as you say you are that this is happening," Leslie had said ten minutes into our phone conversation.

"That's not fair."

"Jane. He heard you say you sometimes wonder why you two ever got married. He heard you say you wonder that if you had stood up to Mom and Dad, if you might've married Kyle instead."

"But you're the one who brought it up! I was just scooping sherbet into the punch bowl! You brought it up."

"And you're the one who didn't deny it."

"For heaven's sake. It was just one stupid comment in an unplanned conversation. I didn't mean anything by it."

"Brad thinks you did. I actually think you did."

"Leslie!" I'd been incredulous. It wasn't like I had been waiting to get Leslie alone at that party so I could tell her how mixed up I was feeling about my marriage. It was a comment made off the cuff.

"What?"

"I *didn't* mean anything by it."

"Brad's right."

"What do you mean, Brad's right?"

"You have doubts, but you pretend you don't."

"Hey, I'm not the one who walked out."

"Yeah, but we're not talking about what he did, Jane. We're talking about you."

"You think I have doubts that I married the right man?" I challenged her.

"Noooo," she said slowly, casually. "I think you love Brad, but maybe you just don't know why. For the longest time, you haven't had to know why, but now you do."

Her words somersaulted in my head long after we'd said good-bye. Yet I still went to bed as keenly aware of Brad's absence as I had been since the first night he left. I woke up five or six times to the sensation of falling, of reaching for the safety of strong arms and finding an empty pillow.

I sipped my coffee as I walked the last few yards to my shop. Wilson was waiting for me under the lavender and white awning, watching the rain fall.

❦

I wore the ring every day to work that week. Wilson and Stacy both asked me several times, as the week wore on, if I'd heard anything from Emma about the ring's origin, their interest growing steadily after I'd shared David Longmont's assessment of the ring's age.

Wilson had whistled when I told him. "Well, that would make it a fairly expensive ring, wouldn't it?"

I'd simply nodded.

"So are you going to sell it?" Stacy asked.

"Well, actually, I want to see if I can figure out where it came from and perhaps who it belonged to. Dumb idea, huh?"

"Not at all," Wilson had said. "It would be different perhaps if the name inside were Beatrice or Katherine. But it's your name."

And then I shared David's other assessment, that the ring showed no sign it had been worn. Neither Wilson nor Stacy jumped to venture a guess as to why not. We all seemed to speculate it could not have been for happy reasons.

Late in the week, I had my second appointment with Jonah Kirtland. There was nothing in the bowl as I sat down at the glass-topped table in his office. No pistachios. Nothing at all. The bowl had been wiped clean.

"No snacks today?" I asked as I settled into my chair.

He smiled. "Are you hungry for some?"

I wasn't.

I began with telling him about the weekend at my parents' and then Brad's surprise visit to the apartment. And then I told him about Brad's accusation, based on the punch-bowl discussion, that I had the same doubts about our marriage that he did.

"The thing is, it was a dumb conversation while I was making punch. I had no idea Brad heard any of it." I leaned back in my chair. I had been talking for close to fifteen minutes with little interruption from Dr. Kirtland.

"Why do you think it was a dumb conversation?" he asked.

"Because it was! I didn't bring it up. Leslie did. And I never would have said what I did if I had known Brad was listening."

Dr. Kirtland now leaned back in his chair. "No, you probably wouldn't."

"But I didn't mean anything by it."

He shrugged. "Then why do you think you said it? Do you still think about this guy Kyle?"

"I never think about him!"

"So he's perhaps a representation of what you wonder when you think about why you married Brad? Maybe you wonder how your life would be different if you'd made different choices? That's not so odd."

I stared at the empty bowl on the table.

"Who do you think you risk disappointing by being honest, Jane?"

Only for a second did I entertain the thought of continuing to insist the punch-bowl chat had been silly talk and nothing else. "Well, Brad, of course."

"You sure it's Brad?"

"My parents too, I guess."

"You guess?"

I lifted my head. "I don't have all the answers. That's why I'm here."

Dr. Kirtland sat forward in his chair. "I'd like for you to think about that. Who do you risk disappointing by being honest about how you think your life is playing out?"

Molly's revelation sprang to my tumbling thoughts. "Look. I know what you have figured out about me. I know you've figured out I've let everyone make all my decisions for me, and I admit you're right, and honestly, I'm glad you've figured it out, but I can't undo the past—"

He cut me off. "Where did you get that?"

"What?"

"Where did you get the idea that I think you've let everyone else make all your decisions?"

I wasn't about to tell him Molly told me. "Isn't that what I have done?"

"Did someone tell you that's what you've done?"

My cheeks bloomed with heat. I thought I had marked a milestone by embracing this uncomfortable knowledge about myself and that Dr. Kirtland would be proud of me for admitting it. But he was hacking away at the notion with a calm voice and disarming questions.

"But…but it's true," I said. "I don't like it that it's true, but it is. Isn't that what you were getting at last time I was here? That I needed validation from my parents and from Brad and that's why I let them make my choices for me?"

Dr. Kirtland was silent for several moments. "I have a little assignment for you. A couple, actually. I want you to make a list of all the qualities you appreciate about your husband. Don't ask anyone else for input on this, okay? No one. Not Molly. Not your sister. All right?"

I nodded.

"I also want you to make a list of things you like to do. Or things you would like to try. Or things you would like to learn. Again, no outside help. Will you do that?"

"So you're not going to answer my question."

He smiled. "You are."

"By making lists."

"The lists are a start, yes." He stood.

"So we're done?"

"For today."

"And what about this weekend when I go to New Hampshire to see Brad? What am I supposed to do?"

"You told me you were going to New Hampshire so that you and Brad could watch your son compete."

"Well, yes, but—"

"One thing at a time, Jane."

The empty bowl seemed a challenge to me then. As if it were up to me to fill it.

On Friday evening I locked up at eight and headed to Molly and Jeff's to stay the night to make it easier to get to the airport the next morning. Molly invited me over with that rationale, and I accepted her invitation, but the truth was she knew I was nervous about the next day. The plane ticket Brad bought for me had my return flight on Sunday. He called me midweek and asked if I could stay overnight since the last flight back to Newark on Saturday left Manchester too early. We'd miss seeing Connor after the meet. I told him I could stay, but I didn't know if he meant we'd be at a hotel near Dartmouth and did that mean separate rooms or would we be driving back to his place? And where would I sleep then?

Meanwhile, I had started Dr. Kirtland's lists over a caprese salad at lunch. At that moment Brad's looked like this:

Brad
Gentle
Smart
Good father
Careful
Strong
Th

I had started to write *Thoughtful.* Brad had always been a consider-
ate person. Polite. Even to people who didn't deserve it. But I didn't finish
it. His gentle cruelties of late kept me from writing the rest of the word.

On my own list, I had written only one thing. Only one thing had
come to mind.

> *Things I want to do:*
> *Find out where the ring came from*

I carried the lists with me as I walked the seven blocks to Molly and
Jeff's, and as I walked, I wondered what Brad would write on his list if he
wrote one about me.

Molly looked at the clothes I'd brought to wear to Connor's track meet—
jeans and a loose-knit blue sweater Brad gave me for Christmas the previous year—and promptly escorted me into her bedroom to find
something else to wear.

"But Brad gave this sweater to me," I protested.

"Yes, but think about when he gave it to you. Six months after hearing you tell Leslie you wonder why you married him."

I plopped onto her bed. "Why do you and Leslie have to keep bringing that up?" I had already decided I wouldn't mention that she and I
were both off somehow in our conclusions about what Dr. Kirtland
thought my underlying problem was.

She ignored me. "You want to wear something that doesn't remind
him of last year at all. Or any of the last twenty-two years for that matter."

"They weren't all terrible."

"I didn't say they were. I am just saying you want to wear something
that doesn't remind him of the past. Here."

She tossed me a pair of silky taupe capris and a pink shell the color of cherry blossoms. As I caught them, she threw a summer-white fitted jacket at me and a striped scarf in pale teal, rose, and cream.

"It's a track meet, Moll."

Molly turned from her closet to face me. "No. It isn't."

And she left me with instructions to try them on.

Later, while Molly, Jeff, and I were watching a movie, Molly's cell phone trilled. She reached for it on the ottoman next to her.

"It's my mom." She rose and took the phone with her into the kitchen.

The twins were watching something else in their bedroom, so Jeff and I were alone in the living room. It was the first time since Brad moved out that I'd been with Jeff when the girls weren't in the room with us, and I was sure he'd subtly planned it so that he didn't have to be alone with me. I looked over at him, and his eyes darted to Molly standing in the kitchen with her back to us. I decided to be completely honest. I had nothing to lose.

"Shall I just ask it and get it over with?"

He jerked his head back to face me. "What?"

"Shall I just ask what you and Brad talked about when he was here last weekend?"

"I…um…," he faltered.

"Does Molly know what you talked about?"

He had a bit of the deer-in-the-headlights look about him. "Jane, I don't think…I don't think I'm the one you need to talk to about this."

I turned my attention back to the television. "So she doesn't know?"

"I… This is between you and Brad. Really. I don't want to be in the middle of it. I don't want Molly in the middle of it. We think the world of you and Brad."

I turned back to him. "I'm just afraid it's too late. Is it too late?"

Jeff hesitated a moment before he spoke. "I don't think it's too late. But I also don't think anything will change until you two sit down together and decide what you want out of your marriage. I told him that. I can tell you that much. Look, I think it's good that you're going up there to see him. You both have too much invested in this relationship to let it just...evaporate."

"I don't know what I'm going to do if he tells me it's over," I murmured, though not really to Jeff. "What am I going to do then?"

Molly was saying good-bye to her mother. Jeff eased back into his chair. "I don't think it's up to just him, Jane."

A second later, Molly walked back into the living room with a bag of jalapeno kettle chips, the kind that once you start, you can't stop eating, because when you do, the burn crawls down the back of your throat and refuses to be calmed.

Twenty-Four

Molly's shoes were a bit loose on me as I made my way from the arrival gate to the area by baggage claim. Although I had only a carry-on and a shoe box of cookies for Connor that Molly and I made at midnight the night before, Brad and I agreed to meet in baggage claim anyway.

Brad was waiting for me at the first set of doors to the outside. I could see him studying me as I walked toward him; aware perhaps that I was wearing something he had never seen before and intrigued by the slight hitch in my step from wearing shoes a half size too big.

He wore stonewashed 501s and a heather gray Henley. He had his hands in his pockets, but when I was just a few feet away, he pulled them out as if to wrap me in an embrace. I stopped short, ready to fall into those arms, ready to hand over my overnight bag if he reached for it.

"Hey," he said. He took the step between us, kissed me on my cheek, and took my bag. His other hand rested lightly on the small of my back as he guided me away from the press of people from my flight and several others. "Flight okay?"

"It was fine."

He swiveled his head to look at me. "You look nice."

I blushed slightly. "Thanks." I lifted a corner of the scarf that hung over my shoulders like a priest's stole and a sudden burst of blabbermouth came over me. "Molly."

"Molly?"

The blush deepened. "She didn't like the clothes I had brought to wear today. She actually dressed me. I think she forgot Connor's on the track team, not the polo team."

Shut up, shut up, shut up.

"Well, you look great."

So do you.

We stepped outside and headed toward short-term parking.

"Molly's shoes?"

I was practically tripping over a suitable answer for, "Yes, doggone it, I am also wearing Molly's shoes," when I noticed he was looking at the shoe box I carried, not my feet. "Oh! No. These are cookies I made for Connor."

"He'll be thrilled." He nodded to my hand. "That's a new ring."

I glanced down at Jane's ring on my pinkie, surprised that Brad noticed. "Old one, actually. Found it in a box of old books I bought from Emma. It was hidden inside the binding of an old prayer book."

"Strange place for a ring," he said.

We were a few feet from the Jeep, and I was about to agree that it was, indeed, a very odd place to keep a ring, when he cleared his throat.

"Something has come up at the hospital. I'm afraid I can't go to the meet with you. I'm really sorry."

I couldn't believe what I was hearing.

"I feel really bad about it," he went on. "The guy on call this weekend is sick. I am going to have to go in."

An odd mixture of relief and frustration instantly poured over me. I had been dreading the hourlong drive to Hanover. And yet I wanted to be with Brad. I wanted him to be with me.

"What am I supposed to do?" I asked.

"You can take the Jeep to Hanover. I've already punched in the address on the GPS. You can just drop me off at the hospital on your way out of Manchester and then pick me up tonight when you come back through."

I was envisioning myself driving alone, sitting alone, eating alone in Molly's carefully chosen clothes when Brad continued.

"I've already texted Connor, so you don't have to worry about explaining why I'm not there."

He caught the irony in the last half of his sentence and looked away.

An audible sigh escaped me. I didn't know how to feel about the turn of events. We reached the Jeep.

"I'm really sorry about this, Jane."

And I could see that he was.

He truly was.

I would have to add *Sincere* to the list.

Fifteen minutes later, we pulled into the parking lot of Brad's new hospital, a building completely foreign to me. I stared up at its red-brick height. It looked like a hotel except for the people in white lab coats and green scrubs leaving and entering through the swooshing automatic doors.

"Do you want to come in?" Brad asked, but his voice was hesitant.

"I would like to sometime. But it doesn't have to be today."

He smiled at this, like he was glad he didn't have to give me a tour today and introduce me to any of his colleagues as his wife from New York, as if this was some permanent arrangement we have. Married but living in two different states.

"I am really sorry about this," he said again.

"It's okay."

Brad pointed to the GPS. "When you're ready to come back tonight, just press Reverse Trip and you'll be able to find me."

It was on the tip of my tongue to laugh and say, is that all I need to do? But I didn't. Instead, I asked the question I needed to ask or I wouldn't have been able to enjoy Connor's meet or seeing him participate in it.

"Where am I staying tonight?" I stared at the GPS.

Brad hesitated a second or two before answering.

"Well, I thought you'd stay at my place. I was going to offer to sleep in the guest room. But I can… I can get you a hotel room if…if that's what you want."

He sounded like I felt, unsure and tentative.

"That's not what I want," I answered quickly, my eyes still glued to the GPS.

Brad nodded, filing away my response, I suppose, into whatever system he used to make his choices these days. He seemed satisfied with my answer. Not pleased, exactly. But satisfied.

"Then I'll see you tonight," he said, his hand on the door.

"Right."

I got out of the Jeep to walk to the driver's side as he pulled a gym bag from the back. At the driver's door, we turned to face each other.

He shook his head, another apology for the way things had turned out, this one unspoken. I told him not to worry about it. I almost added Connor and I were no strangers to last-minute changes in plans. But I caught myself in time. I knew what I was getting into when I married a doctor. That was something I did know.

"Call me tonight when you're a few miles out?" he asked.

"Sure."

He swung the gym bag over his shoulder and then stood there for a second, looking at me. I wondered if he was thinking of kissing me good-bye.

"I… Can we talk tonight?" he asked.

I knew Brad and I needed to talk. Everyone said we needed to talk.

Even Connor said we needed to talk. It surprised me that now that Brad wanted to, I was reluctant to agree. Dr. Kirtland had encouraged me to keep this weekend about Connor and his track meet.

When I finally murmured, "Yes," he tipped his chin as if marking a slot on his day planner.

"See you when you get back. Tell Connor I'll catch the next one."

"Sure."

He turned and walked briskly away. I stepped inside the Jeep and reached for the door handle. Molly's scarf billowed toward my hand and obscured my view of Jane's ring as I slammed the door shut.

I didn't get to see Connor before the meet. I arrived in plenty of time before his first event—the four-hundred-meter sprint, but the team was sequestered in a premeet pep talk, so I headed to a shady portion of the bleachers to wile away the afternoon.

I could've befriended the parents sitting around me, but I didn't feel like it, so the hours slipped away in relative seclusion. I cheered when Connor ran, blending my voice with the shouts of other Dartmouth fans. He turned in a second-place finish in the four hundred, took fourth in the two hundred—not his favorite race—and his relay team placed second in the four by four hundred.

When he wasn't running, I read a book I'd brought and occasionally watched the pole-vaulters sail into the sky, arching their bodies like dancers and falling like rag dolls onto the massive cushion below.

It was after six thirty when the last event concluded and closer to seven before Connor came walking across the field to me.

He looked so much like Brad. I wrapped my arms around him when he finally reached me.

"Mom! I'm all sweaty." He tried to pull away.

"I don't care," I muttered, not wanting to let go. "You did great."

"I did okay." He pulled away anyway. "Did you see that guy who won the two hundred?"

"I saw him, but—"

"I've never run against a guy that fast."

"I thought you did great."

Twilight had started to steal across the field, and the promise of an evening chill made me wish, just for a second, that I was wearing the chunky blue sweater instead of Molly's loose-weave clothes. The field was emptying quickly.

"I'm glad you came," Connor said.

"I am too."

My son wiped his brow with the back of his arm, and I marveled at how strong he'd become. The tendons and muscles in his upper arms were distinct and thick.

"I'm really bummed Dad couldn't be here," he said.

"So am I. And so is he. He really wanted to see you compete."

Connor crinkled his forehead. "I'm not bummed for me."

He looked past me to where Brad might have been, had he come. I could see in his eyes the unease he felt about Brad's and my separation. He looked untethered.

"Dad and I are going to talk when I get back to Manchester," I assured him.

Connor's eyes found mine. "What are you going to talk about?"

I couldn't tell Connor that I didn't know what Brad wanted to tell me. I could see that Connor was already worried we might start talking about who would get what in the divorce settlement. I didn't want to consider that prospect either. Connor needed reassurance. And so did I.

"Well, I guess about how to make things right."

My son silently gauged my words and decided, I supposed, he could live with them for now.

He slung his gym bag over his shoulder. "I'm starving."

"Pizza?"

"Sure."

He said good-bye to some friends, politely declined an offer to eat with them, and we headed toward the Jeep.

I avoided the topic of my marriage as we ate a large mushroom-and-black-olive pizza at a local Italian place. Instead, I told him about the ring. He seemed genuinely intrigued when I showed him that my name was engraved inside.

When I took him back to the campus a little after nine, I hugged him until he laughed and pulled away. I handed him the shoe box of cookies and told him I would call him in a couple of days.

Connor watched me pull away in Brad's Jeep, the shoe box in his hands. As he stood there with a tender crease of concern on his face, he looked like me.

On the drive back to Manchester, I alternately listened to the radio, twisted Jane's ring on my finger, and recited the things I appreciated about Brad. I wished I had the onyx rosary too. I found myself whispering prayers to God to make Brad love me again. And to silence the questioning in my own heart. An easy fix.

I could almost hear Stacy, who prayed without a rosary, telling me it doesn't work like that.

I called Brad when I was five minutes away from the hospital, like he'd asked. He was waiting outside for me when I pulled into the parking lot.

I moved over to the passenger side, and we spent the ten-minute drive to his rented town house talking about the meet, Connor, his busy day at the hospital. Just like old times.

I fell silent when we turned onto a quiet, tree-lined street. A black wrought-iron fence was sprawled across the entrance to a housing complex of Georgian design. White accents glistened in the moonlight. Mature oaks rustled in a breeze. Brad pressed a button on an opener on the visor, and the gates opened in a welcoming, sweeping fashion.

I said nothing as we made our way to a unit near the back on a hushed cul-de-sac. Brad pressed another button and a garage door ahead of us began to open. Brad drove into as pristine a garage as I'd ever seen. There was nothing in it except for a garbage can, a broom, and Brad's canoe.

We got out of the Jeep in silence; the only sound was the garage door shimmying down on its rails behind us.

Brad unlocked a door with a red welcome mat in front of it, pushed it open and then turned to me.

"Come on in. I'll get your bag."

I said nothing as I stepped inside the furnished home where Brad had been living for the last nine weeks. The kitchen was tiled in terrazzo. Black granite counters and stainless appliances sparkled under recessed lights, and the walls were painted a warm brick red. An empty juice glass, coffee mug, and plate lay on a wooden dish drainer near the sink. Black and cream striped curtains hung above them. A ceramic bowl of wooden apples graced the center of an island in the middle where two tall stools seemed to wait for us.

"So this is the kitchen," Brad said from behind. He moved past me with his gym bag in one hand and my overnight bag in the other.

I followed him.

We entered the living room. It was decorated in shades of green.

The couches were a calming shade the color of french vanilla ice cream. Mahogany woodwork. Impressionist paintings on the wall. A great vase of silk calla lilies sat on the white marble hearth. To the right of where we stood was an open dining room and a table for eight with all the chairs pushed tightly in.

"There's a study in there," Brad pointed to a set of closed french doors. "And the bedrooms are upstairs. The couple who own this place are living in Saudi for the year. He's a civil engineer or something."

I simply could not speak. Being in Brad's house was like waking up from a coma and feeling like an amnesiac. Brad was watching me, wondering, I supposed, what I thought of the place he'd chosen to live in. He turned to an L-shaped staircase and began to ascend the steps. I mutely followed. He pointed to a room to the right of the landing.

"That's the uh…guest room." Then he stepped inside the other room at the top of the stairs. "And this is the master bedroom."

His room.

I walked inside. More mahogany. More pastoral hues. More French impressionists. I didn't know this room. I saw Brad's shoes on the floor, his favorite cologne on the dresser, and on a chair back the hat he wears when he fishes. But I did not know this lovely room.

Brad stood next to me with my bag and his, surely wondering what he should do with them.

"Why don't we go downstairs? I'll make some decaf," he said.

I heard him, but I didn't answer. I reached out to touch the pole of the poster on his footboard. The wood was smooth and cool to my touch. The bed was made, but the spread was crooked and the throw pillows had no symmetry at all in their placement.

Brad never did have much decorating sense. He never did know how to make a bed or arrange a pillow. And I had always found that endearing.

Must add that to the list.

I opened my mouth to laugh, but a laugh is not what came out.

As a stifled sob erupted from me, I heard Brad behind me take a step and then stop. A second later, the bags were on the floor, and Brad took me in his arms, tentative and slow.

"I'm sorry, I'm sorry…," I muttered through the tears I couldn't seem to stop.

"I'm the one who is sorry."

He stroked my hair and back, telling me he hadn't wanted to hurt me, never meant to hurt me.

"I know," I whispered. Because I did.

Brad was thoughtful.

After several moments I lifted my head from his chest and wiped my cheeks, apologizing again for my meltdown.

He rubbed his thumb across my jaw line where a ribbon of tears had formed. As he was looking at me, regret and tenderness mixed in his expression, he leaned toward me.

And kissed me.

The next moment was a blur of desire, hope, nostalgia, fabric, and the steady practice of two bodies that knew each other.

Molly's scarf was the first thing that fluttered to the floor.

Twenty-Five

I was alone when I woke in a strange bed. My first thought was one of panic—I didn't know where I was. I opened my eyes and nothing was familiar. It was a full second before I remembered whose bed I lay upon.

And what had happened.

I sat up in Brad's bed and turned my head toward his bathroom. The door was open, and sunlight streamed through the skylight. A wet towel hung askew on the glass shower door. I stretched out my hand to his side of the bed. It was cool to the touch.

I eased myself out of his bed, grabbed for my overnight bag, and headed into the bathroom, unsure what to expect from Brad that morning. I didn't know if we took a giant step forward the night before or if we simply gave in to loneliness and desire. We didn't talk, but it seemed to me we reconnected at a level we had not experienced in years. I was afraid to believe what happened between Brad and me was more than just sex. I wanted to believe it was more, but I was afraid to.

I dressed in my own clothes—a denim skirt and a red blouse. I sprayed on a dash of Molly's perfume and ran a wet comb through my hair. My makeup from the day before was still on my face. I fixed the smudges and then slipped on a pair of white flats, anxious to see Brad.

I grabbed Jane's ring from the bedside table and slipped it into my pocket. And then I headed downstairs.

Brad wasn't in the kitchen, but a fresh pot of coffee was on the counter and a black stoneware mug. I poured myself a cup and peeked inside the living room. No Brad. He wasn't in the dining room either, but I could see from the dining room a set of doors that opened out onto a patio. The curtains that hung on them were moving as a morning breeze caught them.

When I reached the doors, I could see Brad seated at a glass-topped patio table with his own mug of coffee. He sat back on the cushions with his legs stretched out in front of him. The morning newspaper was on the table by his mug, but it was still tightly folded. I stepped outside, but he didn't hear me.

"Mind if I join you?" I asked.

Brad turned his head and smiled, but it was a smile with regret behind it. "Sure."

I slipped into the chair across from him and took as deep a breath as I could without being obvious. I set my coffee mug down and waited for him to speak first.

A moment later, he sat forward and folded his hands in front of him. "I owe you an apology. I am really very sorry for what happened last night."

"I'm not sorry."

He held up a hand. "No, you need to know I had no intention of… I didn't bring you here to…" But he didn't finish. He just stopped in the middle of his sentence like an actor who'd forgotten his lines.

"Brad?"

Silence followed for a second or two.

"I wanted you to come here so we could talk," he finally said. "I never should've come upstairs last night. I should've just stayed downstairs."

His softly spoken apology stung a little with the unintended force of his rejection. The sensation silenced me.

"There is something I need to tell you." Brad looked away.

I breathed in and out like a practiced athlete. "What is it?" I asked calmly, though inside I trembled.

"I…I haven't been completely honest with you."

Oh, God. Oh, God.

"You're having an affair?" The words tasted like metal off my tongue.

"No. I'm not."

And I exhaled.

"But I almost did."

For a second, I was frozen to my chair.

"What did you say?"

He cleared his throat and repeated his confession using different words. "I wanted to have one."

I bolted to my feet and walked the length of the patio, unable to absorb what I had heard. This couldn't be happening. Couldn't. A huge container of pansies nodded their heads as I moved past them, and I wanted to grab them by their skinny necks and yank them out of the dirt they grew in.

"You lied to me." My voice was a rasping reprimand.

"You asked me if I was having an affair. And I told you I wasn't. I am not. Whatever it was I had is over. And I never slept with her, Jane."

The word "slept" nearly cut me in two, and I screwed my eyes shut. "Stop it."

"I didn't. I never slept with her!"

Anger and nausea tumbled inside my stomach. I rushed past him and headed for the dining room doors and the billowing curtains, but he stood and grabbed my arm to stop me.

"You needed to know. It wasn't fair to you that you didn't know."

"Fair to me?" I whirled to face him. "You're worried about what's fair to me? Is this what being treated fairly feels like?"

He said nothing.

"Who was she?"

"No one you know."

"Who was she?"

"Someone I worked with at Memorial. Her name is Dana. She's one of the reasons I had to leave. I couldn't work anymore with her there."

I turned from him to face his fence and a hedge of happy forsythia. I felt stupid, ignorant. Duped. Leslie was right. It was better not knowing there was—or had been—another woman. I needed to get myself back to New York. How could I get to the airport? I needed a taxi. I needed to call a taxi.

"We met on a surgical team last year, and we became friends."

I needed a taxi. Where was my purse? Where was my phone? I turned toward the house. My purse was in his bedroom.

"I didn't want anything like this to happen, Jane. I didn't want to be attracted to her." He sought my gaze. "I didn't! When I realized that I was, I knew something was already wrong between us. The doubts were already there."

"That's very convenient," I murmured, and I moved past him into the dining room. He followed me. I needed a taxi. I needed my phone. I needed to get out of there.

He reached out for my arm. "When I overheard you having that conversation with Leslie at your parents' party, I was already struggling to figure out what was wrong with us. Just like you. This thing with Dana started after that, several weeks after that."

I yanked my arm out of his grasp. "This is not my fault! I can't believe you're equating a stupid conversation I had with my sister over a punch bowl with what you have done. How can you compare what I said to Leslie with what you're telling me now?"

"I didn't say it was the same! And I didn't have an affair, Jane. It never went that far."

"Lucky me." I pivoted away from him and headed for the stairs. I needed my phone.

Again, he followed me. "I don't know how it happened. We were just good friends. She was easy to talk to, made me laugh, gave me good advice, asked me about my canoe trips. I didn't want to look forward to those times I spent with her, but I did."

I wanted to plug my ears. I didn't want to hear any more of it. Somehow it was all an indictment against me. All of it. I was on the first stair when, again, he grabbed my arm and turned me to face him.

"It was all one-sided, Jane. It was just me. Not her. I…kissed her one night. In the parking lot. It was nothing I planned. It just…happened."

I reached for the banister. Taxi. Phone. I took another step.

"But she didn't want me to kiss her." Brad's grip was still firm on my arm. "She was upset that I did. She knew I was married. She told me we needed to back off, that nothing good could come from us continuing to spend time together. But I saw her nearly every day. She went out of her way to avoid me. But we kept running into each other. I needed to get out of that hospital. I had to get out of there. So I did."

Tears had sprung and now slipped unchecked down my cheeks. "But you didn't just leave her, Brad! You left *me*!"

The pain in his face tore at me. I looked away from him.

"I couldn't pretend that it hadn't happened, Jane. I had to get out. I had to get away. I needed time to think."

"Do you love her?" I whispered.

"No. I don't know."

I breathed in and out. In and out. "You don't know?"

He hesitated only a second. "I'm not in love with her. I just…I just miss how I felt when I was with her." Brad leaned forward. "I am really sorry. For everything."

"Are you sorry we made love last night?" I didn't look at him.

"Jane."

I wouldn't look at him.

"I knew I was going to be telling you this. I should never have taken advantage of you like that. It was wrong."

A few long moments passed between us. Birdsong from the open patio doors behind us filled the silence.

"I want to go home," I said.

"I'm so sorry, Jane. I...I just don't want to go back to the way things were. Back to where I could be attracted to someone I wasn't married to and like it."

The impact of his words made me shudder. I felt Jane's ring poke me in my hip.

I wanted to go home. I took a step.

"About last night—," he began.

But I stopped him. "Please let me have this one little delusion that you wanted me."

"Jane—"

I released myself from his grasp and ascended the rest of the stairs to his bedroom. I threw my things into my overnight bag and was back down in less than two minutes.

I yanked my phone out of my purse, but I couldn't summon the wits to figure out how to call for a taxi. I felt numb and disoriented. I stood there staring at my phone, crying.

Brad asked me to let him take me to the airport. I asked him to please call a taxi for me.

While we waited in silence for the taxi, Brad brought in our coffee mugs from the patio. He set the two mugs, full to the brim, side by side in the sink.

Molly and Jeff were at Newark to pick me up. They wanted to take me to brunch as we headed over the bridge to Manhattan, especially when they heard I had missed breakfast. I just wanted to go home and disappear for a while.

Molly turned from the front seat, concern deeply etched in her face. She wanted to ask me how things went, but I could see she was afraid I couldn't talk about it with Jeff in the car with us.

Actually, I didn't care. I really didn't. And I had this feeling Jeff already knew about Dana anyway.

"Brad liked the clothes you picked out," I offered as an answer to her wordless question. The sarcastic edge to my voice was grating, even to me.

"Oh, Jane. Did it go terribly?"

I could see Jeff's eyes in the rearview mirror as he looked at me. When he saw me looking at him, his eyes darted back to the road.

"I wouldn't say that." I let out a breath. "It's actually a relief to finally know what made Brad's mind up for him."

"What…what do you mean?" Molly asked.

Jeff probably knows what I mean, I wanted to say. I saw him looking at me again in the rearview mirror.

I told them most of what Brad told me. I skipped the part about the night before, and Brad's attempt to apologize for it. When I was done, Molly looked genuinely crushed on my behalf. Jeff's eyes in the rearview mirror were expressionless.

As we pulled up to my brownstone, Molly asked if I'd like to go to a movie later or shopping. Anything. I declined, hugged her good-bye, and thanked her for loaning me the clothes and perfume. She had tears in her eyes as she got back in their car. Jeff walked me up my steps and handed me my overnight bag.

"Thanks for the lift." I faked a bright tone.

"I'm sorry about all this."

"Me too. But at least you don't have to carry this secret around anymore, eh?" I smiled at him.

His shock only lasted for a moment. "He should've told you before now."

I shrugged my shoulders and blinked back a few threatening tears.

"Molly didn't know," he said.

I nodded wordlessly. If I opened my mouth to speak, I would lose it. I said nothing.

"Call us if you need anything."

"Will do," I whispered.

I waved as they drove away, and then I headed inside my very quiet apartment. Once I was inside, I was aware that my phone was vibrating inside my purse. I'd missed two calls. I wondered if Brad had tried to call me, and I fished out my phone with trembling hands. One call was from Emma. She had left me a voice mail. The other was from Wilson. There was no message.

I punched the button to retrieve Emma's message. *"Hey, love. So I found the vendor who sold me the books. His name is Edgar Brownton. He bought them from the granddaughter of some old pensioner who died last winter. Had a shed full to the ceiling with boxes. She sold it all, by the box, at auction. Brownton doesn't know her name. She doesn't even live in the UK. Canada, he thinks. He bought them in Swansea. That's about all I can tell you, love. You may have to just make up a good story for where that lovely trinket of yours came from. So ring me up when you get home. My offer still stands to come see me."*

The voice mail ended, but I put off working through my disappointment so that I could call Wilson back.

Wilson answered on the first ring.

"It's me, Jane. Is everything all right?"

"Oh. Oh yes, Jane. Say, I've just come across something, and I didn't want to wait until tomorrow to tell you. It's the most curious thing. Is this a good time?"

He sounded excited. As nice as it was to hear a happy voice, it would've been really easy to say it was a crappy time. But I slid into an armchair, kicked off my shoes, and told him his timing was fine.

"Well, my grandson Eric is here today, and he's a political science major, you know. And so I was telling him about the ring you found."

"Yes?"

"He said a person of noble birth would have had her betrothal recorded. You know? There would be a record of it."

"Yes, but this Jane might not have married the person who gave it to her. Remember? The ring appears not to have been worn."

"Indeed. My point exactly."

"I don't know what you mean, Wilson."

"Eric went on his computer, and he typed in the words *Jane— betrothal—sixteenth century* into a search engine."

My next breath wedged in my throat. "Yes?"

"Two names came up over and over. Jane Seymour is one. She was the third wife of King Henry the Eighth. But she and Henry were betrothed within twenty-four hours of Anne Boleyn's execution and married less than a month later. It seems very unlikely to us Henry would've given her a betrothal ring. And it's not likely the ring of an English queen would end up in a tattered prayer book."

"Yes. Go on."

"The other name that came up multiple times is Jane Grey. Remember her?"

The name was vaguely familiar, but I couldn't place it. "No. No, I don't. Who was she?"

Wilson seemed put out that I didn't know who this other Jane was. "Really? Ah, well, she also had a very short betrothal. Less than a month. Just like Jane Seymour."

"Well, maybe young noblewomen didn't wear their betrothal rings for very long."

"Still don't remember who Jane Grey was, eh?"

"No, Wilson. I don't."

"Hold on a minute." I could hear Wilson talking to someone, but I couldn't make out what they were saying. "Eric says he will send you the link. What is your e-mail address at home?"

I rose from the chair and headed over to my desk as I rattled off my home e-mail address. I woke my computer from sleep mode and sat in the swivel chair.

"So do you have it then?" Wilson said a moment later.

The new e-mail landed in my inbox as he was asking. "Yes, I have it. Wilson, do you think this ring was hers?"

"It would be amazing if it was. But no. Still, it's fun to imagine. Well, you have some reading to do. We'll talk tomorrow. Bye, Jane."

"Good-bye, Wilson. And thanks."

I hung up, then pulled the ring from my front pocket and placed it on the desk so that the stones faced me.

I folded my legs under me and opened the link to an online biography of Lady Jane Grey.

I began to read.

Lucy

London, England, 1553

Twenty-Six

The rooms at Richmond Palace were fragrant with the scent of first-of-May roses, but Lady Jane seemed oblivious to the exhilarating aroma.

She paced the carpet in her room with regal beauty, but still she paced. As I stitched a torn riding frock on the floor by her feet, she recited verses from St. John's Gospel; first in English, then in Latin, then in Greek, then in a language I did not know. Her nervousness washed onto me, and I pricked my finger.

I winced and slipped my finger into my mouth. She did not notice.

Her parents were at last making a final decision about her betrothal. They had told her to expect their summons sometime before noon. Finally, after all these many months, there would be a decision regarding Edward Seymour.

I would've been pacing too, had I been in her stead.

At nearly sixteen, she was very much the lady I had called her since the day I met her. She had been eleven then, mourning the death of a beloved queen, alone in a beautiful palace, and surrounded by people who decided her every movement. Today she was in another palace, surrounded by more people who were to decide her every movement.

The months leading up to this day had been fraught with ill news from all sides, starting with the execution of Edward's father early the year before on a gray January morn.

I had returned to London after the Christmas of 1551, betrothed to my dear Nicholas, to the shocking development that the former Protector's sentence would not be overturned as we had all hoped. Jane returned, already vexed, from spending the holidays with the Princess Mary—Jane and her royal cousin were not of the same persuasion in matters of faith. This news of the former Protector's fate only served to increase her melancholy.

Talk below stairs and above, and even among lords and ladies at the breakfast table, was that the Duke of Northumberland had masterminded the elder Edward Seymour's downfall to win the friendship and loyalty of powerful men who did not care for Seymour. Why John Dudley coveted so many influential friends was unknown to me. Nicholas told me this kind of posturing is how kingdoms rise and fall and that, sadly, it has always been this way. It would not have been so worrisome if His Majesty had not taken ill. There were rumors that Dudley, who was the young King's closest confidante, was often in His Majesty's sick chamber, bringing him this document and that document to sign, and at all hours. And some whispered that the Duke of Northumberland might be slowly poisoning the King.

To what end, I could not guess.

Jane did not hear these rumors in her own home, but she did hear them when her parents took her out and about. It was no secret that it was John Dudley who maneuvered Seymour into the hopeless position of being found guilty of conspiracy, a charge difficult for those of us not attached to court to believe.

Jane certainly did not believe it.

Her distaste for Northumberland and his politicking set her to distraction. Mrs. Ellen and I were forbidden to say his name in her presence, though we never had need to. Conversations between her and her beloved Edward, the few times they saw each other, were wrapped in veiled emotion I alone understood. I, of course, did not speak with young Edward on those occasions he called on Jane, but I would see his face from across the hall, or out in the garden, or alighting from his carriage. It was a troubled face; the face of a man who is chained to circumstances he cannot control.

I fully expected Jane's parents to cancel her unofficial betrothal to Edward after the execution, though I said nothing of the sort to Jane. Nicholas told me if the duke's lands and possessions passed to his son upon his death, young Edward would be a rich man, and still a worthy match.

But for many months, there had not been news of the disposition of the dead duke's wealth and properties, and therefore no official contract between Jane and the man she loved.

A full year had passed, and still there was no official contract, and all the while, the King's health continued to fail. In the meantime, Nicholas and I made plans for our own wedding, which was to take place in June. Jane had already decided I should stay with her when she and Edward Seymour married and that Nicholas could be the tutor for their children. I had laughed and told her it would be several years before any children would be ready for letters and sums, and she had said that Nicholas could just tutor us, then. She and I. Jane ever loved to learn. Were it not for her books and translations and correspondence with learned theologians on the Continent, she would have gone mad in those many months, waiting for her marriage to be decided.

It remained to be seen what I would do after my wedding to Nicholas. A position as the head seamstress in a married noblewoman's home was enticing. And Nicholas would no doubt be an excellent tutor to Jane and Edward's future children. But there were no children as of yet. My future husband would need a position before then. There was no guarantee he would have one at his uncle's school in Worcester.

Mrs. Ellen stepped into the room at that moment, followed my lady's footsteps with stern eyes, and then raised her hands to her hips.

"You shall wear out the carpet, lass." Her tone, despite her set arms, was soothing.

"I care not for the carpet, Ellen." Jane recited the first beatitude, in English.

"Perhaps you would like to write some letters, then. You love to write your letters."

"No letters today." Jane sighed and settled onto the couch in front of me. "Tell me again what your dress looks like, Lucy."

"Not this again," Mrs. Ellen murmured, and she moved away into Jane's sitting room.

My wedding gown, which I was stitching by candlelight every night before bed, was a design of my own making. It was not finished enough to show anyone, not even dear Jane, but I had promised I would show her when it was done. In the meantime, I had described for her how I envisioned it.

I began to describe it again.

"Well, first, there is a long flowing skirt of the softest golden lawn, gathered here and there in billowy pleats like clouds. On the bodice, I will embroider, with silver thread, tiny thistles that will glisten like diamonds. Over the shoulders, there shall be puffings of white and silver gauze. And a needlepoint collar with more silver thread and trimmed with a length of Venetian lace."

"And your veil?" Jane asked, smiling.

"It shall look like a waterfall, and there shall be tiny white roses and pink asters and larkspur, tumbling down from it onto my train."

"I wish you would wear some of my jewelry." Jane's voice was wistful. "My necklace with the diamonds and amethysts would look splendid with that dress."

She said it to tease me. Jane knew I couldn't possibly wear any of her jewels at my wedding. She likely would not even be permitted to attend.

Jane rose from the couch. That day, she was wearing a gown of plain velvet with just a bit of lace at her throat. It was all she ever wore since turning fifteen, unless her parents took her out and insisted on opulence. She wore black, gray, and bottomless brown. As her dressmaker, it had been saddening to see her attired in such somber hues by choice. But Jane had begun to turn inward as her destiny hung day after day like a broken pendulum, swinging neither to the left or right, and her gowns reflected that. The duchess didn't care much for Jane's attempts at extreme modesty, but there was much the duchess didn't seem to care about when it came to Jane. Though a Reformer herself, the duchess didn't understand her daughter's wish to be free of all things vain and impious and arrogant. I didn't truly understand it either—beauty to me was also a creation of the Lord God—but Jane and I existed in different worlds. I knew this. And so I respected her choice. Even admired it.

"I wish you were the one who would be making my wedding dress." Jane turned to face me. "It should be you. Mother will no doubt insist on her own dressmakers."

"I am sure it will be lovely, my lady. I am sure of it. What shall it look like?"

She exhaled heavily. "How would it look were you to make it, Lucy?"

Her gaze on me was laden with equal parts trepidation and desire. It was a look that seemed out of place for a young woman about to be married. I spoke carefully.

"Perhaps a gown of Italian fashion, hmm? A skirt of silver tissue, with an overlay on the bodice of silvery netting sparkling with your favorite gems. Gently puffed sleeves to match—"

"And no farthingale," Jane intoned. "I don't want to look like a bulbous turret."

I laughed. "So. No farthingale hoop. Instead, your skirt shall be made of narrow panels of silver tissue bordered with golden passamayne and laced together with pearled cords."

"And no ruff. And a simple veil. With flowers. Like yours?"

"Of course."

Jane again settled onto the couch. I went back to my stitching, expecting her to describe for me what Edward would wear. After a moment or two of silence, I looked up at her. She was staring at me.

"Are you afraid?" she said.

"Afraid?"

"Of…of being alone with Mr. Staverton?"

I colored slightly. As the weeks approached for Nicholas and I to be together at last, I had wrestled with a strange kind of anxiety that was more akin to yearning than fear. But I could see that Jane was afraid to lie in a man's bed, even a man she was attracted to.

"My mother says 'tis natural to be scared of the unknown, my lady. Do not fret over it. 'Tis God who made the way between a man and a maiden, yes?"

She nodded. "Yes." But she seemed far away in her thoughts.

"What is it, my lady?"

Jane hesitated for a moment. Then she looked about her room. "I have never known any life but this one. Mama and Papa have always decided everything for me, who I associate with, who I don't, even where I lay my head at night. I have never been alone with a man behind a closed door. I have never been outside my parents' wishes and control. It seems very strange to me that soon I shall not be under their roof. Or under their thumb."

She was quiet for a moment before continuing.

"I wonder what it will be like to make the kind of choices Mama makes," she went on. "She does make choices, you know. She is a woman, like me, and subservient like I shall be to the will of her husband, but she makes choices. She makes choices every day. I wonder what that will be like."

Her spoken thoughts fell away, and I said nothing. She did not expect me to. Over the years, I'd been privy to many of Jane's innermost thoughts. Most of them she did not voice for me. She simply said them to hear them said. And have them heard.

A moment later, Mrs. Ellen swept back into the room. A page had been sent from Jane's parents.

They were ready to receive her.

Jane rose slowly from the couch and smoothed her skirt, and I got to my feet as well. She closed her eyes and breathed in deeply. As she let the breath out of her lungs, she opened her eyes and the sixth beatitude fell from her lips, in Latin.

"Beati mundo corde, quoniam ipsi Deum videbunt."

The English translation floated into my head. *Blessed are the pure in heart: for they shall see God.*

She took two steps toward the door and then turned to me.

"Wait for me here."

I curtsied. And before I had completed it, she had turned again to the door and was walking away from me.

Mrs. Ellen went with her.

I waited for her on the couch, unable to take up my sewing. My thoughts were a jumbled weave of excitement and dread. It seemed my own future was being decided as well, at least the near future.

Mrs. Ellen and Jane were not gone long. When I heard footsteps rapidly approaching the closed doors, I stood. Someone was running to the door. My heart began to skip with anticipation.

The doors flew open and Jane swept in, clutching her breast, her face streaked with tears. She flew past me, her swishing skirt of black the only sound that came from her. She went into her bedchamber and closed the door, and then the first sound came from her: a sob racked with anger and hopelessness.

My own eyes were already moist with empathy, even though I did not know yet what had happened. I turned from Jane's closed door and saw that Mrs. Ellen had entered the room too. She was biting her lip, shaking her head, and fighting back an emotion that might have been sorrow, might have been fury, might have been exasperation.

"What has happened?" I said.

Mrs. Ellen closed the doors behind her and eased her back against them.

"The duke and duchess have not chosen Edward Seymour," she said.

"Someone else?"

She closed her eyes and nodded.

"Who?"

She said the name slowly as if it tasted sour on her tongue. "Guildford Dudley."

John Dudley's son.

Twenty-Seven

❦

I did not see Jane for two days. She stayed in her bedchamber and did not summon me. I was, however, sent to her sister Katherine's rooms. The fluttering thirteen-year-old had also been betrothed, the same hour as Jane, and the girl was anxious to be about her prewedding wardrobe.

"Has Jane told you?" she gushed when I arrived at her room the morning after the news had made the rounds of the household.

I had curtsied. "Yes, my lady."

"Isn't it most exciting?"

"Indeed, my lady."

"Have you met Lord Herbert? He is older than I, you know. He is nineteen. But he is quite handsome, don't you think?"

I had never met Henry Herbert, but I knew he was the Earl of Pembroke's son. And I knew Katherine barely knew him. Talk on the stairs was that Lady Katherine's marriage was a hastily planned political maneuver.

As was Jane's.

"Yes, my lady," was all I said in reply.

"Can you let out these seams, please, Lucy?" She showed me a peach-colored bodice of satin and ermine. " 'Tis tight on me now that I am a woman!"

She pushed out her chest, tiny though it still was, and I told her it would be my pleasure to let out the seams. I asked her if I could take her measurements.

"Jane is not happy, though," she said as she lifted her arms so I could measure her bosom and waist. "I suppose you know that. She oughtn't to be so glum, if you ask me. Guildford is the most handsome man in all of London. He's had eyes for her for the longest time."

I didn't know what Jane would have me say to Katherine. But I did not wish to keep saying, "Yes, my lady," to everything she said. Jane deserved to have some sympathy from her family, especially Katherine.

"She is fond of someone else," I ventured.

Katherine had her back to me, but she swung her head around. "You mean Edward Seymour? I'm the one who wanted to marry Edward. She knew that. Did she not tell you? I've been pining away for Edward since before his father got into all that trouble. Long before then."

Jane had not mentioned Katherine's infatuation with Edward. It was like her not to. I said nothing.

"But the Seymours are in such dreadful straits," Katherine went on. "I daresay they shall never recover. And if I cannot have Edward, then I am lucky to have Lord Herbert. Jane is luckier to have Guildford. His father is counselor to His Majesty. Did you know that?"

"Yes, my lady. He is indeed a very powerful man."

"Oh!" Katherine said suddenly, twirling around again. "Did you hear His Majesty is having our wedding gowns made? Mine and Jane's? Can you believe it? And we're to be married the same day. At Durham House."

My heart fell when Katherine said this, even though I had no delusions that I would be making Jane's wedding gown.

"When are you to be married?" I asked.

"Whitsunday! In three weeks!" she said gaily.

At this, my heart truly sank to my feet. Three weeks.

Katherine chattered on as I set about opening the seams, readjusting them, and closing them again. As soon as I finished, I asked if there was anything else I could do for her, and I prayed there wasn't.

To my gratitude, she dismissed me, and I went back to my garret room to await a summons from Jane that did not come that day. While I waited, I penned a note to Nicholas, apprising him of the events of late. I still had no idea what to expect as to the matter of my employment. I also wrote to my parents that I would likely be returning to them at the end of May, a month before my own wedding, if I could find no other post in London.

I had no desire to be in the employ of the Dudley family. I did not trust John Dudley.

I knew Jane also did not, and I ached for her that she would soon bear his name and be married to his son.

But I would not work for him.

I did not think for a moment he would ask me.

On the third day, the duchess called me to her room. The Duke of Northumberland and his son Lord Guildford would be calling that day, and I was to see to it that Jane was properly attired to greet them.

"Absolutely nothing in black." Her harsh tone was accompanied by rolled eyes and a wave of her hand.

I curtsied and left to carry out her orders.

I found Jane in her sitting room, seated at a round table where she sometimes took a meal. But today, the tabletop was covered with letters and bits of sealing wax. She was absently picking at a broken seal as I came in.

I curtsied. "Good morning, my lady."

"I can stomach everyone's patronizing tone except yours, Lucy."

I searched for words to reply and nothing seemed appropriate. After a moment of silence, she bid me to approach the table.

"These letters," she said. "They speak of the Jane that no one knows. Not even you. I don't think even you know this Jane."

I looked down at the spread of parchments. I saw the flowing script, the lengthy pages, a couple of signatures. Henry Bullinger. John ab Ulmis. Theologians on the Continent whom Jane had been writing to since she was fourteen. I had never read the letters she wrote, nor the ones laid out before me, but I knew that Jane had come to a place where she saw her faith not as an extension of her position but the essence of her very soul. Faith to Jane was not something to be bargained with or leveraged. It was to be as subtle and unstoppable as the beating of your own heart.

"I fear this Jane is about to disappear," she whispered.

"No, she shall not," I whispered back.

"How can I honor God and yet marry this man?"

"You will find a way."

A tear slipped out of her left eye and ran unchecked down her cheek, followed by one from the other eye.

"And what of Edward?"

I had no answer for her.

"He asks too much of me," she murmured.

I had missed something. "Your father?"

She picked at a bit of wax, and the seal broke away in her fingers. "God," she whispered.

An hour later, we heard carriages outside in the courtyard. Mrs. Ellen appeared to tell Jane it was time to receive her guests. Jane left the room in a dress she had chosen; a brocaded gown of verdant green.

Edward Seymour's favorite color.

I watched from a distance that afternoon as the duke and duchess entertained their guests, slightly jealous of the serving staff being privy to every conversation at the tables in the garden. I could only watch Guild-ford speak to Jane from my window. I could not hear his voice; I could see that he was indeed very comely, but he seemed attentive to Jane only at intervals, as if the conversations between his father and Jane's father were his true interest. His attentions were always drawn to the hushed conversations between the two dukes. Jane barely looked up from her lap. Once I saw her raise her gaze to the windows, my window. I raised my hand and pressed it to the glass. She looked away.

In the days leading up to Jane's marriage to Guildford Dudley, I learned my employment with the household of the Duke of Somerset had come to a successful completion, and that I would be given sterling recommendations upon my leave. I was expected to stay through the month of May to see the Lady Jane's wardrobe safely to her husband's home at Syon Park on the Thames. After that I was free to pursue my next post.

My parents were happy to have me home to make preparations for my own wedding and to dote on me for a few more days as their remaining unmarried daughter. The year before, Cecily had married the fowler's son at the manor house where she was installed as seamstress.

Nicholas had secured a post as instructor at a boys' school at Whitechapel, just outside London, though without my income, we'd be living in the dormitories with the lads. I began to write letters of inquiry, hoping a merchant tailor in Whitechapel needed a seamstress until God would favor us with a nobleman's household who needed a dressmaker and a tutor.

Since I was not involved with the construction of Jane's or Katherine's wedding clothes, I busied myself with a dress for their little sister, Mary, who would not be attending the wedding, as the duke and duchess were increasingly embarrassed by their younger daughter's physical ailments. And at night, I stitched my own wedding dress.

When I was with Jane, I endeavored to take her mind off what lay ahead. But it was always before her, looming ahead like an appointment with a gaoler.

I had the rare opportunity to meet Lord Guildford once during the days of preparation. Again, I noted that he was strikingly handsome, but I could tell in a moment, he lacked Nicholas's humility and Edward Seymour's gentility. He seemed very much like his father. Ambitious. Self-assured. Cunning. And to my shame and disgust, he followed the curves of my body with his eyes as I moved away from him on the stairs.

I had to gather my composure after turning onto the landing. And rein in my revulsion. I said nothing of this to Jane.

The day of the wedding, Whitsunday, dawned cloudless and vibrant. I came to Jane's rooms early with a small token, a lacy undergarment, stitched with silver rosettes, asters, and larkspur since she would not be having the veil of gauze and flowers. Everything else she would be wearing that day had been sewn by His Majesty's tailors and dressmakers. Her gown was resplendent in gold and majestic white, with diamonds and pearls glistening at every seam. The farthingale hoop, which Jane did not truly expect to escape, was bell shaped and enormous.

Tears came to her eyes when I gave her the chemise to wear under the great folds of wedding fabric.

"It is beautiful, Lucy." She fought to keep the tears at bay and was successful. I marveled at her courage.

"I am…I am glad he will not see it. Not today." Jane fingered a silvery rosette.

Her words confused me. "My lady?"

"The marriage is not to be consummated today. Nor shall Kate's."

Color rose to my cheeks. "'Tis a mercy, my lady. Yes?" I said, after a moment's pause.

"Yes, for today. It will happen soon enough. My parents will see to it. So will his."

The heat on my cheeks intensified. I had no words for her.

"His Majesty cannot come to the wedding," Jane said, swallowing her raw emotions and moving away from the subject of her marriage bed. "He is too ill."

"We must pray for him, my lady."

"Yes."

A stretch of silence yawned before us.

"Mama says you are to be released at the end of the month," Jane said at last, speaking aloud what we both knew, and I hadn't the valor to address—we were to be parted.

"Yes."

"But she says that you will be in London after your wedding to Mr. Staverton." She blinked back tears.

"Yes, my lady."

"Then perhaps I shall see you again, dear Lucy."

"You can be sure of it."

She sighed. "Perhaps you would consider future employment, you and Mr. Staverton, when…when this arrangement I am beholden to comforts me with children?"

I could only nod. The young lady needed a dream on that day. I could give her that one.

She stood and held the chemise to me. "Help me dress, Lucy."

Without a word, I obeyed.

Twenty-Eight

I married Nicholas on the eighth of June in my village church, surrounded by my family. A brilliant sun chased away fog that had arrived in maiden white in the wee morning hours, and the air was filled with birdsong and the scent of lavender. My father's health had rallied in the late spring, and color had returned to his cheeks, even if only for a few weeks.

There were many moments during my wedding when my thoughts turned to Jane, though the only event I could adequately picture was her dressing to become Guildford Dudley's bride. That was the only event of Jane's wedding day that I was privy to. I did not see Jane again that day.

As I put on the gown I had sewn while the Grey household slept, I was keenly aware of the differences, not similarities of the two days.

I was breathless with happiness as I walked into the church and could scarce contain tears of joy as I vowed to cherish Nicholas to the end of my days. Jane left her chambers resolute and expressionless, the few stray tears on her cheek silent evidences of her mourning the loss of a life with Edward Seymour that was not to be hers.

I thought of her when Nicholas and I knelt and prayed before God as the vicar blessed our vows. I thought of her when we left the church as husband and wife, and again when Nicholas took me in his arms that night and together we discovered the unspeakable beauty and splendor of the marriage bed.

I knew that nothing about my wedding day was akin to hers. Love brought me to the marriage altar. Duty brought her.

We were both married, but for wholly different reasons.

I had never been more grateful to Almighty God that I was born a commoner than the day I married the man I loved and who loved me.

It did not matter to me that Nicholas and I returned to London to make our home in the upper rooms of a dormitory, that I spent my days mending little boys' torn breeches and doublets, tending to scraped knees, assisting Cook in the kitchen, and soothing the fears of young lads who missed their mothers.

In the evenings, after Nicholas had put away his students' work, and I put away his students' torn garments, we walked the walled garden under splashes of moonlight, read poetry, laughed, dreamed, and then returned to our tiny room and our shared bed.

In my prayers, I interceded for dear Jane; I could only guess what her first few weeks of marriage were like. I didn't know if her marriage had been consummated yet, but I knew that it was only a matter of time. I could not imagine partaking of the marriage bed with someone I did not love, and there were moments when I cried for her. Nicholas did not know why Jane's marriage was not consummated the night of her wedding. He guessed that just as there were political reasons for her marriage, there were political reasons for that as well. It was not because of her age; she was fifteen and certainly old enough to be wedded.

I had asked Nicholas what might be the reason for Jane's parents' hasty decision to marry their daughter to John Dudley's son, a mere three weeks after announcing the betrothal, when they had delayed the announcement of her betrothal to Edward Seymour for more than a year.

He thought perhaps they were reacting to their disappointment that they'd waited too long to see if Edward Seymour would retain his father's lands and possessions.

But why Guildford Dudley? I asked. Jane was a Tudor. Fourth in line to the throne. Guildford was not a royal; he was the son of a duke.

Not just any duke, Nicholas had said. John Dudley was not just any duke.

Nicholas and I had been at Whitechapel for three weeks, and it was nigh unto July when I received my first letter from Jane.

> *My dear Mrs. Staverton,*
>
> *Would you be so good as to call upon me this Friday afternoon at Syon House? I should like to discuss the matter of your services in the construction of a new gown. A carriage shall be dispatched to fetch you at one o'clock.*
>
> *Yours very sincerely,*
>
> *Lady Jane Dudley*

I brought the letter at once to Nicholas. "I would very much like to go see her," I said.

We were alone in his classroom, and he kissed the top of my head. "Seeing her will make you sad, I think."

"I am sad already for her."

His arms went around me. I ached for Jane that she likely did not know what it was like to be in the embrace of a man who did not like to see you sad.

"If there is a gown to be made, would you be opposed to my making it?" I asked.

"Not if you truly wish to do so. But your home is here with me, Lucy."

"I do not wish to be anywhere else. I shall sew it here or not at all."

❦

I was restless the days leading up to my visit to Jane. When Friday finally arrived, I was ready for the carriage a full hour before it came for me. Nicholas assisted me inside, despite there being a footman who had been sent along for that purpose.

"You cannot change what Providence has willed," Nicholas reminded me as he kissed my hand. "She is Dudley's wife, for good or ill. Guard your own happiness, dearest."

I laid my other hand against his cheek. "I shall be careful."

He closed the carriage door and smiled at me as the driver slapped the reins and the coach rolled away. An hour later, we pulled in front of the Duke of Northumberland's Syon House residence, a stately hall of honey-gold stone and bordered with sloping lawns and mature oaks.

When I alighted from the carriage, Mrs. Ellen was waiting for me on the steps. Her face was careworn, and she seemed both pleased and irritated that I was there. I found it strange that it was she who was there to greet me. She was Jane's nurse and principal attendant, not a house-keeper. But I moved toward her with a smile and warm tone.

"Mrs. Ellen! How wonderful to see you!"

"Indeed, Mrs. Staverton." She nodded to me nervously. "If you will follow me."

We had no sooner stepped inside the great hall when a woman in red silk and jewels approached us from just inside a set of double doors leading to a gilded parlor. She looked to be my mother's age. I curtsied.

"What is this?" the woman boomed as I rose from my bended knees.

"My lady, this is Lady Jane's former dressmaker, Mrs. Lucy Staver-ton," Mrs. Ellen replied, licking her lips. "Lady Jane has sent for her now that her illness has passed. She would like a new gown for her entrance back into court as a new bride."

Guildford's mother, the Duchess of Northumberland, narrowed her eyes as she scrutinized me. This was the first I'd heard that Jane had been ill. But I said nothing.

"We have dressmakers here," the woman said. "Send her home."

A voice from the top of the stairs called down to us. "I sent for her." Jane.

She looked pale. And older.

The duchess frowned. "We have dressmakers here," she repeated, this time to Jane.

Jane began to descend the staircase. "Not like Lucy. Her designs are exceptional."

The duchess's frown deepened. "But His Majesty saw to your trousseau. You've gowns you've not even worn yet."

"And all of them hang on me since my illness."

Jane arrived at the landing, and I fell to a curtsy. "My lady."

"Please escort Lucy to my chambers, Mrs. Ellen." Jane's voice was tired and unsure behind the authoritative words. She had indeed lost weight.

Mrs. Ellen motioned to me to follow, and I curtsied to Jane and her mother-in-law, but both of them were looking only at each other.

"If I might have a word." The duchess showered Jane with fake politeness as I walked past them to follow Mrs. Ellen.

The two women disappeared behind the closed doors, and I heard the beginning of their conversation. It began with the duchess's demanding from Jane an explanation for bringing someone into the manor without her consent.

I did not hear Jane's muffled reply.

Mrs. Ellen said nothing as we continued up the stairs and into a bedchamber decorated in rich tones of green and scarlet. She motioned me into a separate room, Jane's dressing room, and closed the door.

"My lady has been ill?" I asked, before she even turned around to face me.

"Aye."

"Is she well now?"

Mrs. Ellen lifted and lowered her shoulders. "As well as can be expected. The fever is gone. She is eating again." She cocked her head as a look of sorrow washed over her. "And her husband's...visits have resumed."

"Visits?" But I knew what she meant. "Has... Is my lady...?" But I could not finish. My face flushed crimson.

"Yes, the marriage has been consummated." Mrs. Ellen shook her head, and her eyes turned glassy. "Poor wee thing. It is not how it should be. Not how it should be."

Something akin to familial fidelity flared up within me. "Was he unkind to her? Did he hurt her?"

Mrs. Ellen wiped her eyes. "Of course he hurt her."

"Is...Is that why she was ill?"

"Her illness was a blessing from God to keep him away from her until she can accept what has befallen her. It was too much for the wee lass. She knew nothing of the way of men. Her mother told her nothing! If I had not prepared her..."

She stopped. We heard movement on the other side of the door. The door opened and Jane stepped into the room. Again, I curtsied.

"Ellen, would you give me a few moments with Lucy, please?" Jane asked.

Mrs. Ellen admonished me with her eyes to please do whatever I could to cheer young Jane. "Of course," she said. She left the room and closed the door behind her.

We stood there for a moment, silent, both of us attempting to grasp how different it was now between us. I didn't know my place. I didn't know what I should do. What she would want me to do.

She looked as sad as the day I met her, when she crumpled into my bosom, and I held her as she poured out her grief. I nearly expected her to do the same just then.

But she turned from me, walked over to a bureau, opened it and withdrew a box I recognized from her bedroom at her parents' house. She opened it, and I saw her take out Edward's ring. Tears began to slide, unbidden, down my face as she walked back to me. I hadn't the courage to even wipe them away.

"I need for you to do something for me, Lucy." Her voice was wracked with emotion that she was somehow able to keep in check. "I need you to keep this ring for me. Please."

"I cannot!" I breathed.

"Yes, you can."

"My lady!"

"Please keep it for me. It cannot stay here. Guildford will see it. His mother will see it. His father will see it. They will take it from me. I don't want any of them to touch it. Especially his father. Especially not him."

The disgust on her face pained me. But still I persisted. "But if anyone finds me with it, they will think I stole it from you!"

"Who will notice that it is missing? My parents have forgotten Edward even gave me this ring."

"But…what about Mrs. Ellen?"

She smiled ruefully. "Do you honestly think dear Ellen will tell Northumberland the ring Edward Seymour gave me has gone missing? Please do this for me, Lucy. You are the only one I can trust."

"But, Jane…" I had not realized I had said her name out loud until a second after I said it. Mortification swept over me.

A tender smile had replaced the rueful one. "You've never called me that before."

"I am so dreadfully sorry, my lady. Please forgive me!"

Her smile grew wider. "I can only forgive you under one condition." She held out her hand.

I hesitated.

"Take it and all is forgiven," she whispered. Desperation shone in her eyes along with tears she refused to release.

I held out my hand, and she pressed the ring into it.

"What shall I do with it?" I murmured.

"Keep it for me," she whispered, each word punctuated with emotion.

"For how long?"

"As long as you must."

I could not help it any longer. I pulled her into my embrace. "I shall keep it safe for you."

Her small frame began to quake in my arms. Measured sobs leaked from her, though I sensed she fought to rein them in.

"You are strong. You are brave," I soothed.

"Oh, Lucy! Sometimes I think they are trying to poison me!"

I stroked her back, hiding my shock at her words with silence. Surely she was overwrought.

"There are meetings here, other lords, councilors, people I don't know, and they whisper about me. They watch me and whisper."

"My lady…"

"The duke! He says things behind closed doors that he thinks I cannot hear. He says things like, 'It's just a matter of time,' and, 'Everything is in place,' and, 'She shall bend to the will of her sovereign; that is her nature.' That is what he is saying, Lucy! What can he possibly mean?"

"Sh, my lady. I do not know. 'Tis most likely nothing that has to do with you." Her ramblings made no sense to me. I would have wondered if she was still feverish except she felt cool in my arms.

"There are moments when I cannot bear it anymore!"

"And then those moments become moments when you can," I said gently. "You are brave and strong. God will protect you."

"I feel so very weak." She eased her body away from me, a sure sign of strength. I told her so.

She smiled then, tiny but genuine. "I miss having you near me."

"I miss you too. You've been my only companion for so long!"

Her countenance turned wistful. "But now you have Nicholas."

I sought no words in response. How could I tell her how wonderful it was being married to Nicholas? I couldn't.

But I didn't have to. She knew.

"I wonder if I will ever know that kind of happiness," she said. "I wonder if I will ever be able to choose my destiny like you have done."

I looked at her ring in my hand. "You chose to entrust me with this," I said softly.

She smiled and nodded. "Yes. That's a start, isn't it? Hide it away, now."

I slipped the ring into my sewing bag.

"You must go," she said. "Guildford will be returning soon."

"What about the dress you wanted me to make? What if I am asked about the dress?"

"I commission you to make any sort of dress for me you please, Lucy. I don't care what it looks like. Ellen will see to it that you have whatever fabric you need. Is that all right?"

"Of course."

"Thank you, dear Lucy. For coming. For doing this for me."

"You are most welcome, my lady."

"Perhaps you will come see me before the end of July for a fitting?"

she said, the traces of tears and fears now safely tucked away somewhere. A wisp of hope replaced the cloak of sadness.

I told her it would be my utmost pleasure to come back for a fitting. And she seemed to revel in the thought that she had something to look forward to in the coming days.

But I did not see Jane at Syon House in July.

Instead, to my absolute astonishment, I saw her in London less than a fortnight later, paraded down the banks of the Thames, accompanied by Guildford, soldiers, cannons, banners, and the Duke of Northumberland.

His Majesty, the ailing King Edward, had died.

And in his will, which he had rewritten just before his death, he had named as his successor, his cousin, Lady Jane Dudley.

The new Queen of England.

Twenty-Nine

It is always a gray day when an English monarch dies. Edward the Sixth passed from this life to the next, riddled with consumption of his lungs, and his subjects did not know of his death for nearly three days. His demise was not altogether a surprise, though certainly no one wished him dead. He had long been ill; King Edward was just fifteen, the same age as my Lady Jane, and he hadn't ruled long enough to allow us to see the kind of man he would have been.

When the news hit the streets of London that His Majesty had died and that his appointed successor was to be Lady Jane Grey Dudley, the response was nothing short of stunned silence. Jane was no stranger to the people of London and certainly not to the lords and ladies of the court, but she was no princess either. As fourth in the line to the throne, no one dared dream she'd reign in their lifetime.

My own heart nearly stopped beating when news reached the school of the King's death and Jane's succession. I begged Nicholas to tell me how this could be. It made no sense to me.

From all that I had already told him, Nicholas reasoned that John Dudley surely had a hand in convincing the King to rewrite his will so that Jane would succeed him and that he probably did so for two reasons. First, it was well known John Dudley and the Privy Council did not want a Catholic on the throne, and Princess Mary, King Edward's much older half sister, was devoutly so. England had been free of Rome's traditions and power for twenty-four years. The Church of England wasn't perfect, but the liturgical reforms that had birthed it had not come without sacrifice. I didn't wish to see more blood shed in the name of Christianity either. And most of England did not want to return to Catholic rule.

To effectively write Mary out of the line of succession, however, the King and his councilors had to somehow alter Parliament's Statute of Succession and make the case that His Majesty's half sister was the illegitimate issue of an annulled marriage, and therefore an unbefitting successor. Princess Elizabeth, a devout Reformer, would have been a more ideal successor, but she was the daughter of a queen who'd been beheaded for adultery. If Mary was to be bypassed, Elizabeth had to be also. Next in line was Frances Brandon Grey, Jane's mother. Here is where Nicholas surmised that John Dudley's plan began to take shape. Frances Grey was beyond the age of childbearing, and she had no sons. Her daughter Jane, however, was young, healthy, of childbearing age. And an impassioned Reformer.

Dudley surely told Jane's parents back in late April that he had a plan in place to put their daughter on the throne and that part of that plan included Frances deferring to Jane as the successor as well as securing the marriage of Jane to Dudley's son. That would explain the hasty betrothal, the quick wedding, and even Jane's overheard whispered conversations in the Dudley household after her marriage.

John Dudley had known for months that the King was dying.

There was a second reason Dudley counseled His Majesty to rewrite his will. With Jane on the throne, and his son as her husband, little stood in John Dudley's way in terms of power and influence. With this plan he would effectively keep papal influences out of the affairs of the Crown, and he'd have a son sitting at the right hand of the Queen of England. And one day there would be a Dudley heir on the throne.

Everything Nicholas supposed made sense to me. And I knew Jane had been used in the most appalling of ways.

"Poor Jane!" I lamented.

Nicholas said it would behoove us to pray for her. And for our country. The days and weeks ahead would not be without incident.

I asked him what he meant, and he said it is never a trouble-free transition when a monarch dies without an heir.

On the tenth day of July, Nicholas and I left the quiet school grounds—all the lads had gone home for the summer holiday—and took a carriage to watch Jane's processional on the banks of the Thames. Jane was escorted from Syon House to the White Tower by barge, and the riverbanks were teeming with men and women of all ages and stations curious to see the young lady whom King Edward had chosen to succeed him.

The crowds were quiet, subdued. There were no joyous shouts or happy music to accompany the procession. I could barely see Jane as she made her way from the barge to the steps of the Tower, flanked as she was on all sides by the powerful men who had orchestrated this strange turn of events. She walked with difficulty, wearing a richly appointed gown I did not recognize. At one point I saw that her feet had been shod with thick wooden clogs to make her appear taller.

"She looks afraid," I whispered to Nicholas.

Ahead of us a man in a merchant's cape turned to another man. "She's not even the daughter of a king."

"Watch your tongue!" the other man rasped.

"Princess Mary's the rightful heir!"

"Hush! I'll not be listening to this. You'll have us both hanging by ropes!"

"It's not right what Northumberland has done. He'll not succeed. Mark my words."

The second man shook his head and moved away from the merchant and his treasonous diatribe.

I reached for Nicholas's arm, and he led me away, back to our carriage and our quiet rooms at the school.

Over the next two days, the news on the street and in the pubs was that John Dudley had attempted to abduct and imprison Princess Mary before she learned of the King's death and Jane's succession. The plan was thwarted, however. Mary escaped the snare Dudley had set, and from a secret hiding place, she had written the Privy Council promising clemency if they renounced their actions of the last few days and swore allegiance to her, their rightful sovereign.

On the fifteenth day of July, I received my second letter from Jane.

> *To the esteemed Mrs. Staverton,*
> *Her Grace, Queen Jane of England, requests your*
> *presence at the Tower on a matter of the royal wardrobe.*
> *A coach will bring you to Her Majesty at half-past*
> *noon today, Saturday, 15 July.*

I handed the note to Nicholas, speechless.

"I don't want you to go," he said, his eyes never leaving the parchment, the heavy black ink or the rich royal seal.

"Nicholas! How can I not? She is the Queen!"

"She is a pawn in a very dangerous game. I do not want you part of it." He handed the letter back to me.

"But how can I refuse?" I asked.

Nicholas looked away, his brow crinkled in thought. "I shall come with you. I will ride in the coach, and I will accompany you inside the Tower. I will wait for you outside the room where you meet her. That is how it must be."

"But what if her guards do not allow you to come with me?"

"Let them arrest us both, Lucy. If Jane wishes to see you, she will no doubt pardon us for insisting on my escorting you. You know her better than I. Do you think she will punish you, of all people?"

I did not think she would. But Nicholas's fear alarmed me.

When the coach came for me, I told the footman that Mr. Staverton would escort me. And I said the same to the guards who attended us when we arrived at the Tower. And though they frowned with displeasure, they did not forbid Nicholas to accompany me inside.

Nicholas was made to sit along a row of chairs upholstered in green velvet. Other lords and ladies were milling about, and they stared at him. He was not one of them, and they knew it. He looked after me as I was led away from him. I turned once, and he dipped his head toward me, an unmistakable gesture that he would be waiting for me when I returned.

I was taken past other rooms where men and women scurried about, dizzily attending to matters like ants defending a hill of dirt. I recognized no one. We made our way to private apartments, and then the attendant escorting me turned to a woman whose back was to me.

"Mrs. Staverton is here," the attendant said to her.

She turned and I was relieved to see Mrs. Ellen.

"Lucy," she said, almost a whisper. "Come with me."

I followed her into a room decorated in rich tones of Tudor green and white and gilded with gold. At a far window, in a gown of creamy pink, Jane stood, much like she stood the day I met her at Sudeley Castle. Alone. Silent. Yearning for the world outside the glass.

She turned and I fell to my knees.

"Your Highness," I said.

I heard Jane say Ellen's name, and Mrs. Ellen silently left us, closing the door behind her.

I was alone with the Queen.

She came to me, then reached for my hands and bid me wordlessly to stand.

I rose unsteadily.

"I am so glad you came," she said.

I laughed. "It's not as if I could refuse, Your Highness."

She smiled too, but it seemed to lack any form. "So. About that fitting…"

"We can try for August instead, Your Highness," I quipped.

Her smile seemed to gain weight for a moment and then just as quickly deflated. "Quite. Come sit with me, Lucy."

She led me to a long couch upholstered in heavy brocade fabric, and we sat.

I waited for her to speak, like always. After a long moment of silence, she did.

"Every morning I wake up thinking surely I am back at Bradgate, and I've only been dreaming an outrageous charade that I am Queen."

"Sometimes I do too, Your Highness. Sometimes I think it must be a dream that my dear sweet Jane is my Queen. But it is a good dream, Your Highness. England is blessed of God to have you on the throne. I know that."

She looked past me then, her gaze on the world outside the panes. "I can feel it crumbling, like a house of sticks." Jane spoke as if alone in the room. "I can feel it starting to collapse."

"What…what is crumbling, Your Highness?"

Jane inhaled heavily and turned her gaze from the window. "My resolve."

"Your resolve?"

"When my parents and Northumberland told me the King was dead and I was his chosen successor, I told them they were mistaken. Horribly mistaken. Princess Mary was the heir to the throne. They insisted the King wanted me to take his place, not Mary, not Elizabeth, not my mother. Me. The King wanted me to keep England from falling back under Catholic rule. 'Only you can do this for England, Jane,' they said to me. 'Only you.' I alone was to save England from mindless allegiance to creeds that do not embrace grace. I alone. God had put me here to save my country. And I believed it."

"Is it not true, Your Majesty?"

Jane looked down at her folded hands in her lap. "I do not think now it was God that put me here, Lucy. I think I may have stepped ahead of him."

"But the King wrote in his will…"

"What Northumberland told him to."

"Your Highness…"

"Guildford wants me to name him King. Can you believe that? He wants me to petition Parliament to make him King. His mother expects it. Northumberland expects it."

"Oh, my lady!" A queer revulsion swept over me to think of it. Guildford as my King.

"I refused, of course. I shall continue to refuse. He tried to leave the Tower. Guildford did. He wanted to go sulking back to his mother, because I won't make him King. I had to have guards fetch him back. Can you imagine how terrible it would look if the Queen of England can't even manage her own marriage?"

"They…cannot make you, can they, Your Highness?"

"No, Lucy. They cannot. There are things no one can make me do.

I have finally realized that." She said it like she had always had this privilege. I stared at her in awe.

"There were moments, on the first day, and on the second, when I thought I would make my parents, Edward Seymour, even you, Lucy, proud of me. I imagined I might do some good with the power and influence that comes with the title of queen. But every hour since I agreed to this plan, there are forces mustering against me, within and without."

"Your Highness?"

But she moved on. "Lucy, did you put the ring in a safe place?"

"The ring is in my bureau drawer, Your Highness."

"Perhaps you should hide it away somewhere? And please tell no one it is mine. I would very much like to have it back one day. I do not know when that will be. But I am afraid for what the future holds. Would you do that for me?"

Her voice sounded childlike and afraid for the first time since I had come into the room with her.

"Of course, my lady."

She stood and I rose to my feet too. I bowed.

"Thank you, Lucy. I am sorry I had to tell you to come on business for the royal wardrobe. I did not want anyone asking questions."

"I did start on a dress for you, my lady. It's very soft velvet, the darkest of blues; it looks like the sky at midnight. Nearly black. With tiny pleats and tapered sleeves with cuttes of ebony satin."

Jane smiled. "Perhaps then we will see each other for a fitting in August after all?"

"I will come whenever you call for me, my lady."

She leaned forward and kissed my cheek. "Pray for me, Lucy," she breathed.

"Always," I whispered back.

When I returned to Nicholas, he wore a troubled look on his face. He said nothing as we were led back to the coach nor as we stepped into it. It wasn't until we were safely away that he leaned forward and took my hands.

"You cannot come back here, Lucy. Princess Mary is gathering forces and support. I heard talk of it in the rooms beyond the chairs. I do not think the lords inside knew how far their voices carried. She has been named Queen in East Anglia and Devon, and several of Jane's councilors tried to flee during the night. Princess Mary is said to be marching on London."

"Where are these supporters coming from?" I asked him. "I don't understand any of this! I thought England was decidedly Reformed!"

"It appears the people are decidedly feeble; they follow whatever creed keeps them on the winning side."

"Is…Jane not on the winning side, Nicholas?" Dread for her, for all of us enveloped me.

He did not answer me.

Four days later, on the nineteenth of July, Mary Tudor, with thousands upon thousands supporting her, acceded to the throne. Jane's councilors, one by one, abandoned her. Bells pealed across London when Mary finally arrived in London the third of August. And everywhere she passed by, the crowds cried out, "God save the Queen."

My dear Jane had reigned for just nine days.

Thirty

I learned, before Princess Mary arrived in London, that my Lady Jane had remained in the Tower when Dudley's scheme finally and fully disintegrated around her. On the ninth day of Jane's reign, when Mary's claim to the throne was made official across England, Jane was taken from the royal apartments in the Tower to a very different kind of room. She was put under arrest, as was Guildford, John Dudley, her father, and many others. The Tower which had been her palace was now her prison, and she was to be charged with crimes against the Crown.

Nicholas was at once worried for her. He told me it was by the new Queen's command that Jane was imprisoned in the Tower, albeit in a nicely appointed room.

"But she did not want to be Queen!" I told him. It was an angrily hot morning in mid-August, and we had just finished preparing his classroom for the imminent return of his students.

"She may not have wanted it, but she did not refuse it," Nicholas replied.

"But the King named her his successor! The Council approved it!"

"Parliament did not, dearest. And, yes, King Edward named her his successor, but the King is dead. A dead monarch cannot issue orders. His will had only been in place two weeks before he died. Parliament never saw it."

"But Mary is fond of Jane. They are cousins! You should see the dress she sent her two Christmases past. It was extravagantly beautiful."

"Then we must hope and pray Mary is lenient. That she sees what all of us see. That Jane was leverage to Northumberland and she was coerced to accept a plan she did not devise."

This initially set me at ease. Of course the Queen would see that Jane had been used by powerful men and was guilty only of youthful naiveté. It was only a formality that she remained in the Tower.

But on the eighteenth of August, John Dudley and five others were tried, convicted of treason, and sentenced to die.

Four days later, John Dudley, the mastermind of Jane's dreadful circumstances, was executed at the Tower. It was said that he converted to Catholicism in the hours before he lost his head, and that the imprisoned Lady Jane watched him walk to the scaffold from the windows of her room after the formerly staunch Reformist celebrated the Mass. It was also said that Edward Seymour was in attendance. I could only imagine what terrible emotions roiled about in that young man's head and heart as he watched John Dudley be dispatched to the Judge of all souls. And it pained me to think that if Jane saw John Dudley walking to the ax, surely she saw her beloved Edward standing in the crowd of spectators.

I could neither sleep nor eat in the days that followed. I wanted badly to visit Jane, but I knew that was impossible. Visitors to high-ranking prisoners in the Tower needed permission from the Privy Council. I was no one to them. I could only pray for Jane, which I did, asking God to be merciful to her.

With the swiftness of John Dudley's trial and execution, I expected to hear any day that Jane had been pardoned. Her father had been pardoned, and he had far more to do with Dudley's plans than Jane did. But day after day went by, and there was no news on the streets of anyone leaving the Tower.

Instead, Queen Mary set about beginning her design to return England to Catholicism, as Dudley, arrogant though he was, said she would. Her first act was to ban the printing and preaching of all treatises that did not have the court's approval, and she forbade any disparagement of the Catholic faith. By September, talk in the streets was that the Queen, who was thirty-seven years old when she ascended the throne, was seeking a marriage with Prince Philip of Spain, a Catholic. This caused much uproar, though why it did surprised me. What did her Council or anyone else think she would do in the matter of her own marriage? Marry a Reformer?

October came and with it a cracking end to the oppressive summer heat. Jane had turned sixteen as autumn began. But there was no pardon.

Finally, on the thirteenth of November, my Lady Jane and five others, including Guildford and the Archbishop Thomas Cranmer, were taken before the court to face charges of treason. In my heart I knew Jane was innocent and that the Queen surely must also know this. I reasoned with myself that it was just a requirement, this trial. Surely at the trial she would be pardoned, like her father had been.

When the news came that Jane and the others had been found guilty and sentenced to death, I fell to my knees in shock and fear. Nicholas had to bear me up and take me to our rooms where he consoled me as best he could.

"A death warrant was not signed," he said. "The Queen signed no death warrant!"

And indeed no warrant had been signed, but we soon learned the new Spanish ambassador was pressing the Queen to have young Jane executed. In his view, Jane posed a conceivable threat, since there was no small outcry to the Queen's plans to marry a Catholic.

I wished to send letters of encouragement to Jane, but Nicholas would not allow me to put myself in a position so dangerous, that of being a confidante to a convicted traitor to the Crown. He assured me that was why Jane sent no letters to me.

We spent the Christmas holidays with my parents. We celebrated as best we could, not knowing what would befall us in the days and months to come. I had ever known only the Reformist way of devotion to God, as had Nicholas. My family was understanding of my compassion for Lady Jane, but they exercised caution. Uncertain days lay ahead.

She's just a young girl, I wanted to tell them. But I was smart enough to know this had never been about Jane's age or her sex. It was her position that men had lusted after. And now others feared that position.

We returned to London in the first days of the new year. I schooled myself to remain optimistic.

But in late January, in a senseless uprising designed to thwart the Queen's plans to marry the Spanish prince, Jane's father led a revolt in Leicestershire, proclaiming Jane as rightful Queen of England. A warrant was issued for Henry Grey's arrest, and his little band of supporters quickly dissolved. He was captured, arrested, and imprisoned.

I knew the moment this news reached us, that Jane's father had sealed her fate with his selfishness. As long as Jane lived, a plot for the Queen's overthrow could quickly be assembled. He had proven that. The death warrant for Jane was signed soon after.

I took to my room when news of the warrant reached me. I was drained of prayers. I could only kneel and sway in silent supplication for Jane.

Four days after the warrant was issued, I received the third and final letter from Jane. The letter was not actually from my lady, it was from Mrs. Ellen, and was sent to me by way of a servant of Mr. Partridge, her gaoler. Mrs. Ellen wrote:

Lucy Staverton
Seamstress
Whitechapel School

Dear Mrs. Staverton,
    Lady Jane Dudley requests the dress she commissioned
you to sew for her be brought to her at the Tower. You
may bring it to the living quarters of the Tower gaoler,
Mr. Partridge. The servant who has brought you this letter
shall accompany you.
    Kindest Regards,
    Ellen MacIlvray

Nicholas was hesitant but gave in to my pleadings on the condition that he would accompany me. I had to see her.

The dress had been finished for months, and I had kept it in a trunk, not knowing what else to do with it. As I drew it out to bring to Jane, my breath caught in my throat. The gown looked blacker than ever before. In the gray light of early February, all traces of blue had been swallowed as if by pitch.

The quickest of thoughts entered my mind, and I shooed it away not a second later. I could not even for a moment dwell on whether Jane asked for this dress to wear to her execution.

Mrs. Ellen was there to meet us at the gates of the Tower. She would not look into my eyes when I came near her. With her were two guards who searched the folds of the dress and my sewing bag for items I suppose I could've smuggled to aid in an escape. The dress and bag were handed back to me.

"Good of you to come, Mrs. Staverton," Mrs. Ellen's voice was emotionless, as if I had come to merely mend a torn hem for a visiting gentlewoman from the Continent.

We followed her silently into the massive structure of stone and mortar.

I had never set foot inside the Tower before, nor had Nicholas, and I was glad that he was with me as we made our way to Mr. Partridge's apartments. The expanse of the Tower was foreboding in the hushed bleakness of midwinter, and I wished for even a smattering of bluebells in the cracks of the stones, but there was not a spot of color anywhere in the dreariness. Our breaths puffed away from our bodies like little ghosts, spinning away as if eager to disappear into the shadows.

When we entered a second courtyard, Nicholas took my arm and whispered to me to close my eyes, that he would guide me. I knew without him telling me that were I to open my eyes, I would see the platform where John Dudley had been executed, where others had been executed, where others still would be. I scrunched my eyes shut, buried my face in the folds of the dress, and leaned into my husband.

Soon Nicholas whispered to me that I could open my eyes, and I saw that we were entering a building. We climbed two sets of stairs to a hallway. Nicholas was bade to sit on a bench just outside the gaoler's rooms.

"Ten minutes," one of the guards said to me as I was let in.

He did not follow me inside.

I walked in behind Mrs. Ellen into a comfortable room where a cheery fire blazed in the grate. Jane was seated at a writing table, dressed in a gown of dove gray with just a bit of french lace at the throat and wrists. Her lovely brown hair was pulled away from her face in a lacy net, decorated with a single strand of pearls. She rose and came to me, and I fell to a curtsy, unable to speak. The dress in my arms nearly fell to the floor.

"Lucy," she said, her voice soft and sad.

I could not rise to my feet. Jane reached for my arms and pulled me to stand. Tears had already begun to slide down my cheeks, and they fell like raindrops onto the dress. She clasped her hands on to the fabric.

"Take this, please, Ellen."

The gown was now out of my hands, and I felt myself begin to shake. The first words out of my mouth were an anguished cry for her forgiveness.

"There is nothing to forgive, Lucy. Come sit with me."

She led me back to the writing table and to a chair opposite the one she had been sitting in. I reached into my sewing bag and groped for a scrap of lawn to wipe my eyes.

"I am so sorry, my lady," I muttered. "I wish I were stronger. I should not be weeping."

Jane merely inhaled gently. "Do not be sorry. Not today. I don't want sorrow today."

I blotted at the tears and begged God to brace my heart. When I finally looked up at her, she was sitting there, with her hands in her lap, waiting for me.

"Surely there will be a pardon," I whispered.

Her answer was quick. "No, Lucy. I do not think so. My cousin the Queen has sent her confessor here these many days to win my pardon with my conversion to Catholicism. But as I am not persuaded, I daresay she has given up on me."

"My lady?" She answered me so quickly, I barely understood the implication of her answer.

"If I were to recant my faith as a Reformist, the Queen would have a tidy excuse to pardon me. Her councilors do not want her to. And she certainly can't if I do not recant."

"She would spare your life if you...if you converted?" I could not keep the edge of repugnance from stretching across my face. And the moment it did, I knew Jane would never reduce her deepest beliefs to political posturing. I sank deeper into my chair as the truth closed in around me. Jane was doomed.

"Perhaps she would not spare me anyway," Jane went on, toneless. "My father-in-law certainly denied his convictions to no gain. But then, he never was a man of conviction, was he, Lucy? He was a man of ambition. Very different, those two things. At least to him."

"Oh, my lady!"

Several long seconds of strained silence hung between us.

"My life would mean nothing, *nothing,* if I were false about that which matters most to me," she finally said. "If I am to die for anything noble, should it not be for that which I hold most dear and most true?"

I did not answer her.

She leaned across the table and grasped my hands. "Lucy, just think of it!" Her voice was animated and childlike. "I have been given a second chance to make a grand choice. It was my arrogance that let me think I could be Queen. I should have refused. But now I have a second chance to choose. I can choose. Do you see how marvelous this is? *I can choose.*"

My tears had begun to fall again. Jane squeezed my hands, willing me to rejoice with her, that the decision that would define her life—more than the one she made to accept the crown—awaited her, and she alone could make it.

"Is this why you made me bring that dress?" I rasped, looking at the dress in Mrs. Ellen's hands and hating it just a little.

" 'Tis a beautiful dress, for a beautiful day. And you made it for me. I am not afraid to die, Lucy."

I jerked my head up, appalled.

"I did not say I was not afraid of the ax," she said. "I am frightened to my core of the ax. But I am not afraid to die. I can die like this."

I began to weep, and Jane pulled me close. We reversed the roles we had played the day I met her. She stroked my hair and whispered to me that all would be well.

"You have been a true friend, Lucy. I am grateful to God for having known you."

"And I, you."

"What about Edward's ring?" I whispered a moment later.

"I want you to keep it hidden for now. Someday, perhaps, you may find a way to give it back to Edward. If you cannot, do not fret. If he marries another, do not give it back to him. Keep it, then, Lucy. You keep it. To remind yourself to thank God every morning that you have Nicholas and he has you."

The guard opened the door and announced it was time for me to leave. I kissed Jane's cheek.

"You are so brave, my lady," I murmured.

"Call me Jane," she whispered. For the first time since I arrived, her eyes glistened. "Pray for me, Lucy!"

"Always, Jane. Always."

My friend Jane was taken from this life at the Tower of London on the twelfth of February 1554 at nine o'clock in the morning. She was sixteen.

I did not attend her beautiful day.

Jane

Upper West Side, Manhattan

Thirty-One

❦

The ring rested on the acquisitions table under the warm glow of a gooseneck lamp. Wilson stared at it, with his chin resting comfortably in one hand. A bit of breakfast was glued to his blue hibiscus shirt, and he frowned. Stacy gazed at the ring with a look of restless hope on her face, her head slightly cocked in the pose of one who has chosen to imagine what others won't. I knew what they were thinking.

Wilson didn't think the ring belonged to Jane Grey.

Stacy wanted to believe it did.

And I stood in between them.

Wilson coughed. "It just doesn't seem likely, Jane. Not likely at all."

"Just because it's not likely doesn't mean it's not possible," Stacy said.

I sipped my coffee, my fourth cup of the morning, and then set the cup down on the table. "I was awake half the night thinking you are right, Wilson. And I was awake the other half thinking *you* are right." This I said to Stacy.

"Well, it's of course amusing to suppose it could be hers," Wilson said. "That's why I called you. But Eric and I read the same online biography as you, Jane. There's no mention that there was a betrothal ring given to Jane Grey by anyone."

"Doesn't mean one wasn't given to her," Stacy interjected. "Just that no one mentioned it."

I picked the ring up and turned it in my hands, studying its old stones. "I read several other articles on the Web last night. Dozens, actually. No one mentions a ring like this."

There were only three men recorded as Lady Jane Grey's betrothal hopefuls. King Edward the Sixth—and nothing ever came of those discussions; the Duke of Somerset's son Edward Seymour—and that arrangement was never official; and Guildford Dudley, the man she married less than a month after their engagement was announced.

"Well, maybe Guildford gave her the ring," Stacy offered.

"Maybe. But their marriage was so quickly arranged. Several accounts suggest that she didn't even like him. Why would he give her a ring with that kind of inscription?"

"Maybe Guildford loved *her,*" Stacy said, after a moment's thought. "Maybe no one else knew. Maybe he loved her in secret."

"But why should it be a secret? He married her. And if he did give her this ring, it wouldn't have been in secret."

The three of us stared at the ring in my hand

"If Guildford gave it to her because he loved her, then how did it end up stuffed inside the binding of a prayer book?" I mused, not expecting either one of them to answer me.

"My point exactly." Wilson folded his arms across his loudly patterned shirt. "If it's Lady Jane Grey's ring and Guildford Dudley gave it to her, then it would have been in her possession when she was arrested. If her jewels were seized from her, the ring would have likely been taken."

"But maybe they let her keep it since it wasn't a Crown jewel?" Stacy suggested. "It was her ring, after all. Hey! Maybe…maybe she wore it the day of her execution, and one of the men who buried her body took it."

"And how did it end up in a prayer book, then?" Wilson asked.

"And why?" I set the ring back down.

"You see? Those are things you can never know." Wilson took a sip of his coffee.

"I still wish it was her ring. Such a sad story. I'd like to think there was someone who loved her," Stacy murmured.

"Well, you can think whatever you want. You just won't be able to prove it to anyone." Wilson stepped back from the table.

"It's hers." The words fell from my lips almost of their own volition, surprising even me. But the minute I decided the ring was Jane Grey's, I believed it.

"But you can't know that for sure," Wilson was quick to respond.

"It's not about what I know. I just have this…hunch."

"I do too!" Stacy echoed. But I was pretty sure she believed it because it made for a good story. It was different with me. I couldn't quite put my finger on how it was different, but I knew it had nothing to do with wanting to improve the details of Jane Grey's sad legacy.

Wilson walked away, lecturing me that hunches only matter in police work and horse races.

"What are you going to do now?" Stacy asked.

I slid the ring onto my pinkie. "Somebody, somewhere has to know more about Jane Grey than people who write articles for the Internet. I need to find those people."

"I'll help. I can ask at NYU. Someone in the history department might know of an expert somewhere. Or maybe there's a book you can get at the library or a bookstore."

"I already looked!" Wilson called out from ten feet away. "There's no book about Jane Grey's personal life written at the academic level. It's all speculation by nonscholars."

Stacy turned to him. "Does it have to be at an academic level?"

"It does if you wish to believe it."

"And hey," Stacy continued, "her personal life was her public life."

"Nothing. At. The. Academic. Level." Wilson punctuated every word with force. "There's a huge difference between conjecture and fact, Jane."

Wilson shuffled off to turn on the floor lights. It was almost time to open.

"Don't let it ruin your day, Wilson," I said as my phone began to vibrate in my pocket, and I reached for it.

"Don't let it ruin yours!" he called over his shoulder.

I looked at the tiny screen on my phone. Connor.

Finally returning my call.

Connor had called Brad after I left New Hampshire to ask him if we had talked. Brad had decided to drive up to Dartmouth and tell Connor the truth about why he had to get out of New York City, that it was more than just needing a break from Manhattan and me. They met at a coffee shop, and Brad told him about the affair that wasn't an affair.

When my phone rang, I was in bed with my laptop, reading the last of many Web entries on Lady Jane Grey. I could see on the display that Brad was the caller, but I waited for four rings before picking up. He had only just that morning told me the truth, and I was still swimming in troubled thoughts. Still, I didn't want his call to go to voice mail. I wanted to know what he had to say. I wanted to hear his voice. I wanted him to hear mine. I flipped the phone open and said hello.

"You got back to New York all right? Everything go okay?" He sounded like he was pacing perhaps. I leaned back into his pillow.

"Yes."

"And Molly and Jeff were there to meet you at Newark?"

"Yes."

"Look, I know maybe you don't want to talk to me right now, but you know I saw Connor. I told him everything, Jane."

I grimaced. "What did he say?"

"He wanted to know if it was over with her. I told him yes, it is."

Silence.

The only light in the room was coming from my laptop, and at that moment, it had reverted to standby mode. I wiggled the mouse, anxious for light, even just a spill of it, to return to the room.

"What else did he say?" I asked a moment later, wondering if Connor had asked if it was over between Brad and me as well.

"He didn't say much else. I think...I think he needs some time to absorb this. I think he's disappointed in me. I told him he didn't have to say anything else."

"So then you just left him?" I didn't mean for it to sound accusatory.

"He said he had a paper to write. I told him to call me later, if he wanted. He needs to process this his own way, Jane. But I don't regret telling him. After...after you were here, I knew I had to tell him. He needed to know."

"Did he?"

"You both did."

I had said nothing, but in my heart, I knew he was right. For Brad to be Brad, he had to tell me what he had done. Brad was thoughtful and sincere—two qualities that I admired about him. Plus, I'd already begun to understand that Brad's confession had moved me to a different place. A place of decision rather than limbo. I would need to forgive Brad if our marriage was going to survive. And forgiveness is always a choice.

Then Brad told me he'd call me if he heard from Connor again. He apologized again for everything. And then he said good night.

I hung up and immediately called Connor, but he didn't pick up. I left a message telling him to call me back and that I didn't care what time it was. He didn't.

But he was calling me now.

I flipped open my phone. "Hi, Connor."

"Hey, Mom."

Awkward silence.

"You okay, honey?"

"Are you going to get a divorce?" He sounded mad. But it wasn't the tone of his voice that startled me. It was the question. The word "divorce" sounded hopeless and terminal in my ears and in his voice. Like a diagnosis of cancer.

"No one's said anything about getting a divorce."

"Are you?"

I said no, and it struck me that up to that point, I had only fearfully wondered how I would react if Brad said he wanted to divorce me. It hadn't yet crossed my mind that I could decide if I wanted to divorce him. Even as I realized this, I knew that wasn't what I wanted. Brad had wounded me, but I did not want a divorce. Divorce seemed a bottomless abyss.

"Mom, do you still love Dad?" Connor's tender question pulled me from my introspection.

I heard him, but I still said, "What?"

"I said, do you still love Dad?"

As I stood in my antique store, surrounded by hundreds of remnants of past lives, both blissful and unfortunate, I knew that I did. I loved Brad. For a million little reasons, not for one big obvious one, reasons too subtle and numerous to count. We were like two people in an arranged marriage who were complete strangers on their wedding day, but who woke up twenty years later, unable to imagine a life of happiness without the other beside them. At least that is how I felt. And I knew I needed to open my eyes to those myriad little reasons. We both did.

He had hurt me, but I still loved him.

They were wonderful, they were awful, those two truths.

"Yes," I said, and I heard Connor sigh on the other end of the phone.

"What happens next?" he asked.

I was about to say that I wasn't altogether sure when the door to the shop opened and in swooped my mother with a large wicker laundry basket and a weatherworn Macy's bag. I needed to cut the call short. Especially this call.

"Grandma's here, Connor. I'm sorry, but can I call you later tonight?"

"Yeah. Sure."

I told him I loved him and we hung up. My mother walked briskly toward me as both Stacy and Wilson called out a hello to her. The basket in her arms was half filled with fabric. I recognized one of her old Christmas tablecloths. She set the Macy's bag down by her feet.

"Jane! I'm staging a town house in Brooklyn, and I need to borrow your Blue Willow dishes. Please? They will look perfect in the dining room."

"Hello, Mom, good morning to you too." I slipped my phone back into my pocket.

"So may I?" She was wearing a melon green linen suit with a creamy white shell underneath.

"I only have service for six."

"That's perfect. That's all the chairs they have. And may I take that marble chess set? The little one. I tore up some old tablecloths to wrap everything in. I don't need the whole set of china, just the plates, cups, and saucers. Please? This one's going to sell by the end of the month. You'll have it all back in no time."

"Sure. Come on. I'll help you wrap it."

We headed to the oak barley twist table where the Blue Willow china currently spent its days and nights.

"Yes, this is perfect," she cooed, picking up a plate. She looked over her shoulder and saw that Wilson was helping a customer who'd just walked in and Stacy was on the computer at the back of the store. "So. How did it go this weekend?" she asked.

I picked up a plate and set it in the fragmented corner of a faded fabric poinsettia. I knew what she wanted to know. But I told her Connor did great.

She pursed her lips. "I don't mean that! I mean with you and Brad! Did you talk? Did you fix things? Leslie said you stayed at his house."

Thanks a lot, Leslie.

"Of course we talked, Mom."

"And?"

"And we have some things we need to work out."

"Like what? What things?"

"Mom."

"What? I am just saying if you would admit you need help, you wouldn't be trying to fix your marriage while being two hundred miles away from your husband!"

I folded the aging poinsettia scrap over a blue dish and took a measured breath. "Mom, this is not just about me, it's about Brad too."

"That's exactly what I mean! How are you going to figure out how to fix this if you don't get professional help?"

I set the wrapped dish down hard on the table. "Please, Mom. We're not going to talk about this right here, right now."

"You never want to talk about this."

"It's not something you and I need to talk about!" I grabbed a cup.

"Well, you should talk about it with someone. A professional certainly. That's what marriage counselors do. They help couples work out their differences."

I nearly tossed the cup onto the floor. "Brad and I aren't quibbling about differences, Mom! He almost had an affair! There! Now you know."

My voice was a rasping whisper that made me sound a little like

Dorothy's witch, but it was out. All of it was out. Brad was in New Hamp-shire because he had almost had an affair.

Mom's eyes were wide in her head. "Brad…had an affair?"

"I said almost. That's why he moved to New Hampshire. To get away from her. Not away from me. Away from her. Because he was afraid he was falling in love with her."

My mother looked down at the wrapped dish in her hands. "I don't believe it."

But I could see that she did. The disappointment in her face was chilling.

"Did…did you kick him out? Is that why he left? Is that why he's in New Hampshire?"

"He left before I even knew about this."

I wrapped another cup while my mother stood statue-stiff with a dish in her hands.

"Why?" she finally said. "Why would he do that?"

Anger filled me, and I placed my hands on the table. Jane's ring winked at me. It was almost as if the ring on my finger made me bold. "Are you suggesting this is somehow my fault?"

She gazed up at me. "Is it? Did you push him away?"

My mother didn't want to believe Brad was practically unfaithful to me, but she was seconds away from believing I had pushed him into an-other woman's arms. I looked down at my hands pressed to the wood, and I saw the ring. The blue stone in the middle looked like a bit of ocean, the rubies like blood. I couldn't help but think of the woman who I wanted it to have belonged to. The woman robbed of choice. The spurt of anger swirled away.

"Why did you want me to marry Brad, Mom? Why did you like him so much?"

"What? Why are you asking that now?"

"Why?"

"I can't believe you're asking this!"

"I'm asking."

"Because we wanted you to be happy!"

"Happy."

"Yes. Happy! All your Dad and I have ever wanted for you was for you to be happy. Brad was a wonderful young man with a bright future. We just wanted you to be happy! Is that so terrible?"

"But you aren't responsible for my happiness, Mom!"

She stared at me, speechless.

And I was speechless as well.

My parents weren't responsible for my happiness.

Nobody was.

Except me.

Everything about my life suddenly shifted into focus. It was like time froze, and I was given a dazzling moment to comprehend the difference between that moment and the one before it. This was what Dr. Kirtland had wanted me to understand. No one made my choices for me. I made them. If I took no risks in the choices I'd made, it was because I didn't have the courage to take them or didn't want to live with the consequences. I didn't want to risk disappointing myself. It had been safer to defer than to strike out on my own. It had been safer...

The bright moment dissolved as my mother angrily snatched up the last dish. Her movement seemed to set the world back to spinning. I reached for a chair back to steady myself as she placed the dish in the basket. "I have to go."

She swept past me with the laundry basket and headed for the door, swishing past the Macy's bag that she'd placed on the floor when she had arrived.

Wilson, watching her go, reached for it and called her name. "Sophia. Your bag."

She turned her head but kept walking. "That's Jane's." Her tone was clipped. "I wanted to surprise her."

My mother was out the door.

Wilson turned to me and lifted the bag. Wordlessly I walked toward him, took it, and looked inside. The mantel clock she had borrowed for the town house lay wrapped in several folds of gray fleece. The *Titanic* clock. I drew it out of the bag.

It was ticking.

I sat at the acquisitions table with a cup of Earl Grey and a bottle of Tylenol. The clock rested on the table next to my cup, marking the minutes in a slow, cadenced dance. Whoever had fixed it had also shined its brass fixtures and oiled the mahogany blooms. The wood glistened like melted chocolate under my store lights.

Wilson stood next to me. He held something in his hands, but I didn't raise my eyes to see what it was.

"I can't believe she got it fixed," I said.

"I'm sure she didn't know how much you liked it broken."

"I *told* her I liked it broken. I told her I didn't want it fixed!"

I sensed him shrugging. "Then break it," he said.

"It's not that simple, Wilson. It was…special."

"It's still the same clock, Jane."

I rubbed my left temple and raised the teacup to my lips. I took a sip. Wilson touched my shoulder. "She forgot one of the saucers."

I turned to look at his hands. He held a Blue Willow saucer.

"Great," I muttered.

"Maybe you could take it to her," he said gently. "On your way to your appointment. And then you can tell her she's ruined your life by fixing that clock."

I snapped my head up to look at him.

"I never said my life was ruined because of it."

"Oh." He handed the saucer to me and winked. "My mistake."

Thirty-Two

A New York City subway train is one of the few places where you can be hemmed in on all sides by a press of people and still feel like you're alone.

As the train ambled across the river into Brooklyn, I felt elbows, pant legs, and thighs of fellow passengers who seemed oblivious to this strange phenomenon. They jostled against me and the other people around them, but their attention was on their newspapers, laptops, cell phones, or the rushing nothingness outside the window. Each of us was holed up in our own private laboratory of thought and speculation.

My mother was grateful that I offered to bring the saucer to her, though she intimated indirectly that it was my fault she'd forgotten it in the first place. Our argument had distracted her. And wounded her a little bit. She sounded hurt when I called to tell her I was coming with the saucer and needed the address.

The condo my mother was decorating was located in what locals call Dumbo—Down Under the Manhattan Bridge Overpass. A century earlier, before the Brooklyn Bridge was built, the Dumbo blocks were known as Fulton Landing. When the ferry was discontinued, the district became the kind of windowless warehouse district that made you want to run for cover when the sun went down. Like so many warehouse districts that won the hearts of the artistic community, the old Fulton Landing neighborhood was lovingly adopted in the late seventies by creative souls. It was now home to art galleries, loft apartments, ethnic restaurants, and a chocolate factory. Something beautiful had been forged out of something forgotten. As we neared the Dumbo landscape, I thought of the clock that now kept time back at the store, rhythmically celebrating its second life.

Wilson was right. It was still the same clock. The past hadn't been erased just because a new future had been handed it. If anyone should understand that, it should be an antiques dealer like me. I shook my head, annoyed with myself. The woman sitting across from me arched an eyebrow and then looked away.

I got out at the York Street station and walked five minutes to the complex on Gold Street, and my mother buzzed me inside to the fourth floor. She was waiting by the elevator when the doors opened.

"You didn't have to bring the saucer down here, Jane. But I'm glad you did. The table looks ridiculous without it." She took the saucer from me, and I followed her inside the sparsely furnished condo.

"Actually, Mom, I wanted to apologize."

The condo was painted a pristine and saintly white. Every surface—floor, wall, ceiling, light fixture, and curtain—was a brilliant white. Blue was the only accent color. The brocade pillows on the white leather couch were blue, as were the cushions on the dining room table chairs, and the area rug. And, of course, the Blue Willow dishes were blue. It was an odd blend of contemporary and classic.

Mom placed the saucer on the table and set the coffee cup on top.

"I don't know why you got so upset with me, Jane. You, being a mother, should know exactly what I mean about wanting your child to be happy."

"I do. I do know what it's like to want your child to be happy."

"Well, then." She fluffed a bunch of silk delphinium blossoms in a bone china vase in the center of the table.

"What I meant to say was, I'm finally beginning to understand it's up to me to be happy with the choices I've made. And to realize that I am the one who made them. It's always been up to me."

My mother's forehead was crinkly in lukewarm consternation. "What on earth are you talking about?" She gave the flowers another fluffing.

"I've always thought you and Dad pushed me into marrying Brad. Like I didn't have a choice." I fingered Jane's ring on my hand. "But I did have a choice. I could have said no when he proposed."

"Which would have been a mistake. Despite his flaws, he's still been a good husband to you and a good father to Connor."

Brad had dropped but a few percentage points in her eyes. "Mom. What if I told you Brad doesn't know if he loves me anymore?"

Her hands fell away from the flowers, and she simply stared at them.

"Love isn't something you know or don't know. You decide it. If he's not happy being married to you, you need to find out why not."

"He told me he doesn't know what is keeping us together other than Connor. He told me that!"

"Well. There's your problem." She shrugged her shoulders and walked past me into the living room. "A child isn't marriage glue."

"Marriage glue?"

She turned to face me. "Yes. If you both really think what keeps a couple together is a child or even a feeling, then no wonder you two are floundering. What keeps a couple together is determination."

It just wasn't that simple. "But I can't *make* Brad happy."

"But that doesn't mean if he's unhappy, you just sit around and do nothing. If you love Brad, you don't give up on him. You stand by him."

"Even when he walks away?"

"Especially then."

"He was practically unfaithful to me!"

"Well, it doesn't sound like he wishes he had been."

A tear was beginning to slide down my face. I brushed it away. "You make it sound so incredibly easy."

"Who said it was easy?" she exclaimed. "Really, Jane! Open your eyes. It's hard work. You have to want it more than anything. And be ready to give up everything for it."

She turned from me, like she was deeply disappointed in me. But I saw her reaching up to her face. And flicking something away. She hurt for me. Ached for me to be happy, like all mothers do. It was a side of her I'd never seen or perhaps looked past. And I couldn't help wondering if in her fifty-one years of marriage, there weren't times she wanted to walk away but chose not to. Not because it was the easy thing to do, but the right thing.

"You don't give up on someone just because that person is unhappy," she said, her back to me. "And you don't let them give up on you."

I stood there, staring at her back and pondering those words; words that came from some deep, private place in my mother's soul, but yet also seemed to have rushed up from within me too, from a hideaway inside my own spirit.

Brad told me we had to find out if there was anything strong enough to keep us together. Something as strong as attraction. Stronger. I finally knew what that was. It was us. He and I had to be the strong ones. We had to start counting the little reasons. And he and I had to fix what was broken.

I walked to my mother and put my arms around her from behind. She stiffened at first and then slowly relaxed.

"Thank you."

"For what?" she said, her tone unconvincingly indifferent.

"For fixing the clock."

"You're wrinkling my suit."

A smile broke across my face.

"I need to head back." I gave her shoulders a squeeze.

She nodded, not quite ready to turn around.

I took a few steps toward the front door, and she called my name.

I turned around. "Yes?"

"Your business cards?" she said impatiently, waving toward the Blue Willow dishes.

I sat across from Dr. Kirtland with the lists in front of me. In between us, yogurt-covered raisins sent up tendrils of unseen sugared air from the wooden bowl. The aroma was too sweet for me. I had just told him about my weekend with Brad. And what I'd realized while arguing with my mother as we wrapped Blue Willow dishes in scraps of tablecloth. Dr. Kirtland had sat quietly and listened.

I hadn't added anything to either list since my return from New Hampshire.

Dr. Kirtland pointed to Brad's list. "So, knowing what you now know, not just about you, but about Brad too, are these still things you appreciate about him?"

I looked at the qualities I had written before I knew Brad had clawed his way out of New York to get away from another woman.

Gentle
Smart
Good father
Careful
Strong
Thoughtful

I traced the word *Gentle* at the top of the list with my eyes. And then *Strong.* "I don't want to give up on him. On us. Even now. I know he's not perfect. I know I'm not perfect. And maybe we didn't marry for the right reasons, but I'm thinking it's possible to stay married for the right reasons. That's possible, isn't it?"

Dr. Kirtland folded his hands in his lap. "This is one of the reasons I had you make this list, Jane. You may have married Brad for convenience—even as a way to please your parents—but your marriage most likely has produced the feelings of deep affection and attraction that may have been missing when you married Brad. And that's why you are so troubled that he has left you, and why you are not willing to walk away from it, even though he has hurt you. So, yes, I think it's possible."

"But I'm not responsible for Brad's happiness."

"No."

"So what am I supposed to do? I know I can't make him happy by wanting him to be happy, right?"

"Brad is the only one who can make Brad happy."

"So I just wait?"

He pointed to the other piece of paper on the table. "You only have one thing on that list."

"I didn't know what else to write. I really don't know what I'd like to do or try."

Dr. Kirtland smiled. "Then don't you think it's time you found out?"

I looked at the sheet of paper with just the bit about the ring at the top. A couple of moments of silence hovered. He waited.

A tiny stream of possibilities began to bubble up inside me, from a faraway place. "I'd like to go back to school and get my master's. I'd like to not be afraid of deep water anymore. I'd like to see Nova Scotia." I stopped.

Dr. Kirtland reached into his shirt pocket and handed me his pen.

Thirty-Three

I left Dr. Kirtland's, arriving at the Eighty-sixth Street station a little after three. I emerged onto the street, and I stood like a lost tourist for several long seconds, pondering the busyness and the weight of the new list in my jacket pocket. I should've headed back to the store, but I saw a snippet of the awning of my favorite bookstore a block away. A few minutes later, I was walking toward it.

The smell of new paper and coffee and leather journals filled my nostrils the moment I stepped across the threshold. From behind the sales counter, a thin twenty-something with his hair gelled to stony peaks asked if he could help me find something.

I asked him to show me everything he had on Lady Jane Grey.

And canoeing.

And Nova Scotia.

Wilson was eating a hot dog from the vendor who often parked his mobile business by our street corner when I finally returned to the store.

"Don't tell my cardiologist," he said, as he wiped a bit of mustard off his chin.

"It's just one hot dog, Wilson."

"It's actually two hot dogs. This was my second."

I smiled at him. "You only live once, right?"

He smiled back. "It might even be three."

I set the bag of books on the acquisitions table where he was seated. Stacy watched me from her post in the front where she was ringing up a sale. She mouthed something to me. I couldn't make out what she was saying, but her expression was animated. She obviously couldn't wait to be done with the customer so that she could talk to me.

"I thought you went to Brooklyn to deliver a saucer." Wilson nodded to the bag on the table.

I pulled the books out and positioned them so he could see their spines. "I did. And then I had an appointment. And then I went to a bookstore."

He set his hot dog down, and I watched him scrutinize the titles. "I told you so," he said a second or two later.

"Told me what?"

"That there is nothing at the academic level about Jane Grey's personal life."

"Wilson. There's bound to be *some* truth in these books," I said defensively.

Wilson picked up the first one. "This one is fiction."

"Historical fiction."

He picked up the next one. "So is this one."

"They're *historical* fiction."

"Fiction."

He reached for the third.

"That one is written by a very well-known and respected historian," I said.

He pointed to the subtitle. "It's about the effect of Jane Grey's reign on the English Reformation. I doubt there is much in here about her love life."

"There are two whole chapters on her marital prospects."

"And how they affected the English Reformation, no doubt. I really don't think you will find anything in here about a ring, especially a ring that no one else has ever mentioned."

He reached for the fourth. A six-hundred-page volume on the Tudors. "This one looks like a very well-written book, actually." He studied the back cover. "Two Oxford professors wrote it."

"There you go. At the academic level. Just like you said."

"Yes, but of all the Tudor monarchs, Jane Grey's was the shortest of very short reigns."

"I know that."

"Do they give her even her own chapter in here?"

My hands flew to my hips. "Were you this much of a kill-joy with your students when they had new ideas?"

He cocked his head. "I am a historian. Something is either historical fact or it's not. History is not like science where you make a hypothesis and set out to prove it is true. You start with historical record, you analyze it, and you question everything for which there is no record. It's as simple as that."

I took the Tudor book from him. "I don't see why you are so against this, Wilson."

He picked up his hot dog. "I don't see why you are so for it." He pointed to the last book on the pile. "That's a book on canoeing."

I snatched it from the pile as Stacy walked toward us. "This is for something different."

"What are all the books for?" Stacy asked.

"Jane's a scientist," Wilson quipped.

"Oh! Books on Lady Jane Grey. Cool!" Stacy ignored Wilson's comment and turned to me. "Hey! I got an e-mail back from one of my history profs at NYU. Well, not from him actually, but from his assistant. He knows a gal who did her doctoral dissertation on the female

Tudor monarchy. He met her last fall at a symposium or something. He said she specifically mentioned having spent considerable time studying Jane Grey's life."

"Well, of course she would. There were only three female Tudor monarchs. Jane being one of them." Wilson tossed a catsup-stained napkin into the trash.

Stacy was only momentarily taken aback by Wilson's interruption. "Anyway. He gave me her e-mail address. I bet she'd know if Jane Grey had been given a ring. Or if she *might've* been given a ring." This last sentence she directed to Wilson.

She handed me a slip of paper with a name and an e-mail address.

Claire Abbot. A professor at the University of New Hampshire.

New Hampshire.

"This guy said she's really nice and quite passionate about Tudor history," Stacy continued. "And she's already published a book for children on the kings and queens of England."

Wilson laughed at this. "I wonder if she had trouble with the illustrations and all those beheadings."

When Stacy and I didn't laugh in return, he mumbled, "Sorry."

Stacy turned back to me. "You should e-mail her. I bet she'd talk to you."

A customer walked in, and Wilson eagerly offered to wait on her. He walked away.

"I think I will." I put the slip of paper inside the canoeing book so that I wouldn't lose it.

"Canoeing?" Stacy peered at the cover of the book in my hands. "I thought you didn't like the water."

I told her usually I didn't.

But I was choosing to see if I might learn to like it.

Leslie didn't quite know what to say when I told her the real reason Brad left New York was to get away from the woman he feared he was falling in love with.

"Do you believe him?" Leslie asked.

"That that's why he left?"

"That he didn't sleep with her."

The thing was, I did. I did believe him.

"Sounds like you want to forgive him," she said.

In my mind, I saw my mother with her back to me, telling me you don't give up on the people you love. Not even when they walk away from you. Not even when they hurt you.

"I guess I do."

"Won't that be kind of hard?"

"But isn't wanting to half of it?"

"I suppose. But what if that's not what he wants?" Leslie asked. "What if he doesn't want you to forgive him?"

I leaned back on the cushions of my couch as the setting sun turned my living room amber. "I can't control what he wants and what he doesn't. I can't make him happy with me if he doesn't want to be."

We were both quiet for a moment.

"So what are you going to do?" Leslie finally said.

"Actually, it was Mom who helped me figure that out."

"Get out of town."

"I'm serious. I think maybe Mom's resilience comes from a place she has never shown us. We think her tough exterior comes from her arrogant and meddlesome ways, but I'm wondering now if it comes from another place altogether."

"I don't know what you're talking about."

I didn't elaborate. It seemed a private thing, what I witnessed with my mother. "I want to stand by Brad, Les. I want to support him and be his best friend. He's having a really hard time. I'm going to let him mend, let him have his space, and let him think. But I am not going to let him go."

As soon as I said this to my sister, I realized I was happy with the choice I'd made to find out what it meant to love someone without physical conditions. I felt brave for the first time in a long time.

"But what if, in the end, he wants to let *you* go?" Leslie's tone was tenuous.

I tested my new resolve. "I am not giving up on him." I hadn't really answered her question, and we both knew it. But she let it go.

"So. You have a plan for how you're going to do all those things?" Leslie asked. "I mean the supporting, standing by stuff, since you live in two different states?'

"Well, for starters, I am going canoeing on Saturday."

"You? On a canoe?"

"I signed up with an instructor today who has guaranteed I will learn to enjoy the water. He's also a fisherman who is going to show me how to set a line and unhook a fish and sit for hours on end waiting for a bite. Brad feels very at home on the water. I've never thought about how much."

Leslie was silent, and for a second, I wondered if our call had been dropped. "I don't get it," she finally said. "You just said you aren't responsible for Brad's happiness. And yet you're going to learn how to canoe. Something he loves. You hate the water."

"But I don't want to hate it anymore, Les. I don't want to be afraid of it anymore. I'm not doing this for him. I'm doing it for me. I don't want there to be fear in between Brad and me. Not even this little one."

My sister said nothing.

I continued, "And I'm looking into going back to school and planning a trip to Nova Scotia in the fall. I've always wanted to go there. I am going to stay busy learning how to be me, and I'm not going to ask Brad when he's coming home."

When I said the word "home," a light seemed to click on in my head, and the glint was brilliant. I couldn't believe I didn't see this before.

Home for Brad would not be Manhattan.

If we were going to reinvent our marriage, I was probably the one who was going to have to pack my things.

And move to New Hampshire.

Thirty-Four

T he plan to be there for somebody who isn't there turned out to be
harder to implement than I thought. The first time I called Brad
was three days after the phone conversation with Leslie. He answered,
spoke politely with me, answered my questions about how his week was
going, how the job was, if he'd been fishing, if he'd be able to go to Connor's track meet that weekend. Ten minutes into the conversation, he
asked me if there was something I needed. I think it threw him off when
I said I just called to see how he was. I then told him I was looking at
graduate programs, that I was thinking of getting my master's, maybe in
history. He grew silent when I started talking about me. I think he wished
I had been angry with him. Dr. Kirtland told me Brad might not be emo-
tionally ready for forgiveness from me; that it could make him feel worse,
not better, and keep him attached to the distance between us. Guilt was
made bearable by anger from the offended. A peace offering from me
messed with that.

When I called the second time, just to chat, I prepared for the call by
having a list of things to talk about that would keep the conversation
moving. Did he see that PBS was airing a biographical film on Wilhelm
Conrad Röntgen, the Nobel prize–winning doctor who discovered the
x-ray? Did he want me to share with him the simple recipe I found for
making *rouladen*? Did he hear that our friends Noel and Kate were expecting their first grandchild?

He seemed to relax somewhat as we talked, but I still sensed unease. The third time I called, I told him I'd been reading books on Lady Jane Grey, since I was convinced, for no other reason than sentimentality, that the ring he'd noticed on my hand when I flew to New Hampshire was Jane Grey's betrothal ring. He listened to the story of how I found it, the fact that my name was inside, and the sad details of Jane's life.

"So why again do you think it's hers?" he asked, not unkindly.

"I don't really have a valid reason for thinking it. I just do. It's a beautiful ring. Someone with a lot of money had to buy it. It's from the mid-sixteenth century—her time period. And it has her first name engraved inside."

"Couldn't it belong to someone else who had been named Jane?"

"Yes," I had said. "Yes, it could."

"But you don't think so?"

"I really want it to be hers."

"How come?"

It took me several seconds to piece together an answer for him. It was the first time he had asked anything about how I felt.

"I'd like to think that even though she was denied the chance to choose her own destiny, there was someone who loved her. Someone in secret. Someone not mentioned in the history books. And that she loved this person, and that the ring and their love had to be kept hidden."

"Sounds like the plot for a fairy tale."

I laughed. "I like fairy tales."

And though I wanted to, I did not add, "and happily-ever-after endings."

I didn't tell him that I'd booked a plane ticket to Nova Scotia for early October or that I'd been out on a canoe and that I'd learned to handle bait, cast a line, and remove a hook. Or that on my third time on the lake, I had begun to realize deep waters are intensely blue, sapphirelike.

Majestic. Not easily disturbed. The very antithesis of shallow and super-ficial. Worthy of my awe.

The bit about the canoe needed to come up naturally, somehow. Otherwise he would think I was trying to make him happy.

And I was not.

I was trying to make me happy.

Three weeks after I e-mailed Claire Abbot, I received a reply. I'd begun to think she had no time for my silly notions. I had mentioned in my e-mail the details of the ring, all that I knew about it, which was not much. I told her I wondered if perhaps it had belonged to the unfortunate Lady Jane Grey. When I saw Claire's name in my inbox on an early Monday morning, I opened her message before anyone else's.

> *Dear Mrs. Lindsay,*
>
> *Sorry for the delay in getting back to you. I've been in England on a research trip but am back and now sifting through my many e-mails. I would, of course, be happy to look at your ring, as well as the prayer book in which you found it. I don't plan on being in New York City until the fall, but as you mentioned you have family in New Hampshire, perhaps you would be able to come my way.*
>
> *Looking forward to meeting you,*
> *Claire Abbot*

I wrote her back immediately, asking if it would be too much trouble if I came to see her that Friday afternoon. My son had a track meet the following day in Hanover.

I waited all day to hear back from her.

Stacy was excited for me. Claire Abbot didn't say there wasn't a ring. Wilson was cautious. Claire Abbot didn't say there was.

Finally, at a little after three o'clock, Claire e-mailed back. Her reply was short. She asked if I could meet her at her office at the university at three thirty on Friday.

I accepted at once.

Then I called to reserve a rental car for the weekend.

When I hung up, I considered what my options were for housing.

I could stay in a hotel.

I could ask Brad if he'd again be amenable to my staying at his place. And I could tell him that I could sleep in the guest room. And then we could go to the track meet together.

I decided to text this request to him so that he could process it his own way. And because I really didn't want to hear hesitancy in his voice. He might have it, but I didn't want to hear it.

As I walked home three hours later, he texted me back.

I'll be out of town Friday night. Conference in Providence. But please feel free to stay at my place. Key under the mat.

So.

That was that.

The drive to Manchester was enjoyable once I was well away from the frenetic commotion in the city. I rented a Mini Cooper. Red with white racing stripes. I had always wanted to drive one.

I arrived at the University of New Hampshire campus fifteen minutes early, so I took my time parking, making sure the prayer book and ring box were safely inside my purse, and finding a rest room.

I found Claire Abbot's office at the Horton Social Science Center and was standing outside her door at precisely 3:30 p.m. I knocked and a woman's voice from within told me to come in.

Claire Abbot was a little younger than I was, petite and slender, her short hair cropped close to her head. She was wearing denim pants and a madras blouse with her sleeves pushed up. Her office was in a state of organized clutter. Little stacks of books, papers, and magazines were everywhere, but they were very neat little stacks.

She stood when I came in. "Jane Lindsay? Hello, I'm Claire Abbot. Please have a seat."

"Thanks for seeing me on such short notice, Dr. Abbot. I really appreciate it." I took a seat across from her desk. I noticed that on her walls were pictures and lithos of castles, cathedrals, and English nobility. Tall bookcases on either side of her desk were top-to-bottom filled with colorful spines, some of them obviously very old. At her elbow was a cup of tea on a saucer.

"Well, I am glad it worked out for you to come today. And please call me Claire." She settled into her chair. "Would you like some tea?"

"No, but thank you. I...I almost expected you to have a British accent."

"My father was British," she said, lifting her cup to her lips. She took a sip. "And I was born in London. I haven't lived there since I was three. But I still feel like British history is in my blood." She set her cup down. "How about you? You have an interest in British history? Is that how you came by your ring?"

"Not exactly. I manage an antique shop in Manhattan, and I have a lot of Victorian and Edwardian antiques in the inventory. But I've never come across anything this old before."

"May I see it?"

I reached into my purse and handed her first the prayer book, which

I had wrapped in a piece of cotton flannel, and then the ring. I removed it from its box and placed it on her desk.

She spent a few minutes looking at the prayer book, murmuring that whoever had owned it should have taken better care of it.

Then she set the book down and examined the ring. I watched as she held it under her desk lamp. She reached for a small magnifying glass in a pencil cup and held it close to the inscription inside.

"Vulnerasti cor meum, soror mea, sponsa," she recited. "That's from the Song of Solomon."

"Yes."

"This ring is beautifully made. Has a jeweler seen it?"

"A friend of mine who's an antique jeweler on Long Island looked at it. He said the stones are top quality and expertly cut. That's why I think it had to have been purchased by someone of nobility and given to someone of nobility. And that it's Elizabethan or older."

"And that's why you think it was Lady Jane Grey's ring?"

"Well, the time period is right. The quality of the stones fit her station in life. And her first name is inscribed inside."

Claire nodded slowly. "How much do you know about Jane Grey?"

"I've read four books about her and an entire volume on the Tudors. I know the only betrothal that was official was the one to Guildford Dudley."

"Whom she married."

I leaned forward in my chair. "But this ring shows no sign of wear. What if she didn't wear it because she felt like she couldn't. What if...what if it wasn't a betrothal ring so much as a declaration ring. What if the person who gave it to her was in love with her, and this was his declaration to her?"

"What if, indeed?" Claire smiled at me.

"You think it's a crazy idea."

"Crazy? No. Intriguing? Very much so. Likely? No one can say, really."

"Could it be hers, though?" I asked.

Claire held the ring up to the light again. "Well, you probably know as well as I that it's of course possible. But in all my studies of Jane Grey's literary remains, and those of people who knew her, there is no record of who she might've loved, if anyone. And then there's the matter of this ring being hidden inside a prayer book for who knows how long. If it was hers, how did it end up in a forgotten prayer book?" Claire handed the ring back to me. "It would be nice if the ring could talk."

I took the ring and fingered the stones. "When you held it, did you think perhaps it really could be Jane Grey's ring?"

Claire toyed with the handle of her teacup. "No. I can't say that I did."

"I do, though. Every time I touch it, it feels like it's her ring."

"Well, then, if I were you, I'd stop asking experts like me our opinion and just live like it was hers." Again, she smiled. But not in a mocking way.

"You don't think it's…silly, do you?"

"It really doesn't matter what I think, does it? It's your ring, now. And it has your name in it. But I don't think you'll want to sell it in your store under a placard that identifies it as Lady Jane Grey's ring. You might end up on the front page of the London tabloids."

She laughed gently and I joined her.

"I'm not selling it." I slid the ring on my pinkie.

"I wouldn't either, if I were you. Besides, I think maybe you were meant to have it."

I gazed up at her. "Meant to have it?"

Claire lifted and lowered her shoulders. "I don't believe in coincidences. It doesn't seem like it's an accident this ring fell into your hands and that you feel this way about it." She took a sip of her tea. "Do you think it's mere coincidence?"

I shook my head. "No. I don't."

A couple of quiet seconds passed between us.

"I wonder if she knew any happiness at all," I said. "She never got to make any choices for herself. She was a pawn. To everyone."

Claire set her teacup down carefully. "Actually, you're only half right. Jane Grey was indeed used by people like the Duke of Northumberland, and even her own parents, but she made many choices, and she gets far too little credit for having made them."

"I don't know what you mean. She was forced to marry a man she probably didn't love and forced to accept a crown she didn't want and then was executed because of it."

Claire crossed her arms in front of her desk. "Yes, she married a man she probably barely knew, but all aristocratic girls of that day faced that possible dilemma. But think about it. She could've run off before her wedding day. She could have disguised herself and run away. And if she did love someone, like you are supposing, she could've fled with that person. They could've escaped into the wilds of the North and lived as lovers and paupers. It would have been irresponsible and scandalous, of course. But she could have done it. Instead, she chose to stay and fulfill her duty."

I could think of nothing to say. Claire went on.

"And, yes, she had no desire to wear the crown, and at first she declined it. But the men who wanted her on the throne instead of Mary persuaded her to accept it, which she did. She could have refused. But she truly thought she could do some good for her country. That made her naive, but not without choice.

"And when Mary kept sending her confessor, John Feckenham, to the Tower to try and convert Jane to Catholicism, Jane would not bow to it.

Guildford did, as did his father. But Jane would not. She didn't believe in the tenets of Rome, and she wouldn't perjure herself by confessing that she did. That, in itself, is the most amazing of all the decisions she made. So I don't think of her as a young woman robbed of choosing her own destiny. I know there are many who do think of her that way, but I don't. And if you are going to live your life believing you are wearing her ring, I suggest you don't either."

In that moment, everything seemed to crystallize for me.

I thought it had been easy thinking my life to that point had been one long bend toward the will of others.

It had been punishing.

And I was through with it.

Thirty-Five

I t was still light as I pulled into Brad's driveway. I found the key under the mat and a note.

Jane,

> *Sorry there's nothing to eat. Was going to go grocery shopping. Too many emergencies. I think there's a can of tomato soup in the pantry. Should be home in time for the track meet tomorrow. But don't wait for me.*

I crumpled the note and slipped it into my pocket. Once inside, I went from room to room and opened windows, a facade for letting in fresh air, but my true intent was to test my presence in each room.

What if this were my house? What if I lived here with Brad? What if this were my kitchen? My living room. My dining room. My patio.

I went upstairs and into the guest room and imagined Connor sleeping there during Christmas vacation and his summer break. I pictured his posters of the Boston Marathon and New Zealand on the walls and his trophies from high school on a shelf above the dresser. And his ball caps on the posts of the bed.

Then I went into the bedroom. And I pictured a different bed. Not that one. And not the one that is in our apartment in Manhattan. A new bed.

I pictured our black-and-white photos of Boston and Quebec on the walls. I pictured my shoes lying askew in the middle of the floor, my jewelry on the bedside table, my scent in the unseen air.

I walked over to the bed and sat on it slowly, closing my eyes and imagining being in a house like this one when it rained and when my parents came to visit and when one of us had the flu and when we celebrated our twenty-fifth wedding anniversary.

I pictured coming into this room at the end of the day, after locking up a little antique store in downtown Manchester. Or maybe not.

Maybe there was no little antique store in downtown Manchester. Managing an antique store wasn't on my list of things I liked to do. I hadn't written anything about owning or managing a store on that list. Treasures from the past still wooed me but selling them on the retail market obviously did not.

Perhaps, instead, I would take some classes from Professor Claire Abbot. Maybe someday I would teach history, like she did.

Perhaps I would check out the pretty white church near Brad's new hospital. Contemplate what Jane Grey staked her life upon. Get a dog. Learn how to waltz.

My list was expanding.

I headed back downstairs to the kitchen. I was hungry.

Brad was right. There was practically nothing in his fridge. I got back in my car and headed to the corner grocery store on the other side of the boulevard that led into his gated complex. I decided not to overdo it. Just a few basics. Bread. Eggs. Cheese. Bananas. Frozen pot stickers, because Brad liked those. Rice. Baby carrots. Cheerios. Milk. A microwaveable entrée for me for dinner. And all the ingredients to make a red velvet cake, including the nonstick cake pans, since I was sure Brad didn't have any. I love red velvet cake.

I returned to Brad's, put the groceries away, and started on the cake.

While it baked, I ate my dinner and did the crossword puzzle in Brad's newspaper. After frosting the cake and cleaning up my mess, I watched an old movie. At ten o'clock, I headed up the stairs, stopping when I got to the landing. Brad never told me where he wanted me to sleep. I hovered at the guest room.

I had no desire to sleep in there.

Pivoting on my toes, I headed into Brad's bedroom. I didn't know much about that house. But that was a room I did know a little about.

I lay in bed a long time before sleep finally came to me. I felt like I was heading into the vast unknown on an open sea. Ahead of me lay the uncharted territory of my marriage where no one had dropped a boundary marker. I heard a ticking clock in the darkness of Brad's bedroom, and I thought of the clock my mother had fixed, as a gift to me; an unintended reminder that things that last always have second, third, and fourth beginnings. That is why we have antique stores. That is why past beauty has a sure home in the future. I didn't know what time it was when sleep overtook me.

Sometime in the middle of the night, I awakened suddenly. I knew where I was, but I was afraid nonetheless. I felt like I wasn't alone. I sat up in bed, my heart pounding. Across from me, in an amply stuffed armchair, Brad was asleep. His head was cocked to the side, and his feet were crossed at the ankles on the matching ottoman. An empty wine glass rested on the table beside him.

It looked as though he'd sat there, watching me sleep and sipping a glass of wine until he, too, fell asleep.

Part of me wanted to wake him and ask what made him leave the conference early. What made him sit in a chair and watch me sleep? I wanted to ask if he was beginning to understand, as I was, that our relationship had roots we hadn't seen, buried deep below the surface of our routine lives.

Part of me wanted nothing about that serene moment to change.

I sat there for a full minute before I slowly lay back down. I rested my head on Brad's pillow and watched him, until sleep again returned to me.

When again I woke, moonlight was just giving way to pearly day. The chair across from me was empty. I turned in the bed to see if Brad had slipped in beside me, but I was alone in the room.

Had I dreamed it? Had I dreamed he was there? It seemed so real.

I got out of bed and dressed, unsure. Then I heard a noise downstairs.

I made my way to the door and quietly opened it. More noises. In the kitchen.

I tiptoed down the stairs. The kitchen light was on, and coffee was brewing. The clock over the sink read a few minutes before six.

I heard noises now from inside the garage. Then the door to the garage swung open, and Brad jumped slightly when he saw me. He was wearing a fishing vest and faded jeans.

"Jane. You're up."

"You're here." I kept my tone light.

"Yeah. I...I left the conference last night. It just wasn't doing anything for me, and I wasn't teaching at it, so I left."

"Get home late?" I walked over to the cupboard and pulled out two coffee cups.

"Um. Yeah. After two."

I didn't ask him where he slept. I knew where he'd slept. And I was done with pretense. I poured him a cup of coffee. "Going out in the canoe this morning?"

He took the cup from me, and his fingers brushed across mine. "Yes. I... I'm sorry if I woke you up. I'll be back in plenty of time for us to drive together to Dartmouth."

I carefully poured my own cup. "Is it okay if I come with you?"

"To Dartmouth? Sure. Sure, we can drive together."

I turned to him. "I meant, can I come with you right now?"

He blinked at me. "You want to come fishing? In the canoe?"

I nodded and sipped my coffee.

"Um. Well…"

"I've been out a few times with an instructor. I know how to get in and out and where to sit and how to paddle. I even know how to bait a hook and reel the line in. I promise I won't be in the way."

Brad's wordless stare was impossible to read. "How…?" But he didn't finish.

"I started meeting with an instructor a few weeks ago. I know I still have a lot to learn. I just didn't want to be afraid of the water anymore, Brad. I wanted things to be different."

Brad just nodded.

"So. Is that yes? I can come?" I asked.

"Yes." His voice was barely audible.

"I'll just run up and put my hair in a ponytail. Is it okay if I borrow one of your sweatshirts?"

"Uh. Yes. Of course." A slight smile rested on his lips.

I left him to gather his thoughts, and I took my coffee with me. I needed to gather mine.

Brad seemed happy I wanted to come canoeing with him.

He seemed happy.

I sipped my coffee as I brushed my hair, slipped on my Keds, and rifled through his dresser drawers for a hoodie. Brad seemed happy.

When I came back downstairs, he was standing by the sink, waiting for me.

"You made a red velvet cake," he said.

"I did."

"I've missed those." He opened his mouth to say something else, but he stopped.

"Ready to go?" I asked.

He smiled and nodded.

We headed out to our canoe-laden Jeep in the garage and the hushed stillness of dawn.

Brad backed slowly out of the driveway, and there was no other sound but our vehicle and the music of birds. The garage door closed with a quiet thud behind us, and we turned toward the breaking day.

Lucy

Thirty-Six

S pring came reluctantly in the weeks following Jane's death. Or perhaps it came as it always did for everyone but me.

I did not want the sun to shine on London. I did not want color to burst on the hillsides or riverbanks. I was angry at the forces that wished Jane dead and aggrieved that no one save a few understood the immense pleasure my lady had at choosing, at last, her fate. A traitor is capricious in his or her allegiances. Jane was no traitor.

Guildford was executed the same morning as Jane. Her father, a few weeks after. Her mother swore fealty to Queen Mary and was reinstated at court. I chose never to look upon Frances Grey again. In the midst of all this, my father's illness bore him to heaven, and my one consolation was he did not suffer the dismal state of Mary's sway.

Jane's sister Katherine, whose marriage to Lord Herbert was annulled before consummated, spent the years of Queen Mary's blessedly short reign as a prisoner, as did the Princess Elizabeth. Threats to the Crown, they were. Katherine secretly married Edward Seymour, and I have long wondered if the two found a bit of consolation for their many woes, including the loss of sister and soul mate, in each other's arms. I honored Jane's request and never sought Edward to return the ring to him. And since no one knew the ring's whereabouts—not even Mrs. Ellen knew I had it—no one asked about it.

The spring that I had despised brought one bit of wonderful news. Nicholas and I learned I was with child. Our daughter, Jane Margaret, was born the following January, and it was her timely arrival into our hearts and lives that kept us from quaking within at the bloody horror of Mary's reign.

Nicholas continually reminded me, as he had done when I first met him, that religion was not the true end of many a monarch's horrific schemes, but power. Always power.

Mary was a hungry ruler, desperate for control and posterity. Her marriage to the Spanish prince brought her neither. He did not love her, and she did not produce an heir with him. He left her.

Nearly three hundred souls, Reformers who would not yield to her demands, were executed under her reign. Nicholas and I left London for a safer life and home for Jane Margaret the winter of Queen Mary's second year on the throne. Nicholas took a post at a school in Bristol, far from London's chaotic atmosphere. A year later, our Thomas was born.

When the Queen died four years after wresting the crown from Jane's innocent head, no one mourned. Her half sister, Elizabeth, ascended the throne, rebirthed the Church of England, and a calm return to Reformist rule. She was not a perfect ruler, of course, but she brought a measure of peace. Many daughters born in the years of her reign were named Elizabeth, including two of mine; one who lived and one who did not.

My dear little Jane Margaret did not care for needle and thread, and try as I might to teach her to sew, she would not have it. She was forever getting into tussles and spats, with boys, not girls. And she ever hated to lose an argument with anyone. She is, even to this day, truthful to a fault. She has never bent to the will of anything or anyone but her own. She married a ship's captain who often takes her on voyages that leave me breathless with worry. Jane loves the sea; it is the image of God to her—vast, beautiful, unknowable, powerful, and steady. Her sons are just like her. Lovers of the ocean, respectful of its command, mindful of their own limitations with regard to it.

My Thomas followed in the way of his father and became a teacher. He is now a tutor to an earl's sons. Elizabeth has become a better seamstress than I ever was. She and her tailor husband live in London where they own a tailoring shop. They are the parents of three beautiful girls.

Nicholas and I stayed in Bristol where I sewed party dresses for young ladies and old women. My dearest lived to see his last grandchild born before a wasting sickness bore him away from me. My days are lonely and long now without him beside me.

I feel my own mortality treading upon me now. Through the years, I have often wondered if Lady Jane would still be my friend had she lived. Would her reign have been peaceful had Mary not been successful? Would she have reigned for many long years or would illness or violence have taken her? Would she have borne England a son? And would that son, a Dudley, have a heart like his mother or like his father? Sometimes I would wonder these things aloud to Nicholas, and he would kiss my head and tell me it is impossible to guess what the will of God would have brought us in a different turn of events. The course of history had already been written by Lady Jane's choices, not all of which were made for her. Not all.

It is Christmas, 1592, and I am in my fifty-ninth year. Jane Margaret and her family are coming to Bristol to spend the holidays with me. I have made what preparations I can, but I feel my spirit weakening within me. I had to ask my good neighbor Eleanor to help me prepare rooms for my family's arrival. My breath wants to skip away from me at the oddest times.

I had Eleanor climb the ladder to my attic, sweet thing, to retrieve a small wooden box I have kept there for many years.

"What, pray, would you need from an old chest at Christmas, Lucy?" Eleanor says to me as she now struggles down the ladder with the dusty box under her arm.

I help her down and take the little box. "Just something I need to give to Jane, Eleanor. Come have a posset for your trouble."

"I daresay you shall only find spiders in there," Eleanor scoffs, brushing off her skirts. "It can't weigh very much, whatever it is."

We sit down at my table, and I pour her a warm drink. "It is quite small, actually," I tell her. "'Tis only a ring that belonged to a very dear friend of mine. I want to give it to Jane."

"A ring? In your attic? Are you sure Jane will want it?" Eleanor laughs.

I laugh too. "Oh, yes. I think she will want this one. There's a story behind this ring. A secret story. A lovely story that Jane will want to hear."

My Jane knows only that I once worked for a duke and that I sewed dresses for his daughter. But I believe she deserves to hear whose daughter it was that I sewed for. And why Nicholas and I named our firstborn Jane. I have always believed Jane should know. And I have always known a time would come when I would tell her.

Eleanor sips at her drink. "What have you been doing with a secret ring in your attic, Lucy? Of all places!" She looks at me as if I have the daft notions of an old woman whose mind is thinning.

I smile and sip my own drink.

"I have been waiting."

From Jane Margaret Staverton Holybrooke
Heather Downs
Castle Road, Bristol

3 May 1619

To Mrs. Alice Holybrooke
Great Heath, Liverpool

Dearest Alice:

I am aggrieved I shall not be able to see you and Charles and the new wee babe. A cough has settled into my lungs and the doctor here has forbidden me to travel. And I would not want to share my cough with the little ones.

I am afraid God will soon call me hence to join my dear captain and, while you do not need to mention this to my son Charles, I must tell you why I am sending this package to you. Inside the little leather sack that accompanies this letter is a ring that I would like for you to give to Philippa when she is older. The ring has my name engraved inside but it has not always been mine. Its original owner is now many years deceased. It is my desire to live long enough to tell Philippa the story someday. It is too lengthy for a letter. My mother gave it to me when I was about your age, dear Alice. Suffice it to say that it is a ring meant to be worn by someone who is loved and gives love. Please keep it safe for Philippa until such time as I may see you or her again. There is much I need to tell her.

I remain very sincerely,
Your mother-in-law,
Jane

From *Miles Fenworth, Solicitor*
Covent Garden
London

10 September 1665

To Miss Audrey Tewes
Chesterwood House
Devonshire

Dear Miss Tewes:
    I regret to inform you that your great-aunt Philippa Holybrooke has fallen victim to Plague. It was her expressed wish that you be sent this prayer book upon her death. The prayer book was not kept upon her person during her illness, but was in the keeping of the nuns who cared for her while she lay ill. The rosary is also a gift from your great-aunt to you, as are the gold coins in the bag. Miss Holybrooke was most adamant that you take the prayer book and keep it safe. As the illness devoured her, she became convinced soldiers of His Majesty were in search of it. She asked that you guard it carefully. I write this to you because I promised her I would.
    Again, my most ardent condolences on the passing of your great-aunt. She spoke often of you.
    Your faithful servant,
    Miles Fenworth

From Andrew Bolling
Butterworth Township
Rochdale Parish
The Salford Hundred, Lancashire

November 12, 1715

To Messrs. Tinley and Harper
Booksellers
High Street
Oxford

*As we agreed by earlier post, here are the contents of my
mother Audrey Tewes Bolling's library. I apologize for the
condition of the books. Her house was unoccupied and unheated for several years. It is my understanding that the
prayer book and rosary belonged to her great-aunt Philippa
whom was taken by Plague and my mother was resolute that
the book and rosary stay together. If you cannot find a buyer
for both the prayer book and the rosary, keep them for me and
I shall buy them back from you and perhaps give them to my
niece if she would have them.*

    Yours respectfully,
    Andrew Bolling

December 2, 1715

From Tinley and Harper Booksellers
High Street
Oxford

Dear Mr. Bolling:
    You will be pleased to know that a Mrs. Charlotte Meade
has purchased the prayer book and rosary along with many
other titles from your mother's library. She was quite moved
when I told her the previous owner, a Protestant, had died
childless of Plague, with a rosary in her possession.
    If we may be of further assistance, please do not hesitate
to let us know.
    Yours most sincerely,
    Henry Tinley

To Chester Hadley, Locksmith
Cornmarket Street
Oxford

March 22, 1754

Dear Mr. Hadley:

I am sending to you this copper box that belonged to my mother, Charlotte Meade. I have searched her house from top to bottom and cannot find the key. I plan to settle her estate the day after tomorrow and shall return thence to Leeds. If you could perchance work the lock open I would be much obliged. I do not know what she has placed in the box.

I shall come by your shop before I leave. If I should miss you, you may send the box to me at Park Row, No. 12, Leeds, Yorkshire.

Respectfully,
John R. Meade

To John Meade
Park Row, Number 12
Leeds, Yorkshire

March 26, 1754

Dear Mr. Meade:

    Please be advised, good sir, that my establishment was
looted two nights ago following a dreadful fire and the box
that belonged to your mother was most likely stolen.

    Since the lock had not yet been opened, I do not know the
contents of the box, nor do you, so I am sending you five
shillings for your loss.

    Respectfully,
    Chester Hadley

From Priscilla Colley
Charlton Kings
Cheltenham, Gloucestershire

June 14, 1801

To Esther Waddington
Marshes
Chipping Norton
Oxfordshire

Dearest Mum:

Albert and I are settled into the cottage. It is small but since it is just us two—for now!—we can make do. We found no small amount of rubbish when we moved in. Indeed one whole room upstairs was filled with boxes and crates and spider webs. Most of it we burned in the yard. But there were a few trinkets worth keeping. We found a metal box that is locked. It is green and blackened with age and soot and smells strange but Albert is going to try to open it anyway, though I told him not to bother. We should just burn it with the rest.

We also found a cradle! It was full of old newspapers and horseshoes. Can you imagine?

Must be off now. Love to Papa,
Yours affectionately,
Priscilla

From Isabell Colley Manning
New Bridge House
Kings Street
Gloucester

June 14, 1862

To Sarah Manning Swift
West Halifax Street
Baltimore, Maryland

My lovely Sarah:

I received your letter, dearest Sarah, and am grateful to almighty God that Robert survived the battle at Shiloh. I so long to see you and the children, and I worry so for you, but I fear this War of the States will outlast me, my dear daughter. I am selling the house and the furnishings and moving in with Aunt Josephine. I am afraid I am not well enough to attend to the attic. I have all my parents' belongings there from when they moved from Chipping Norton to live here with me. My mother refused to part with anything after your grandfather died. I do not want you to have the burden of sifting through it all, dear Sarah, on some future day. I am having the lot sold at auction. I shall send to you the locket you had as a child and the doll Papa made for you. I pray I see you soon. Please be safe, my dearest.

With love always,
Mother

To *Aubrey Templeton*
Rosewood Manor
Chapel Gate
Cirencester, Gloucestershire

August 16, 1862

Dear Mr. Templeton:
   I am writing on the matter of the lot you purchased at the estate sale of Mrs. Isabell Manning. The steamer chest has been deposited, as you requested, to your carriage house at Holywell House in Bristol.
   Jeremy Stokes

To Mrs. Annabelle Templeton Ashley
Bridge Street, No. 12
Chepstow, Monmouthshire, Wales

January 17, 1901

Dear Mrs. Ashley:

It has been some time since I wrote you to tell you your father's things are still in storage at the carriage house at Holywell in Bristol. There are a number of boxes of books, chests, and letters. Would you please be so kind as to direct me as to where they shall be sent? I hasten to remind you that the new owners of Holywell House are anxious to get on with the repairs.

Simon Cardwell, Solicitor

From Dora Ashley Hughes
Summer House
Swansea, Wales

August 21, 1940

To Mrs. Annabelle Templeton Ashley
Bridge Street, No. 12
Chepstow, Monmouthshire, Wales

Dear Mum:
    I got your letter yesterday. I shall try my utmost to come for you at the end of the month if the Germans haven't bombed the whole of Britain to kingdom come. Don't toss anything out. I don't care what Leo says about your father's junk. We may need all that old rubbish to live off of. Don't toss anything out! Must run. Martin's awake and hungry.
    Affectionately,
    Dora

NOTICE OF SALE

———∗———

The Estate of Martin Hughes

February 6, 2010

Swansea Auction House

Sale starts at 8 AM

Many unique items

Stored boxes sold by the case

ALL SALES FINAL

From Swansea Auction House

To Mr. Edgar Brownton
13 Collier Close
Cardiff, Wales

February 14, 2010

Dear Mr. Brownton:
    As per your correspondence of February 8, the condi-
tions of the lots were made clear on the bill of sale. All sales
are final. I am sorry you have been unable to open the little
lockbox you found in one of the boxes you purchased. We are
in possession of no key, nor do we know the contents of the
lockbox. As you were told at the sale, the boxes have been in
unheated storage for forty years. Like as not, there is not
much inside the box but dust.
        Samuel Llewellyn
        Swansea Auction House

From the desk of
Emma Downing

Janie:

 I am sending you the letter from the man who sold me the boxes at the jumble sale, Mr. Edgar Brownton. He wrote to the auction house after he first bought them and asked about a key for that lockbox where you found the ring, but as you can see, that search went nowhere.

 No one knew about the ring, love. No one has known about it for a long time.

 You were meant to find it, I think. You know I am right. And you were meant to keep it.

 Glad to hear you are sleeping well for a change. And enjoying a bit of canoeing. You should come visit me this summer. We shall punt the Thames and I will show you the place where Queen Jane rode on the same water. You can wear her ring.

 Lovingly,

 Em

AUTHOR'S NOTE

While much of the account of Lady Jane Grey's life in *Lady in Waiting* is based on recorded fact, there is no evidence at all that Lady Jane Grey had been in love with anyone at the time of her death. The character of the dressmaker Lucy Day is fictional, as is the idea that Jane was given a betrothal ring. Is it possible that Lady Jane Grey was indeed in love with Edward Seymour, and is it also possible that no, she loved the man she married instead of him? Her literary remains do not give us a glimpse into that part of her heart. *Lady in Waiting,* then, is a book that explores the question "What if?"…one of the lovelier aspects of fiction.

Visit the author on the Web at www.susanmeissner.com.

READERS GUIDE

1. Did you find yourself drawn more to the story of modern-day Jane or long-ago Lady Jane? Why?

2. Why do you think Jane conditioned herself to defer to others when an important decision had to be made? Can you relate?

3. What have you learned about yourself or life or God when you've had to wait? Do you consider yourself a patient person?

4. A quote by the French philosopher Diderot is mentioned in chapter 3. "What has never been doubted has never been proven." Do you think that is true? Do you think this quote holds any significance to Jane Lindsay?

5. Do you think it's conceivable that Jane truly saw no signs that Brad was unhappy? Why or why not?

6. Does Jane Lindsay's mother have any redeeming qualities? Is there anything about her personality that makes her admirable? What about Lady Jane Grey's mother?

7. What do you think Lucy Day's strengths were? Why do you think she gave personality traits to the dresses in Jane's wardrobe?

8. When Jane Lindsay's mother has the clock fixed, Jane has a hard time thinking of it as the same clock. Is it the same clock? Do you approve of what her mother did? Would you have had the clock fixed? Why or why not? Why do you think some people are drawn to antiques?

9. In the end, Jane decides to stand by Brad during his crisis. What do you think of her decision?

10. If you had lived during the sixteenth century, would you have wanted to be a commoner, a noble, or a royal? Why?

11. Professor Claire Abbot tells Jane Lindsay that Lady Jane Grey was not entirely without choice; had she chosen to, she could've refused the crown and escaped to the North with the man she loved. What do you think of this suggestion? If Jane Grey had done something like this, how would it alter your opinion of her?

12. Where do you see Jane and Brad Lindsay in ten years? What do you think Jane Lindsay does with the ring?

ACKNOWLEDGMENTS

I am grateful beyond words to:

- the incredibly gifted editorial team at WaterBrook Multnomah, especially Shannon Marchese, Jessica Barnes, and Laura Wright. I'm also grateful to Jennifer Peterson and Lissa Halls Johnson. Their collective insight and refining fire were invaluable to me.

- my agent, Chip MacGregor, for affirmation, encouragement, and candor.

- colleagues James Scott Bell and Vasthi Acosta for helping me see, feel, and breathe Manhattan, and marriage and family counselor Jeff Sumpolec for helping me visualize what a crumbling marriage might feel like.

- my husband and best friend, Bob, who has gallantly denied me the experience of knowing what a crumbling marriage might feel like.

- Judy Horning, proficient proofreader, first reader of anything I write, and mother extraordinaire.

- Pam Ingold, Kimlee Harper, and my book club gals for holding me up when down was easier.

- God, who is patience personified, genteel beyond measurement, and the kindest of kings.

Sometimes we find the truth about ourselves in the lives of others.

Leaving her privileged life and family behind, Lauren Durough learns the consequences of misguided perceptions as she uncovers the story of a seventeenth-century victim of the Salem witch trials.

Secrets smolder even in the nicest neighborhoods

Amanda Janvier and husband Neil take motherless niece Tally into their seemingly storybook life. Yet the family is hiding dangerous secrets—secrets of the past that can't stay hidden forever behind their white picket fence. Will they find their chance for redemption?